Jacob Chance, U.S. Marshal
Johnny Gunn

Cover Art:
Michelle Crocker

http://mlcdesigns4you.weebly.com/

Publisher's Note:

This is a work of fiction. All names, characters, places, and events are the work of the author's imagination.

Any resemblance to real persons, places, or events is coincidental.

Solstice Publishing - www.solsticepublishing.com

Jacob Chance, U.S. Marshal
A Novel
By Johnny Gunn

Dedication

This book is dedicated to my lovely bride, Patty, in my full realization that it would never have come together without her trust and love.

Inspiration for Golden Valley comes from Fish Lake Valley in Esmeralda County, Nevada. It's a lush little valley sitting on the eastern base of the White Mountains. While Golden Valley, the town of Preston, and all the people are a figment of my imagination, Fish Lake Valley is rich and fertile and home to many fine ranches. Given half the chance, I think Patty and I would move there in a heartbeat.

Chapter One

In many areas of the west, sometime around sun up or sun down, you can see two or three hundred miles if you're up on a ridge looking out across an endless sea of mountains and valleys. Mountain ranges layered in the morning or evening mist, one after another, a great sea rolling toward you, and coupled with brisk mountain air and the aroma of freshly boiled coffee, or a rabbit on a makeshift skewer, it's enough to bring tears to the eyes of the hardest of the hard men.

Jacob Chance might have been considered one of those hard men, standing about six feet tall, thin as a reed, and hard as a rock. He wore wool pants tucked into high black leather boots, Mexican style spurs that rarely touched the flanks of Mr. Morgan, his stud of that breed. A buckskin shirt was tucked into those pants, and on warm days Chance draped a Mexican serape over himself. "You get a little sweat going, put your horse in a mild trot, and the breeze cools you right out. Been wearing one of these things for ten years, now." He carried what some called an ironic grin, others called it boyish. More than one woman called it enchanting.

There were other accouterments to fill out the man, like a flowing moustache, floppy hat, and the large forty-five caliber revolver sitting high on his right side, the one with hand carved maple grips, and tucked in a well-oiled, well-worn holster, also hand engraved. He was a man who spends most of his life on the trail, in the saddle, which also carries his repeating rifle in an engraved scabbard.

The grips on his revolver evolved over many campsites, as Chance sat in front of a quiet fire following supper, tin cup filled with hot coffee, his knife, sharp and strong, slowly allowing the wood to fit his hard hand and fingers. He was known to hammer and carve bull hide as well, learned from people he'd met over his long career moving from camp to camp, territory to territory. "The wood knows what it wants to look like, to say to the world," he told people, "I just have to follow along and pay attention."

He was in Abilene a few summers ago and found himself talking about retiring, or as he put it at the time, "Bein' shoved out of the only job I've ever really enjoyed." He would never have been asked to leave-or to quit, but the thought of not doing his job almost frightened the big man. "What do people do when they have to quit a job?" he asked the man he had been working with.

"Don't know, Jacob. Don't think I've ever give it any thought. Hell, boy, as young as you are, what you talkin' 'bout anyway. And-besides, the way you work with leather, you should open a saddle shop somewhere and chase the saloon girls." The two laughed for some time over that, Chance knowing living in a town, not doing what he does best, would just about kill him.

Steel gray eyes that gave one the impression they could burrow into the soul like hardened steel could also turn into buttermilk, soften at the cry of a child or the lilt of a lovely voice. Chance had large hands, the kind that manipulated tools and equipment, more than horses' reins or hammers on a revolver. Fingers - long and tapered, and it was obvious to an onlooker that he did his nails with a skinning knife, like the one at his belt.

He remembered when he became a Deputy United States Marshal, responsible now for the area west of the Wasatch Range on the east and the Sierra Nevada on the west. He talked to himself, to his horse, to the great outdoors regularly, was as observant a man as most have ever met. "Been a good life," he mumbled, tossing another couple of sticks onto his fire, "and it beats the hell out of being a farmer." He snickered to himself over that, remembering back to when he was a boy and those around him were bound and determined to make him a farmer.

"One has to be born to the plow," he had said many times. "I'm not one of them, but I have nothing but respect for farmers and farming. To create great fields of food, to take acres of alkali dust and turn it into wheat and corn, great baskets of squash and beans, I tell you, it's a miracle. Helping that young heifer with her first calf, feeding mama something you grew so she can turn it into milk for something she grew.

"There's more than a miracle at play for the farmer's life. I've been through the agony of drought, lived through devastating floods, and being told by the farmer that the flood is bringing him new topsoil, and feeling good about it. I will never be a farmer, I simply wasn't born to it."

These little discussions with himself happened most mornings while he's on the trail. "Keeps my mind fresh," he told himself, "Gets me going. Strong camp fire coffee, memories from years ago, and I'm ready to face today." He stirred his fire, poured another tin cup full of boiling coffee, and continued to greet this new day.

On the cold days, he wore a bearskin long coat, slit up the back so he could ride, and - doubled across the front. And one other item, a large badge that proclaimed- -*U.S. Marshal*-pinned to that buckskin shirt.

"I never have liked cold weather, ever since I was a child, back in Missouri." There was a mountain chill in the air this morning, and Chance had the fire going long before sunrise, was sipping hot coffee, watching his big Morgan stud roll in the fresh grass of a high meadow. "It's always cold when you're this high. Must be about eight thousand feet going through that pass yesterday." He could see Golden Valley, miles away in the morning mist, and several thousand feel lower.

Chance was again deep in thought, wondering what would be waiting for him when he rode into the big Golden Valley, far below, rich valley colors just coming into early

7

sunlight. The chill also reminded him of many years ago, back along the breaks in Missouri, growing up as a farmer's son, learning how to tend to the land, how to tend to the animals, how to get along with the neighbors. "Chill morning air does something to my brain, I guess. Can't keep from remembering things." He still carried the little boy grin when he said things like this, those hard eyes softened visibly, and he gently added another stick or two to the fire.

He left that farm a long time ago, but what he learned there, when very young, has been a driving part of his life. "Pappy always said, 'First do the job the best you know how, and second, be honest and fair with those you work with or for.' Pappy was a good man, and I guess that's what led me to become a lawman."

When he left the farm and headed deep into the west, territories that were blossoming because of rich ore, some because of good grass and water, some because of location for transportation, he met some good people and some bad. One bad man in particular put him on the road to becoming a-marshal.

"Mean old Ed Brown put me here," Chance was thinking as he poured another cup of boiling coffee, slipped a hard tack biscuit into the tin cup to make it edible, and settled onto the soft ground. "People in Green River called him Big Ed Brown, and he swaggered around, took whatever he wanted from whoever had it, got in fights daily, and was known to use a big knife to kill more than five people.

"He took a great dislike to my wearing a serape one day. We were in a rag-tag saloon, just a couple of barrels holding a plank of wood for the bar, and inside a canvas tent at that, and he pulled that knife. Never forget the look on his face when the two slugs from my forty-five slammed him in the chest. Complete shock that somebody would dare stand up to the man.

"People in the village were pretty happy that the bad man, Big Ed Brown was gone, and asked me to stick around and be sheriff. I had never in my life had such a thought, but they were so intent on making me sheriff, that I did it. Now, look at me, ten years as a deputy marshal." He poked at the fire, downed his coffee and biscuit, and whistled his stud over. "These high mountain mornings with the chill in the air sure do get me going," he said, getting to his feet.

***

Chance pulled the letter from his pocket to read for the hundredth time. "Looks like range trouble in Golden Valley, Nevada Territory. Find Sarah Jackson. Federal homestead laws at risk." To be able to visit Golden Valley was something Chance had wanted to do for years. Some of the best grass, sweetest water, and gentlest climate in the Great Basin, and now–a possible range war. A marshal's territory wasn't dependent on borders between states and territories, but rather–on how many or few men were available. In the 1860s, Chance has found himself covering thousands of square miles, from the Sierra Nevada to the Rockies, much of the land recently acquired when California was taken from the Mexicans.

"We'd have more men in the field," the U.S. Attorney in San Francisco had said over and over, "but with this damn War Between the States, there just aren't very many men available." Because of the civil war, there was always the possibility of an uprising by southern sympathizers, problems between those with differing philosophies, the kind of problems that bring death and destruction, the kind of problems U.S. Marshals were trained to handle.

The great migration west brought people of many backgrounds and made them neighbors, but couldn't put out the fires that drove their passions. Slavery was a southern issue, and those who came west from the south brought the issue with them. Now, with war scarring the eastern states, north and south, those passions have moved west, a west that is mostly sympathetic to the northern cause.

"This is big country," Chance wrote in letters to his superiors, "and it takes a long time to get from here to there. Someday there will be railroads, actual roads that will connect some of these various areas. Someday, Major Randall, but not today." Wagon roads that brought emigrants in also brought in trouble. "Sometimes, major, the only trails leading out from a town or village simply go to a nearby ranch. All these mountain ranges in the Great Basin run north and south, and the only ways east and west are by trails that follow the few rivers and streams. Those pioneers that came through here opened those trails." His letters and conversations were accepted by those in higher positions, but the major and his supervisors knew that nothing would change until the war was over.

"Yes, sir, this is big country," he had said to his boss so many times. Jacob Chance is Deputy U.S. Marshal for this territory, and was the kind of man who didn't tolerate fools or criminals. "It was Pappy that made me the man I am. I sure miss that old man."

Chance lost his parents when he was three years old, and old man Kincaid, Pappy to most, took him and his sister into his home, raised those kids to be fine people, and died just a year ago. "Janey has the farm now, and that's the way it should be. I might want a ranch someday, but I know I could never be a farmer again. Not in my blood, I guess, though Pappy sure did try to make me one."

Chance finished what structured schooling there was in western Missouri, kissed his little sister goodbye on his eighteenth birthday and rode west. Contemplative this morning, he remembered those days, "almost twelve years now. Been home twice, once just because I was headed to St. Louis, and once when Pappy passed on. And now this war is tearing that country to shreds." He worried often about his sister, about the farm, about the country. "I have boyhood friends, good friends that would be willing to shoot me or Janey just because of how we feel about our country. I'm very proud of Mr. Lincoln, and I support this country."

He took his time with his coffee and side meat, one chunk of hard biscuit left for lunch on the trail. "Time to move down the road, old man," he said saddling his Mr. Morgan. He stomped out the fire, packed the bed roll and gear behind the saddle, and stepped into the stirrup for a nice long ride down into the valley. "Don't see grass like this in the Great Basin very often," he was thinking. "Kind of reminds me of home." The tall grass along the rutted trail was nicking at the belly of his horse and he hadn't been in the valley for more than half a mile before he had to ford the first of many spring run creeks. "You smell that, old man?" he asked the stud. "That's the sweetest grass I've smelled in a long time. Makes you just want to roll around in it, eh big boy?" Chance stepped out of the saddle and grabbed a handful of thigh high grass, tiny flowers nestled in the leaves, lupine, maybe even clover tucked away. "I could make a valley like this home."

It had been years since Jacob Chance had a home, someplace that he could call his own, and the thought about having one set him back a step. "A home?" he mumbled, getting back in the saddle. "Now there's a thought that hasn't bounced around before." He put the horse in a long trot, thinking about words like home, ranch, family, not having any of those since leaving Missouri. "Yeah," he said to Mr. Morgan. "Yeah, maybe in twenty years or so," and chuckled gently.

The trail wound through thick stands of cottonwood and quaking aspen, and it seemed that about every fifty feet or so he would raise some game birds, like quail or sage hens. Rabbits bounded away, he kicked out several coyotes, and high overhead a big Golden Eagle soared on warming currents. That chill Chance felt in the high mountains was evident in the leaves changing color here in the valley. "Fall can't be too far away," he told his horse, watching a small band of does looking for their buck. He had stopped for a short rest on the top of a small ridge and off in the high grass watched a large herd of antelope dusting up the air.

He had passed within a mile or two of a couple of large ranch houses, complete with barns, holding corrals, and out buildings. There was smoke coming from the chimneys and on at least one place, he saw a large herd of cattle. "Must be bringing the herds down from the high summer grazing," he muttered, wondering what it would be like to live on a ranch like those he was seeing.

"A couple of those mule deer would be meat for a long cold winter," he said to the great outdoors, watching large deer with oversize ears bound through the grass. "If I live long enough to retire," he thought, "this valley would make a fine home. Man sure wouldn't go hungry here."

The little village of Preston was plunked down in the middle of the valley with Good Hope River running right down the middle of town, and Chance rode up to the livery stable, stepped off his horse, and looked up and down what was the main street. "Just doesn't look like the setting for a range war to me," he whispered to the Morgan stud, walking him into the stable.

"Howdy, stranger. Welcome to Preston. That's a fine looking stallion you're riding. Be with us long?"

"Howdy yourself, Smitty. Yeah, this old boy is one fine ride. Good grass and sweet water is all he needs, and I can tell you for sure, I need a cold beer." That was followed by a rolling laugh his eyes all crinkled up. He pulled the bedroll and other belongings off the saddle, then pulled the saddle and blanket. "He could use a good rub down, friend, and maybe just a touch of fresh grain. Not too much, now, don't want to get him all riled up."

"Looks like you've been on the trail for a spell. What brings you to this fine valley?" The Smithy was giving Chance a good looking over, saw a long, hard, westerner, his revolver tucked neatly at his waist, a good strong knife on the other side, and a repeating rifle leaning on his bedroll.

Was he a buckaroo, an outlaw, or just passing through? The town's blacksmith knew best not to ask those kinds of questions of a stranger.

"Looks like a man could run some fine beef cattle around here." Chance was hoping this would lead the livery operator to say something about range or fence trouble.

"There's some fine grass, good water, and some that wants what others already have. We've got a little bit of trouble being stirred up. Hope you're not going to be part of that."

"That doesn't sound very good," Chance said, and stepped into the shadows of the large livery barn. He pulled his serape up and flipped it over his shoulder. "Afraid I am, Smitty," he said, pointing to his Marshal's badge, "'Fraid I am," and he stuck out his big right hand. "Jacob Chance, U.S. Marshal," he said.

"Well, damn me," the big smith said. "My name's Jerrod Stockton, and I sure didn't believe you would really be coming. Well, damn me, Marshal, I'm one to say I'm glad you're here."

***

There are two saloons in Preston, Nevada Territory, which by itself is remarkable since Preston is part of the old Mormon holdings in the west. This was called Utah Territory just a year or so ago, and it extended from Colorado on the east to California on the west, and the majority of its communities were peopled by Mormon immigrants, so a little village in a beautiful valley with two operating saloons is to be considered rare. Those that run the church told their people to give up their holdings and come back home when this area became Nevada Territory.

When silver was discovered in the western mountains, Nevada Territory was broken off, but many of the Mormons chose to remain, but for most, their church makes the laws and rules. In territorial days, the church was the state.

The "Bucket of Good Hope" was the name of a saloon that referred to the splendid water in the Good Hope River, which the owners used to make their beer and to water down their whiskey. They had a long oaken plank bar, shined and clean, but showing enough wear that one knew this was a busy saloon, exemplary back bar, reportedly brought to the territory from California after being shipped on a three-master from Boston. The bartenders and dealers wear brocade vests with string ties, and the dancing girls wear as little as the sheriff will allow. The Bucket of Good Hope might be considered an upper class saloon.

Often saloons are rated one-bit or two-bit emporiums of vice, the bit coming from Spanish pieces of eight. One piece of eight is twelve and a half cents, so a one-bit saloon sells its cigars for twelve and a half cents, while a two-bit saloon gets the full twenty five cents. The Bucket of Good Hope Saloon is proud to call itself a two-bit saloon.

"I wonder who that might be, riding into town alone." Preston Miller owns the Preston Bank, and lets everyone know that the town was named for his grandfather on his mother's side, one George Preston. Miller watched as Marshal Chance rode up to the livery stable. "Looks like a drifter of some kind."

Preston Miller is a determined man, determined to be the richest in the territory, even more wealthy than the mine owners up north. "Laws and rules were made for the meek," he remembers his grandfather telling him when he came west to join him. Now, this place called Golden Valley is his, this town called Preston is his. Preston Miller doesn't understand that the new federal law called the Homestead Act of 1862 might slow down his ambitions.

Miller is standing on the porch of the Bucket of Good Hope Saloon, talking with Colonel George Dickson, saloon owner. "He's got a big revolver under that serape and there's a rifle hanging on his saddle. Might be a hired gun coming in because of all that trouble with that Jackson woman." Dickson snarled the comment, his eyes narrowed in anger.

Dickson got his rank from riding with a California regiment in the early 1850s, just after statehood for those in the gold state, and fought Indians, Mexicans, and some that owned Spanish land grants. He likes to be called Colonel George, and is known as one fine specimen of that breed known as skinflint.

"Sarah Jackson. Humph. Had to bring up her name didn't you. You know that I own the mortgage to that property, and that I did what had to be done." Miller opened his bank, with Grandpa's help, after settlers started arriving in Golden Valley, after the village of Preston became one. His grandfather had staked claims on many pieces of the finest property in the valley. Land law was vague in the Mormon territory, the leaders in Salt Lake City preferring the land be claimed and staked.

Old man Preston took what he wanted and if somebody complained, they better have a bigger gun and be faster. None were, and young Preston Miller was a fast learner. "This valley is mine and that's the way it is, Dickson, and you know it. We have done well here, and no damned woman is going to take this from us."

This country called Nevada Territory was owned by Mexico even though that country had never come north and settled the vast deserts and ranges. The Indians in the area were Paiute, Shoshone, and Washoe, and in the area of

Golden Valley were primarily Western Shoshone. Old man Preston and young Preston Miller simply staked the land they wanted and to hell with anyone that might dispute them.

The federal government now has other plans, offering quarter sections of land, beginning in 1862, to those that would develop farms and ranches and "prove the land" valuable enough to sustain a family. If they remained on the land, made it produce for their living, in five years they were given the deed to the property.

"Let's go have a drink, Colonel. I don't like what I just saw."

***

Some of the ranches in the valley have come about because Preston Miller would sell portions of his claims, giving the new owner easy access to a bank loan, and the size limits were what the individual felt he could maintain. For instance, Ben Stokes ranches about two full sections, while Clarence Toby holds a quarter section. A section of land is one square mile, six hundred forty acres. A quarter section then is one hundred sixty acres. Banker Miller holds the mortgages on the Stokes and Toby ranches.

Some that picked up some land, cheap by most standards, found they couldn't make the mortgage payments, and banker Miller has sold some properties two or three times, having to foreclose when payments were late. Some of the foreclosures, which of course, made him a rich man, were more than questionable. Some of the means used to foreclose were criminal, Marshal Chance would find out soon.

Sarah Jackson on the other hand, is homesteading her quarter section by way of a homestead grant from the government. She has paperwork from a federal office in San Francisco, with the federal seal attached, showing that she will own this land after five years of continuous presence, thus proving the homestead. She has been in the

16

valley about one year. Miller says the government doesn't have the right to give away what he is claiming as his, and has thrown Jackson and her daughter off the property, with the help of the sheriff and a couple of men to back him up.

Preston Miller uses people, uses their money, offers very little unless it favors him or one of his projects. Many of the men in his employ are lazy drifters, needing whiskey or a dollar or two. Among them is Clarence Toby, and big Jim Stokes. Toby has been accused of stealing more than once, and carries the nickname Raccoon because of it. Like young Stokes, he has a bad temper, can be mean to animals, and has few friends. He works at being Miller's bad dog to help pay his mortgage.

Miller and Dickson, almost opposites, are standing at the bar, two large flagons of chilled brew before them. Dickson stands tall, carrying his weight with an ease that comes from one in good physical shape, always with that military carriage, full head of wavy chestnut hair, hanging long across his shoulders, a full walrus moustache drooping in every beer he drinks, and packing a revolver on his hip and a single shot Derringer in a vest pocket. Miller has spent the greatest portion of his life indoors, at a desk, manipulating numbers, making deals, doing what is necessary to avoid physical exertion. Rotund is a good descriptive word for the banking gentleman.

"New batch, Preston. Tastes good. That river is just sweet, isn't it?" There were several barrels of the new batch brewing, and Colonel George wanted to get the word out that it was ready. Several of the ranches would be paying their hired hands this week, so he had good reason to get this batch ready for consumption.

"You don't really think that Jackson woman would hire a gunslinger, do you Colonel? That would certainly be bad for Golden Valley." Beer wasn't Miller's choice, straight whiskey is more to his liking, but he gave it a go. "Yes, you're right, this is good. I'll make sure to spread the

17

word." He watched as Dickson downed half his pint, wiped a big paw across the moustache, and continued. "It wouldn't be right if she did hire someone. Sheriff Sample has to be told about this right away. I don't like it, I tell you, I don't like this at all."

"I wouldn't worry about it too much, Pres. With the Stokes outfit and Clarence Toby to help, the sheriff will have plenty of back up. What would one lone gunman do against the whole valley?" He smiled at his little joke, and quaffed the last of the fresh brew. "Gotta get back to work. Go see the sheriff, and don't put too much worry on this. You did the right thing throwing that woman off your property. She never paid you a dime.

"Don't forget to pay for that beer." And he walked up the long circular staircase to his office.

Banker Miller went straight to the sheriff's office, muttering to himself about gunslingers and saloon keepers. "Sample," he said stomping into the office. "Some man just rode into town, and I think he might be a hired gun, hired by that Jackson woman, and I want you to check him out right away. We can't have gunmen running around this town." Peter Sample was in his late fifties, out of shape, drank rot gut whiskey at Preston's other bar, the Crystal, and was sheriff in name only.

"Ain't no law against riding into town, Mr. Miller. No, sir, we have people riding in and out of town all the time."

"I hired you to keep the peace, Sample. Now, do your duty and check out this stranger." Miller had indeed hired Sample, there was no election, and in fact, no one else in town wanted the job. Sample gets twenty dollars a month and a room behind the jail, and does the banker's will. Miller stomped out as he stomped in, slamming the door on his way and Sample slowly stood up from behind his desk and sauntered out onto the street for a look at this stranger.

"Ain't no hired guns would come to Preston," he

muttered, "besides, what would I do about it?" He turned to the café instead, and had himself a plate of meat and gravy for midday meal.

Chapter Two

Chance walked to the hotel and checked himself in, putting his gear in the little room at the top of the stairs and found the Bucket of Good Hope Saloon, just a few long steps from the hotel, for that cold beer. Jarrod Stockton saddled his old mule and went for a ride into the valley to find Sarah Jackson.

Stockton gave much thought to things outside his livery stable, is what one would call aware of everything going on around him, and the treatment of Sarah Jackson and some of the other land owners in the valley, along with the business community in Preston, has the large man in a turmoil. There are many that don't cotton to the concept of giving the other guy an equal chance, and if Jerrod Stockton had ever taken the time to think about such a thing, he would not agree.

He was born into the blacksmith trade, studied under his father and grandfather and probably would have had a grand business in a large community. In answer to a question from a friend back east, he said, "The draw of the west, maybe not the lure of gold and silver, but of creating an entire new society in the wilds, and bringing my knowledge of iron and steel and animals to grow that society, that was the lure. And, the way Preston was described, this new town in a lush valley, open my own business with a very sweet deal from the bank, excellent mortgage rates and all, I jumped at the chance.

"Now, I find out that it is possible that the banker and his constant companion, Colonel George Dickson might have some kind of criminal activity goin on. The way that banker is treating Sarah Jackson is just wrong.

"I work hard for what I have, and if some slimy bastard like Preston Miller thinks he has the right to take it away, I'll fight him all the way. That's what makes me so angry about Sarah. Damn it, she has done everything the right way, by the book, according to the law, and Miller shouldn't be able to throw her off what is rightfully hers."

Over the last few years Stockton has found himself at odds with the banker, mostly because of falling behind in his lease payments. No one in Preston is buying their property, they lease the land. Not so the ranchers. Then, according to the contracts, the Preston Bank builds the building that sits on the land, and that cost is added to the lease payments. The business itself is owned, but nothing else is. That, of course isn't the way things were described when Stockton put his name on the dotted line, when most in town put their names on the line.

Stockton is nearing forty, reads a lot, seldom drinks in one of the saloons, but usually has a keg of something in the livery, just for sippin', he'll tell you, and keeps a clean and orderly set of rooms toward the west side of the stables. "Wind blows down this valley from the west, you know," he enjoys telling anyone that will listen. "Keeps the barn smells goin' t'other way." His family moved into Kentucky back in the early 1700s, and he is the first to leave in all that time.

"My papa was one of the best men I've known for working with iron and he taught me from the time I was able to stoke a fire, and his pa taught him. I've still got the first knife I ever made, and it still holds a fine edge. Need a knife, an ax, a set of shoes for your animal? You just come see me," is the way a circular read that he distributed when he set up in business in Preston several years ago.

The iron business has been good, with ranchers needing equipment fixed, specialty items manufactured, and animals taken care of, but lately, with the banker becoming a feudal lord, it has been slacking off. He told Hank Adams that many businesses in Preston aren't getting needed work done because they don't know if their leases will be good or if they will be foreclosed on.

"I'm telling you, Jerrod," Mr. Waggoner, the

mason, was saying. "That Jackson woman has stirred up a hornet's nest, and we're gonna pay for it. I know, I know, Miller is a crook, but he holds our lives in those damn mortgage papers of his.

"Look at you. If he foreclosed on any one of us, do you have enough money to pack up and head for another place? I know I don't." Stockton knew he was right, but he also felt that Sarah Jackson was right, that the banker didn't have the right to throw her off land the government said she owned.

Jackson and her ten-year-old daughter, Georgia, were camped in a little draw that empties into the river, about ten miles out of town. Stockton and his mule were tired and thirsty when they arrived.

"Hi, Miss Sarah. I think I have some good news for you. A U.S. Marshal rode into Preston this morning. Maybe you'll be able to get your ranch back." He walked the mule over to a spring fed pool, knelt down and cupped up a drink for himself, and continued talking to Sarah Jackson.

"He looks like he's about as tough as they come, and said he rode all the way down here from Mormon Station. I guess that letter of yours is getting looked at somewhere."

Sarah felt her knees go weak, wobble about some at the news. "Oh, my," was all she was able to get out. Her mind was spinning, and she called to Georgia. "Honey, come here. Oh, my." She picked the girl up and hugged her, spilling kisses all over the little one's face and head. "Oh, my," she said again, trying to get her thoughts put together. She and the girl had moved to what she called the J bar D ranch two years ago after losing her husband in a terrible accident at their farm in Georgia.

Seems James Jackson was working some cotton, beans, and tobacco on about one hundred acres when some men came to conscript him into the rebel army. Jackson said that he wouldn't fight for something like slavery, and besides, he had a wife and young child. One of the army men slapped him across the side of the head, he fell back from the blow, scared the hell out of his mule, which in turn kicked him in the head. He died two days later from the concussion. His farm was taken, and Sarah and little Georgia were turned out.

"Those were horrible days, Jerrod. I've never been so frightened. They allowed that I could have one small buggy, the mule that killed James, and some of our clothing. Those were the meanest men I've ever met, that is until I met Mr. Miller.

"Oh, Jerrod. Me and Georgia have lost two homes in just four years. We came here and homesteaded our little farm, and it's been so good to us. We don't have to buy hardly anything. We can grow all our own food, raise our own meat and milk and eggs. Oh, Jerrod, do you think I might get my farm back?" Tears were falling and one couldn't tell if they were from joy, or maybe sorrow. She was holding Georgia so tight the girl was trying to squirm free.

In the year that Sarah had lived on the homestead she had put up a cabin, fenced some property for goats and sheep, ran a small herd of about twenty five breeding cows, and had three sow pigs. There were many in the valley that came to her for butter and cheese, and for pork products. Not too many people wanted to raise pigs.

"I've got my milk cow with us, but I'm afraid for the rest of the cows and those steers that were almost ready for market. That was going to be my cash money for the year, Jerrod. And, what about my hogs, Jerrod? What's going to happen to everything we've worked so hard for? Will this marshal really help?" She was crying, part from fear, part from thinking she might finally get some help, and realized that she was also babbling from the wonderful thought that she might get her ranch back.

"If looks mean anything, Sarah, I would sure think

23

so. He looks like the kind of man gets done what needs to be done. I've never asked, but why did you name your ranch the J bar D? I remember putting your branding irons together, but never did ask about the name."

"Oh, that's simple. Jackson and Daughter. James and I named her Georgia because we really loved that state, up till the end, that is, but we did talk about the west and having a ranch. We always played with the name we would call it, so when I ended up here, Georgia and I, alone, I named it for the two of us."

Those first few months were more than just difficult. There were no buildings and Sarah and her daughter lived in a tent and lean-to complex that she put together. "Do you remember helping me build that first cabin? I wasn't very strong back then, was I?"

"Maybe not like now, but you were good help, Sarah. We had lots of trees, good wood to work with, and that cabin grew into a nice home for you two."

"Yes, it did. Old Ben Stokes came over to help a few times, but that boy of his never offered a minute's help. Neither did old Toby. You and Cotton Phelps were life savers. I guess I've never taken the time to really thank you. We wouldn't have made it without your help, Jerrod. Wouldn't have made it. And, now, just maybe, we might get that old place back."

"Miller hired Cotton to run your place for him. Jimmy Stokes wanted the job, but Miller gave it to Cotton. At least you know it's being run right." The two were sitting on chairs in front of the tent Sarah and Georgia were living in. Jerrod Stockton has never been married, never even given much thought to the idea, and even during the first couple of years when Sarah first arrived, spending lots of time alone with the woman, the idea of romance never entered his mind.

"I always thought you and Cotton Phelps would end up being a couple, Sarah. He'd be the man to take care of you and Georgia."

"Yes, I think you're right, he will make some woman a fine husband, but not me. I don't think I'll ever get married again, Jerrod. James Jackson was my husband, died too young, but I still love him. I'm still married, Jerrod. Does that make sense?"

"You're a fine woman, Sarah. I'm heading back to town and with your permission I'll tell the marshal where to find you. I know he will want to talk with you as soon as possible."

"That will be fine, Jerrod. Would it be better if I came to town to meet him?"

"No, I don't think so. Let's let him make that decision. Anyway, back to my forge, and as always, it's been really nice to see you and Georgia. Do you need anything that either the marshal or I could bring with us?"

"No, we're fine. Cotton sneaks over with things when he can, and we did get most of our stuff out before Miller forced us to leave. Tell that marshal just how bad it has been. Please."

Stockton promised, stepped onto his mule, waved goodbye, threw a kiss to Georgia, and headed back to Preston. The ride back gave the big man time to think, to put what was happening in some of kind of order. *"She's a fine woman and tough as the nails I hammer out. Lots of iron in her blood, I guess."* He rode on, the mule knowing the way, and certainly not in a hurry.

"I wonder how banker Miller and his sidekick the colonel are going to take it when they find out the government has sent a U.S. Marshal to clean up their mess. There's gonna be a lot of trouble in Preston, I'm afraid." Since Miller and the colonel own just about everything in the valley, trouble will definitely be on the menu. *"There's something bred into a man to make him act so ugly. Daddy always said that a man with too much money or too much time was a dangerous man, and I think Preston Miller is a*

very dangerous man."

All the way back to Preston, Jerrod Stockton could see many of the ranches that have been developed in Golden Valley. Early fall colors are starting to show in the big trees along the river, a little smoke still curling up from a few of the ranch house chimneys, and signs of cattle being moved down from the high country to enjoy the high grass in the valley before being driven to market up north, come spring.

"Those folks up north, with all that mining activity sure do eat good," he was thinking of fat steers coming out of this valley to feed those hungry miners. *"I heard some of them are even driven into Utah, Salt Lake anyway, and maybe even Wyoming. This valley always reminded me of parts of the Ohio Valley, with high thick grass, clear sweet water, and enough winter snow to make everything work. It would be more than just a crime if all this is lost."*

On the trip back to town, Stockton never once looked at the trail, he was too busy enjoying the sights of that valley. *"Good thing Kitty knows the way,"* he thought as they approached the town. Coming into Preston from the north, it's Stockton's livery stables that are the first signs of the town, and he can't help smiling to himself every time he sees it.

***

Chance stood at the long bar in the Bucket of Good Hope enjoying the first cold beer he'd had in two weeks. "This is good stuff, barkeep. Good stuff."

"We don't bring this beer in, mister, we make it right here. The Good Hope River is the sweetest, purest water I've ever had. Glad you like it."

"Been on the trail for quite a spell. This hits the spot." He was looking around the large saloon, saw several card tables and gaming tables, a small stage for entertainment, and of course, a long circular staircase that probably led to rooms where dance hall girls lived and worked. "Quite a spot," he muttered. "Gets pretty busy in the evening, I bet."

If you want to know about a small community, you go to where the community meets and socializes, and in most of the towns in the west, that's the local saloon. A bartender can fill you in on all the events of the day or week, good and bad. "I've heard stories about this place called Golden Valley for years, traveling about the territory, but this is my first time here. I haven't seen good grass like this in a long time. Ranches pretty prosperous, are they?"

"I think that would be fair to say," the bartender said. "Fat cattle driven out of here every year. You looking for work on one of the ranches?"

"I don't know about work," he offered, "but I do want to meet some of the ranchers and see their spreads. This is a beautiful valley." Chance was looking for some names of the larger ranchers, he knew about Sarah Jackson, but none of the others. "I was raised on a dirt farm and never did much care for that kind of work, but raising cattle and horses might be something I could enjoy."

"If you're around here in a couple of hours, some of the ranchers might be dropping in for a cold one or two. Might be able to meet some of them. We don't get too many visitors here in Preston, but the stage from Ione comes through every couple of weeks on its way south. Doesn't sound like the war is going very well."

"Lincoln is right, but it's gonna be a long bloody war. Well, back to ranching, is there any land available for homesteading around here?" Chance wanted to get back on subject as fast as possible.

"That's a bad subject in these parts, mister, bad subject." The bartender tightened up, was looking around to see if anyone was listening. "The bank owns most of the land, staked it from the Utah Territory people years ago. Some have tried to homestead, but it's getting dangerous to do right now." The man was nervous as a cat caught between two big dogs fighting over who would eat him. Chance watched him change his weight back and forth, foot to foot, look around the large bar room, even pick up a glass for the second time to wipe it down.

"Listen, I can't really talk about it. The man what owns this saloon is really good friends with the banker that owns the land, and I could lose my job."

"We wouldn't want that now, for sure. Where can I get a good meal that I don't have to cook over an open fire?" Despite the smile on his face, Chance knew he just learned what the problem is.

Walking across the street to the café, he was worrying this news in his mind. *"Banker stakes out land, then sells mortgages, but did the territory have the right to sell him that land or give him deed to it? And now, along comes the Homestead Act, and mister banker may find himself without a means of support. I wonder if the sheriff knows anything, or if he works for someone other than his office?"*

It was still early for supper, and Chance took the opportunity to walk through the town of Preston. *"This is a nice little town,"* he was thinking, seeing an arms dealer, farm and ranch supplier, clothing stores for men and women, and found himself standing in front of Preston's second saloon, the Crystal Bar. "If their beer is as good as the other place, I might just have to move here," he mumbled sliding through the swinging doors.

"Howdy, don't think I've seen you before," the bartender said, wiping down the bar in front of Chance. There were a couple of grizzled old guys at the other end of the bar that took notice of Chance's arrival too. It was obvious to the marshal that not too many strangers make their way to Preston, Nevada Territory.

"Nope, you haven't. Just got in town this afternoon. Nice town from the looks of it. How about a cool beer after my thirsty ride." Skirting around subjects can often get people to talk, and bartenders usually know more than anyone in town about what is going on. "Mostly cattle ranching around here?"

"Cattle, some sheep, some farming. We eat well here," the bartender joked, patting his own oversize belly. "We've lost quite a few of the young men to the war, though, and then that fool banker seems to think he owns the whole Golden Valley." The barkeep caught himself and decided not to go further into the subject.

"I heard something about that when I got into town. Something about some woman not being able to homestead some property. Something like that can get pretty nasty pretty quick." Chance didn't want to scare the bartender off, but did want a little more information if he could get it. "What's this banker like? Pretty mean, is he?"

"That's not half the word for it, mister. Threw Sarah Jackson and her pretty little daughter right off their homestead. Wouldn't do it himself, mind you, he had a couple of his "boys" and the sheriff do the bad stuff. Yeah, he's mean," and he aimed a good wad of tobacco juice at a cuspidor behind the bar.

One of the hangers-on at the end of the bar tried to choke back a laugh. "He ain't mean, he's a rotten, filthy bastard is what he is. Miss Jackson is the nicest lady in the valley, and that son of a bitch forced her off her own place. I know, cuz I helped her get her stuff together. Mean? Hell, he's the devil."

"You were there?" Chance asked. "I heard the sheriff and two men rode her right off her property." Chance got the opening he was looking for and dove right in.

"I do a lot of little things for some of the ranchers around the valley. All stove up from working too many cattle on those Texas trails to do any hard work anymore, but I can still be a good hand when needed. I helped Sarah move some of her stuff, and her hired hand, Cotton Phelps helped get some stuff out for her also. That fool banker then put a knife in Mrs. Jackson by hiring Phelps to run her ranch. That's really ugly."

Chance decided that this saloon, the Crystal would be a better place for him to break the news of who he is. Good beer, people who know what's going on, he was thinking the Crystal would be a good headquarters.

"Gentlemen, I want you to understand something," and he flung back the serape. At first, the bartender and the two old men only saw a large revolver on the man's hip, then the badge came into full view. "My name is Jacob Chance, U.S. Marshal, and I'm here to see what can be done about all this property rights problem. I might need to ask you some questions about what has been going on around here, but I'll do my best not to get you in harm's way."

"Look at that," one of the old guys said, pointing. "A real Marshal. Mister, I'm sure glad to see you. You got here just in time, 'cuz what I hear is, old banker Miller is looking to have the sheriff throw somebody else off their property." He looked over at his compadre, saying, "I've never even seen a marshal before. Look at that."

"What's your name, barkeep?"

"Bidwell, Marshal. They call me Tiny around here," and he laughed out loud, again patting that ample girth.

"Good to meet you, Tiny. I'm taking possession of that table right over there," Chance said, moving his beer over to one of the tables, but near the bar. "I love a comfortable old saloon with friendly people enjoying themselves." He looked at the old guys at the end of the bar. "You boys join me for a cold one?"

The two old guys spent the next several hours drinking cold beer and telling each other stories they had heard about marshals and gun fights and bad men, the same any two old men would do spending a quiet afternoon in their favorite saloon.

***

Ben Stokes lives with his son James and daughter Jennifer on a large cattle ranch that spreads across the valley, and up into the foothills of the nearby White Mountains that border California and Nevada Territory. Stokes bought his land from Preston Miller, and now, with the controversy surrounding the efforts of the government to give away land, he isn't sure that his land owner status is clear. He and his children, nineteen year old Jennifer and twenty two year old James, are sitting under a large cottonwood tree in front of the generous ranch house they share.

"Just look at that bunkhouse. When we started here, it was just us, and living there, and now, we have five men working our range, a full time wrangler, and a cook. Makes me proud to see that." Stokes was a large man, well-educated but with a quick temper when crossed. He knew that, and was always aware that he could be dangerous if he let his temper get away from him.

Grasses and shrubs extend all around the house, with barns and corrals off several hundred feet. Along with the cattle, Stokes breeds horses and has some of the finest ranch stock in the area. They raise a small flock of sheep, "never more than two hundred ewes," Stokes likes to say, always with a hearty laugh. He has two men and three dogs on the sheep flock, five men work the cattle, and two, sometimes three, working with the horses. "This is a pretty fair size little operation now," he said, enjoying this time with his all but grown children.

Stokes made most of their furniture, and outside lawn chairs are spaced around the shaded areas. He was a splendid carpenter and cabinet maker in St. Louis when his wife ran away with a local gambler and he pulled up stakes, packed his kids and most of their belongings in an old delivery wagon, hitched a team of mules and headed west.

He hasn't looked back one time, he likes to tell people.

Joining a wagon train out of St. Louis was a rather simple thing in the 1850s, and the trip across the plains, a long hard journey at best, was complicated even more because of Indian problems. Territorial claims by the government, individual claims by people simply taking land, and the army trying to defend things that weren't always defensible, made the trip difficult and dangerous.

"You kids were pretty young when we stumbled into this valley, finding deep grass, and trying to get a homestead started. Preston Miller, what a syrup voiced criminal that man is, had me fully convinced that he owned this property and would be willing to sell me a large portion. The mortgage was simple, to the point, and affordable. I believed that fool, and now, the question is, do we own what we bought?"

From the moment Sarah Jackson was thrown off her property and it became known to everyone that she had documents from the government showing that she was the owner of that land, the question in all the ranchers' minds was, "do I really own this?" since they bought it from Miller, not the government. Some sided with Miller, some dead set ready to kill the man, and most simply in a quandary over the question.

The west is populated with men like Ben Stokes, honest, literate, strong, and willing to do what's necessary to get the job done. He cut and split the wood, dug the post holes, built his post and beam home, post and beam barns, and everything else on the property. Men in Preston look up to Stokes, knowing he is honest, his word is law, and he's fair in his dealings with others. Some are aware of his quick temper. Some tolerate his son James, others wish him gone from the town.

"They was talk around Preston today that a hired gunman is in town, and is going to force Mr. Miller to give that Jackson woman back her ranch. That ain't right, Pa."

"Well, we don't know about that, Jimmy. That banker is a wily old guy, and he's saying that he owns all this land by way of the Mormons when this was Utah Territory, so I'm really not too sure of our own position." Stokes is a large man, probably close to fifty, if he ever stopped to think about it, and one who is well read. He has always believed in the value of law and rules by which to live, and this question of land law is a big worry getting bigger. Much of his education came from his love of books, and the old house in St. Louis was filled with them. Many came west with him, and he can be found most evenings, settled in a large chair with at least one book at hand.

If he hadn't taken to ranching, raising cattle and horses, as well as he did, he probably would have become one of those itinerant lawyers that spread the word of the law through the wild lands of the west.

His son James, on the other hand, also has a fiery temper, spends many hours a week in the Bucket of Good Hope, sitting at a card table or standing at the bar. "Hell, Pa, Mr. Miller says that he has all the deeds from Utah Territory officials, and they are legal. You been paying him for this land ever since Jenny and I were little kids. This is ours, and ain't no gunman gonna take it from me." Not much in the way of a thinking man, James is ready to ride with Miller because Miller has been paying him to do some odd jobs around that need a man with a bad temper and a quick hand at the holster. Ben Stokes is not aware of this.

"I know you like to say that this ranch is ours, and we've worked it that way for many years, but you also know, Jim, that you haven't turned a hand around here in a long time. Jennifer has been overseeing the hands and herds, making sure this place is in running order. If you spent less time in town at that saloon and more time out here in the saddle you'd have more of a right to call this ranch part yours." Stokes was angry that his son simply wasn't ready to work the place, to take his rightful place as the oldest child and operate the Stokes Ranch.

"Besides that, how on earth would one man with a gun take on the whole Golden Valley? You don't think, son. Miller is a devil of a man, we know he would steal from his own mother if he could, but it's the law that counts, and no single man with a gun can change that. You're too much like your mother, I'm afraid. If it's booze and gambling that you want, you're welcome to it, but if you do, don't call this your ranch." Ben Stokes' temper was starting to come to the surface.

Young Stokes jumped out of his chair, stomped around the yard, his temper at full throttle, and spat out some angry words at his father. At the end of his tirade, he said something that caught his father by surprise. "Mr. Miller wants me to go to work for him and help him with his land holdings. He has the deeds, he owns the land, and no one is going to change that."

"The point isn't whether or not Miller has deeds from Utah, the point is, did Utah have the right to give or sell him this land? I tried to teach you and Jenny, but I'm probably not a very good school marm," he said with a soft laugh, relieving the tension of the moment.

"If you had read any of those books I gave you, you would know some of how the law works. Federal law takes precedence over territorial or state law, and Miller might not actually own this land he's been selling." He had tried to get James to read, Jennifer always did, loved reading, has had books sent from San Francisco and New York, but the heaviest reading James did was on the backs of cards late at night in Preston. The old man was getting his temper under control, was doing his best to keep his only son from harm.

"I think you need to spend more time on the ranch, James. We have cattle to move into the lower pastures, we have irrigation ditches that need cleaning, and there's always those fences that get broken down. I need your help.

Old Sam Dawson is a good hand, knows his horses and cattle, but is too old to do some of the work. There's more to owning a ranch like this than having enough men to run the cattle. There's lots of work that we have to do." Stokes has spent years trying to teach the boy, and the boy isn't interested. He likes to say he owns a big spread, he just doesn't want to do any of the work.

"I ain't no rancher, pa, and you know it. I hate this place. Mr. Miller wants me to go to work for him, and I think I will." The boy never did do a full day's effort in his growing up years, and Stokes was always a bit soft on him. "I'm gonna take a place in town, work some in the saloon, and do work for Mr. Miller."

"That's a big mistake, son, but you have to do what you think is best. This ranch, your sister and I, need you here. There's trouble brewing, James, what might be big trouble, and you'll be needed here. Give it up to live in town, you're giving up more than you can imagine."

The boy was gone the next morning and Stokes knew he wouldn't ever get him back. "Jennifer, it's just you and me, now. Sam and I can handle most of the work around here, but we need at least two more hands and soon. We've got cattle scattered all over those mountains out there, and they need to be brought down before the snow starts. That large herd of young horses have to be brought in and worked some before the snow flies, and we've got sheep everywhere." He was laughing through his anger and loss, doing his best to keep his spirits up, and Jenny's too.

"I want you to check with Cotton Phelps and maybe Hank Adams and see if there are any able buckaroos around. Those five we have are good, but we need some more. It's gonna be tough, girl, but we've been tough before." She's just as beautiful as her mother, he was thinking, but a lot different personality. He's known for several years that James is more his mother's son and Jennifer her father's daughter. "Jenny, you're too young to remember, but we had a good life back in St. Louis, but, even as hard as it is out here, our life is much better. We're gonna be hard pressed to protect what we have."

He settled back in his large chair, a cup of coffee at hand. "That damn war back east is sure having an affect around here. We never had problems lining up crews to work the cattle and the place, and now, most of the young ones are off at war. Be glad when that mess gets cleared up." He got mail from time to time from some of his friends back in Missouri telling him of how the war was going, how almost everyone he knew had lost either a relative or property. "The war is taking property from folks back east, and this fool banker takes it out west."

He took another long drought of cooled off coffee, saying, "Sometimes, Jenny, I don't think I understand a single thing that goes on in this world."

"What you were saying earlier, pa, about Mr. Miller and the Utah Territory. Do you think he was right in claiming all that land and then selling off most of it?"

"I'm afraid that's the biggest question, honey. The heart of this is how the law, even maybe which law, is interpreted. Miller is slimy, we've talked about that before, and I don't really know whether he can prove he has those deeds. Up until this became Nevada Territory, you remember I'm sure, Miller supported the Mormon leaders fully, and may have been dealing double aces all along.

"This whole thing could bring big changes in this valley. I don't think your brother is making the right decision here, but it is his to make. Well, see if you can find Cotton or Hank, and see about getting at least two, three would be better, hands for this roundup."

Jennifer Stokes was a pure horse woman, could train the orneriest colt or filly, had the patience to finish every project, and knew she would be leading a crew of buckaroos into the mountains within the next few weeks. "Old Sam is good with the chuck wagon, and dad can chouse out an old steer from any bramble patch, but I'm gonna boss this roundup." She had a grand smile as she rode off to find Cotton Phelps. She was also thinking how nice it would be to be in the mountains for a week or two. *"I sure would like to get to know Hank Adams a lot better than I do,"* she was thinking. *"That man is a born leader."*

* * *

Young James Stokes had a room on the second floor of the Bucket of Good Hope Saloon, was setting up to deal stud at one of the four tables, and giving Millie, one of the dancehall girls the big eye. She wasn't falling for it.

"So, the rancher's son becomes just a card dealer. Big Jim Stokes leaves cowboying for card dealin'. Daddy must be awful proud." Stokes glared at the beautiful woman standing before him, proving how hateful she could be. He stood up from the empty table and strode to the bar.

"Gimme a beer. Seen Miller around this morning?"

"Nope, and if you're on the clock you ain't supposed to be drinkin'." The bartender knew better than to break one of the Colonel's most enforced rules. "You know Col. George doesn't allow that."

"Just give me the damn beer and mind your own business." He flung a coin onto the bar, glaring first at the bartender, then at the girl who seemed to be laughing in his face. Big Jim Stokes, with that quick temper, was big enough to put fear in many a man, and wasn't ready for what seemed to be happening. The difference between James and his father was also obvious in times like this. His father was able to think, able to work out a problem. James simply reacted, never thinking.

Banker Miller, Stokes was remembering, had promised him lots of work, keeping his properties operational, forcing families from their property when needed, and using his strength and brawn to help keep order. All he's done is deal cards as the lowest of the hired hands.

He was hoping he would get close to pretty Millie, but that might not be in the cards either. He downed the beer in one swallow and stormed out of the saloon, headed for Miller's bank. "I'll show them, all of them. They think I care about the Stokes Ranch, but I don't give a damn about it, never have." The anger came from not ever being in charge while all the while he knew, deep down, he was the man that should be in charge.

"That Miller, putting Cotton Phelps in charge of the Jackson property, when he knows I have far more ability. And pop, wanting me to take orders from Jenny, knowing I know more about that ranch than she ever will." He was angry, hurt by what the Dickson woman had said, as upset at banker Miller as at his father, and that fool bartender questioning whether or not he could have a beer. "They just better be careful how they treat me around here. They better be careful." He was kicking dust with every step as he crossed the main street, heading toward the bank and a meeting with his new boss, Preston Miller.

Chapter Three

Chance roused himself out of a deep sleep, first in a bed in many days, and splashed water on his face from the bowl on the table. It wasn't common knowledge yet that he was a marshal and in town to make some changes. He had a good day, yesterday, met some of the right people, and got names of those who he needed to meet. He picked up his horse and rode out of town as the sun made its way into the sky. "I sure do understand why someone wants to live in this valley," he muttered, putting the stud into a long legged lope that ate miles in quick time.

Grass was high and thick in the pastures, dotted here and there with large leafy trees giving hints of the coming fall, and visions from many years ago melded into the picture. He remembered running through high grass as a boy on Pappy's farm, climbing trees, shooting squirrels and rabbits, not having a care in the world. His baby sister learned how to climb a tree, became a better shot with the old twenty-two than he was, but could never run as fast.

"Listen to me, Mr. Morgan," he said as they rode along, "don't let me get too far into this little dream of mine. We have a job to do, first, so give me a kick in the ass if I drift off here." The miles brought real-time visions of well-run ranches, and the thoughts, and maybe even dreams of what might be, streamed through the morning hours. The Good Hope River flowed consistently, fed often by little streams coming down from the mountains to the west.

Following the Good Hope River, Chance passed several small ranches, and as he got deeper into the heart of the valley, the ranches got larger. "That must be the Stokes Ranch," he said, pulling his horse to a halt under a sprawling cottonwood tree. He was looking at a big home, spread out the western way instead of stacked the eastern way. There were neat pastures, wide corrals, and a good-

39

sized barn. He put the horse into a walk and headed for the ranch house, across a broad pasture, deep in grass.

"All these years I've been a lawman, and right now I'd just about give it up to have a place like this." Visions of his boyhood on the farm were playing through his memory, and even though he knew he could never be a farmer, he could remember the smells, the open vistas. "Those mountains just go higher and higher, each range a bit taller, and there's snow on the peaks already. The trees smell good, the grass smells good, the river smells good. Damn me, but I could be a happy man living in this valley." He had a wide smile when he brought Mr. Morgan to the front of the Stokes' home.

"Yes," the big man said, "I'm Ben Stokes. What can I do for you, stranger?" Stokes had seen the marshal coming across a meadow on the way to the house and walked out on the covered veranda to greet him. "If you're looking to hire on, you'll have to talk to my daughter, Jennifer. She's on the other side of the barn there," and he pointed at the large structure.

"No, actually, sir, I wanted to talk to you." Chance stepped off his stud and tied it to a hitching rack in front of the porch. "My name's Chance, Jacob Chance," and he slipped the serape over his shoulder, "Deputy U.S. Marshal. Can we talk?"

"U.S. Marshal, eh? Well I'll be damned. Yes, come in," and he held the door open for him. "Have a new pot of coffee boiling. Get you a cup?"

Chance took his hat off coming into the ranch house, tousled his hair a bit, and said a cup of coffee would be fine. "I haven't seen furniture like this in a long time, Mr. Stokes. I was raised in Missouri and many of the old time farms were fit out like this. Very nice indeed."

"I was a cabinet maker and furniture maker in St. Louis, Marshal. You have a good eye, sir." The two men settled into comfortable chairs in front of a fire, cups of hot

40

coffee in hand. "Are you here for a specific reason?" Straight to the point was the way Ben Stokes liked to do business, and this suited Chance fine as well.

"Actually two reasons, Mr. Stokes. First, there seems to be a problem with property rights here in the valley, and the U.S. Attorney in San Francisco has asked me to settle the problem. The new Homestead Act of 1862 is pretty straight forward, but at least one person in Golden Valley seems to be having a problem keeping her homestead. Secondly, there seem to be questions about the sale of land and the claiming of land dating back to when this was Utah Territory."

Stokes sat forward in his chair. "I've been worried about my own position here ever since we heard about the homestead law." He took a long draught of coffee, settled back in his chair, and looked at Chance. "How much have you heard, Marshal?"

"In some cases I think I've heard a lot, and riding out here this morning, I don't think I've heard enough." Jacob Chance with a slightly ironic grin and crinkled eyes, continued, "I believe that a Preston Miller owns the bank in town, that many years ago, when this was Utah Territory he either purchased or claimed most of the land in the valley, and that he has been selling off large tracts, with his bank holding the mortgages. Am I correct in this?"

"That's pretty much it, but missing many details. Many of us that bought land from Miller are now questioning whether he actually had title to that land. Did he have the right to sell it to us? I've been paying for two sections of very good ranch land for many years now, have invested my life in it, and must testify that I'm worried."

The two men spent the next several hours discussing what had been happening in Golden Valley over the years, including the many foreclosures, the rough treatment of people who argued with the bank, and in particular, Sarah Jackson being literally thrown off a piece of land the government had given her.

"From what I understand, Marshal, Miller says he owns the land that Miss Jackson homesteaded. She has built a fine ranch, sir, with good stock, good soil, even a fine, if rather small, home for her and her daughter. She has not been treated well at all, but no one seems to know whether she had the right to move onto her one hundred sixty acres."

"Well," and Chance almost drawled out the answer, as if he was back in Missouri, "according to the U.S. Attorney, she sure does own it, and according to Utah and Nevada Territorial authorities, Miller surely doesn't. Looks like a pretty good mess for me to try and clear up."

Both men watched as two riders came up to the front porch. "That's my daughter, Jennifer, and the man with her is Cotton Phelps. He was Sarah Jackson's ranch foreman before she was evicted, and is now running the place for the bank." The two got up and walked toward the front door of the ranch house as Jennifer and Phelps came onto the porch.

"Hello, Cotton. Hi, Honey," Stokes said walking onto the veranda, "I have someone here you're going to enjoy meeting. Come in, come in." The group moved back inside the house and gathered at a large table in the kitchen. Chance couldn't help letting his eyes roam all about one Jennifer Stokes.

Just like back home, he was thinking. *Gather around the cook stove in the kitchen, but I do like what I'm seeing right now. This is about the prettiest young lady I've had the pleasure of looking at in a long time.* He saw a tall woman with a fresh and friendly face, delightful body coupled to long legs. She in turn gave him a full going over, smiled at the big rugged man, not provocatively, but rather by way of a welcome to her home, and helped get everyone settled.

More cups were brought out and the large pot of

coffee, boiling away on the wood stove, was all but emptied. "Cotton Phelps, Jennifer Stokes, may I present U.S. Marshal Jacob Chance. He's here to change our lives," and there was just the hint of irony in his voice as he said that, "and I hope for the better." Jennifer and Phelps took deep breaths at the introduction, and everyone sat down in almost stunned silence.

Chance's silence was brought on by Jennifer Stokes. She stood about five foot eight inches, weighed in at about one hundred thirty pounds, and every pound was where it was supposed to be. He saw bright green eyes, giving him the once over as well, short light brown hair, and most tantalizing, long legs. Jacob Chance, U.S. Marshal was a tongue tied ten-year-old boy.

"I hope you're here to clear up the Sarah Jackson problem," Phelps said. "Miller has been terribly rough on that lady. Others in the valley too, but her in particular."

"That's why I'm here, Mr. Phelps. And, I might need some help if what I'm hearing is true."

The conversation went on for several hours, and finally Chance said he had to get back into Preston. He shook hands with everyone, an especially long shake with Jennifer, and headed back into town. "I'm up against some big time crooks," he said to himself and the Morgan stud as they found their way back to the trail leading into town. "And I'm certainly going to make many visits to this ranch. Mr. Morgan, sir, that is the most charming young lady I've had the pleasure to meet in years." The ride back to town was filled with visions, as the ride out had been, but these involved more grown up thoughts.

He pulled himself together after letting his mind wander through several delightful scenes. *I doubt that Mr. Miller has any deeds to the land that he has claimed. I'll get that letter off to Carson City as soon as possible. I think I'm going to need some help on this one.* It took a couple of hours to get back into town, and his mind worked its way through several possible scenarios before he tucked the stud away at the livery stable.

"Well, Mr. Stockton, according to some of the people I spent time with today, you are one fine upstanding citizen."

"That's good to know, Marshal. Who you with?"

"Rode out to meet Ben Stokes, and he introduced me to his daughter Jennifer and a man named Phelps, Cotton Phelps. They seem like honest people caught in the web of conspiracy around here.

"It seems there are many people with considerable larceny in their heart, are willing to hurt, even maim or kill, in order to make themselves richer or more powerful. Is it a natural part of the human being to hurt someone in order to prosper? I think everyone wants to prosper, to have a little more land, a little more money, maybe even a little more prestige, but most would put a cost to that, and it shouldn't include taking from another person or harming another person."

"You 'bout said a whole book full of truth there, Chance. You're right, though. Old Ben Stokes is as honest a man as there is, and Cotton would tear a mountain to pieces to help Sarah Jackson. There's gonna be a lot of trouble isn't there? People getting hurt, people going to jail. Is that what's gonna happen?"

Chance saw the same expressions he found on faces at the ranch, anticipation of possible life-changing danger. Like Stokes, Stockton had spent years building a wonderful business never thinking that the business was sitting in the middle of a huge land fraud scheme, a scheme that could financially wreck his life.

Chance let Stockton's worries drift through his mind, thinking about previous cases, troubles that didn't always end well, and troubles that did. "Well, hell, maybe that's why I'm a marshal, Stockton. Yeah, there's gonna be trouble, but you can bet I'll figure out who the bad guys are and see to it they are dealt with according to the law.

"This has been a long day and I'm about half starved. I hope that café has big steaks and lots of them," he smiled, finishing the job of putting up his horse. "No steer out there is safe tonight," and he said good night to the smithy.

***

Chance was at the café when Peter Sample, Sheriff, walked in, took a look around, and sauntered up to his table. "Need to talk to you, mister."

"Fine with me, sheriff, sit right on down. Don't mind a bit of talk during supper. What's on your mind?"

"Don't get many strangers coming to Preston. What's your business here?" The sheriff was not looking forward to this conversation, he had never pulled a gun on a man, ever, and was looking into the eyes of a man who seemed to be afraid of nothing. "Preston, this whole Golden Valley, is a peaceful place with hard working, law abiding people. We want to keep it that way."

"Well, Sheriff, you have no worries from my end. It's a little warm in here," Chance said, standing up and slipping out of his serape. The sheriff actually gasped on seeing his badge. Sitting back down, Chance continued. "Nope, you have no worries about me. Now, if someone here is breaking federal laws, that might get me riled up a bit, but then, you being the local lawman, I would expect you to join me in bringing the lawbreaker to justice." He stretched a big hand across the table. "Jacob Chance, U.S. Marshal. Glad to meet you sheriff."

"Well I'll be damned. And here Mr. Miller thought you were a hired gun come to make trouble." Sample sat back in his chair, smiled a bit, reached out and shook Chance's hand. "Glad to meet you Marshal. I feel so much better now. There's gonna be some trouble around here, I've felt it coming, and I'm not the man to stop it. Yes sir, if there's anything I can do to help you, just say the word."

The two men talked all through supper, with Chance eating a big slab of local beef with mashed potatoes and at least half a gallon of gravy, sopped up with warm sour-dough biscuits and the sheriff downing a platter full of pork chops, not so much gravy, and just as many biscuits. "Ten days on the trail, side meat and hard tack, and now just a bit of heaven. Man shouldn't eat like this every day, but it sure does feel good once in a while." He sat back in his chair, lit a cheroot, blew a stream of blue smoke toward the ceiling, and smiled to everyone in the café.

Earlier, he had heard all the voices whispering back and forth as it became known that a U.S. Marshal was actually in the café having supper with the sheriff. Chance heard Sarah's name mentioned, Miller's name often, and from time to time, Dickson's. Just as he had found at the Stokes' ranch and the livery stable, there was almost palpable fear in some of the voices.

It was like that often when he came into the small towns and villages in the territories, but this time, the voices seemed more anxious, as if waiting for some kind of explosion. He said to himself, *And there is going to be one hell of an explosion around here if I'm not mistaken.* He didn't have an after dinner satisfied look on his face as he fingered the cheroot.

His very active mind got the better of him, and he found himself reflecting on life in Missouri many years ago. Long hours in the hot sun, behind a mangy old mule, plowing, cutting, harvesting, and then, supper, under the big oak tree alongside a creek, the table so full it sagged in the middle. He remembered great slabs of meat, bowls of potatoes and vegetables, hot bread straight out of the oven, and pies of every color and taste. He had to force himself to get back on the subject at hand.

"So the problem goes back to when this was Utah Territory. Well, territory or state, it is still the federal law that must be followed. I'm not sure that Utah had the right

46

to give or sell this land to anyone, so I'll have to have a visit with Mr. Miller and take a long look at those deeds of his. We can do that first thing in the morning, Sheriff. How about we have breakfast here, then go over to the bank and visit with Mr. Miller?"

Chance watched as Sample cringed at the thought of meeting with the banker. "Is there a problem with that? Are you afraid of that man?" Chance got right down to the basics with that question. If Sample is even afraid of visiting with the banker, he sure wouldn't be much of a help if things turned ugly in the valley, if guns and knives came into play, or if he had to stand up to many men all at the same time. "You need to be honest with me, Sheriff."

From the day he was appointed sheriff of Golden Valley, Peter Sample had been afraid that this day would come, the day he would have to stand up to Preston Miller and Colonel George. He had been approached by the men several years ago when it became obvious that Miller would have to have some kind of "official" to help him evict people. For years he simply hired one or two of the hangers-on around town to do the dirty work, but with the change from Utah Territory to Nevada Territory, he needed something called an official, and the position of sheriff certainly fit that bill. *The ultimate authority* is how Miller described the appointment.

Sample has been using the same bums that Miller used to do the evicting, but now the job was easier when the man doing the dirty work carried a badge. Questions had been raised when Sample was appointed, many asking why the job wasn't filled by way of an election, but Miller and Dickson simply ignored the issue. It was decided that every business in town would contribute money to build the jail and office, and that a special tax had been put into place, again without benefit of an election.

More than one person had found himself in trouble with Miller's bank for arguing about what was taking place, for just about every business in town owed the bank some kind of loan or mortgage on property. Preston Miller did not take kindly to anyone questioning his actions, and late night visitors with big fists and ax handles changed many minds over the issues.

"I'm going to be as honest with you as possible, Marshal," and he spent the next half hour telling Chance his story. It was a sad tale, one that Chance hadn't anticipated, and now more fully understood the problems people in the valley were facing. "Again," he thought, "powerful people taking advantage of those less powerful, only for personal gain." He settled back in his chair, took a sip of hot coffee, and looked deep into the eyes of the man called sheriff.

"It took a brave man to tell me this, Sample, and that leaves me with some problems as well. This town, this valley, needs law enforcement, and generally that is provided by way of an elected sheriff, not one appointed by someone, so I may have to step in as territorial marshal and take over your position. I need to sleep on this, Sample, so don't say anything to anyone, and let's go ahead and have breakfast in the morning. I'll have made my decision by then." The two men stood and shook hands, and Chance decided to visit the livery stable before calling it a night.

"Evening, Mr. Stockton. Glad to see you're still up. Have time for a cup of coffee or a cold beer?"

"I'm sure glad to see you, Marshal. I spent most of the afternoon and early evening with Sarah Jackson, and then we didn't have much of a chance to talk when you got back from your visit. Yeah, let's have that beer, but at the Crystal, not the Bucket of Good Hope."

"Good, because I spent most of today with Ben Stokes, and just had dinner with Sheriff Sample. May take more than one or two beers to get today all settled, eh smithy," and the laughter was genuine from the two men.

The two found there were many eyes following

them as they walked the two blocks or so to the Crystal Saloon. A couple of men sitting on chairs outside the Bucket were watching intently, and two or three more were seen inside the dry goods store watching them through the windows. "Looks like we're a couple of pretty popular fellows tonight, smithy."

"Those two on the porch there are hired thugs working for Colonel George, and the men inside the emporium work for Miller. I've had run ins with all of them." Inside the Crystal, the two got their beer and took the empty table that was now Chance's official office, along a back wall. The two old guys that had been in before were still there and nodded to Chance.

"I just spent a couple of hours with Sheriff Sample and he gave me an earful, Stockton. Businesses are taxed at the will of Dickson and Miller? People get their heads busted for disagreeing with those two? And people are run off their land at will? Listen, smithy, I've been in some rough shod places before, but this tops all. There is no town or county government, there is no rule of law, there is no legal authority in this area. Give me your take on the situation, because I'm not sure I'm willing to believe what Sample told me." Chance knew that he did believe, and on top of what he learned from Sample, he had heard the same story from the Crystal Saloon barkeep and the two old guys earlier. "Stokes introduced me to Cotton Phelps, and I've heard some pretty gruesome tales today."

"That pretty much sums it up, Marshal. Miller and Dickson own just about everything in the valley, or hold the mortgage on the property. A tax has been levied on every business and piece of property to pay for the jail and the sheriff, bringing in far more money than is being spent, and anyone that argues either loses the lease to their business, has their mortgage foreclosed, or is beaten with clubs and rifle butts. There is no law other than what those two men declare.

"It's really more than sad when you take the time to ponder what is happening here. This is a beautiful little valley with a fine river flowing through it. Those big mountains to the west gather as much snow as they can grab all winter, and then come spring, things grow and grow and grow. You know, Marshal, just east of this valley is desert and a rancher has to fight every day to stay alive, and here, we live in heaven. And these two men have tainted heaven."

"Listen to me, carefully, Mr. Stockton. I have the authority to declare martial law in this valley, but I wouldn't live two hours if I did that. I need to meet tomorrow morning with at least five, or as many as possible, men that would be willing to back up my play. It will be dangerous beyond most men's thinking, but it has to happen. I will put a letter on the next outgoing stage to my superiors and they will send help, but that will take days, so I need to make my move now, and I need lots of help."

Chance was thinking that he hadn't talked that much in months, but he could see that Jerrod Stockton understood everything he said. "After you find those men and we meet, I will make my move. Are you up to it, smithy?"

A smile slowly spread across the large blacksmith's face, his eyes sparkled, and he sat forward in his chair. "I've been waiting for something like this. It took four of those bastards to whip me the last time, and now I can say, that was the last time. You bet I'm up to it, Marshal, and I know several men that I can get to work with us."

Chance liked that *with us* part, and figured that just having Stockton on his side would bring many more to the fray. "All right, then. Tomorrow, let's get together after I meet with our lofty banker, and I'll outline what we'll be doing. Emphasize the danger, smithy. If someone isn't up to it, that's fine, but those that get involved have to understand the danger." The men shook hands and

Stockton headed back to his livery stables.

He realized that what was happening in Preston and the Golden Valley had slowly built over a number of years. He was muttering to himself as he walked back to the livery. *It was Sarah that got things started. If Miller hadn't been so damned hard on that woman, she would never have complained to the government. I got to thank her much next time I see her.*

Stockton was among the many who lived in the west who were well read, and proud of the country moving through the vast areas, creating towns and cities, building businesses, and bringing law and order to areas that just a short time before had none. *We are a nation*, he liked to say to himself, and he was proud of the concept. He talked often of how the war between the north and south was destroying everything that the country represented. "One man," he said so many times, "should never be able to own another man. The idea of someone actually owning another human being isn't right under any circumstance."

***

"I'll have one more of your brews barkeep, and then I think I'll call it a night. I imagine the word spread pretty fast about that big old badge I wear, eh?"

"Talk of the town right now, Marshal. And you having supper with the sheriff. Whole town knows you now. Gonna clean up this filthy swamp? Sure does need it."

"Gonna do my best, sir. You willing to help?"

"Not much of a fighter, myself, but I can tell you about a couple that would probably be willing." He took a long look up and down the bar, and gave Chance several names of local ranchers and buckaroos who he could trust. "The men and women that have businesses in the valley sure would want to help, but they are probably afraid to do so. Miller and that Dickson have been pretty tough on us."

Chance had names and ideas working through his head as he rambled back to the hotel. Two men in particular were in his mind: a ranch hand named Hank Adams and the ranch foreman named Cotton Phelps he had met at the Stokes' place. "Those two men seem to be well respected by those that don't have any respect for our banker friend. I hope Stockton has them on his list as well," he muttered going up the stairs.

As he approached the door to his hotel room he heard a rustling from inside, pulled his big revolver out and put his foot through the door, coming inside with a full body roll, ending up on his feet, his gun jammed in the throat of a large man wearing a brocade vest and string tie.

"One little move and your brains are all over this room," and he pressed the barrel deeper into the man's neck. With his free hand he pulled a revolver from the man's holster and shoved him down onto the bed. "Breaking and entering, hell, that's only about thirty days, but threatening a federal officer, that's many years." He slapped his gun barrel across the man's skull, opening a large gash.

"You got a name?" The man was trying to stop the bleeding, pulled his vest up to wipe some away, but didn't answer. Chance raised the gun to swing again, and the big man started talking.

"Name's Stokes, Jim Stokes. You got no right to hit me," he started to say when the gun barrel slammed into his head again. Chance had him on his feet and down the stairs and out on the street in short order.

"I got every right in the world, you stupid little boy." He prodded Stokes with the revolver and marched him down the middle of the street to Peter Sample's jail. "With a little luck," he thought, "the whole town will see this little parade." He pushed and shoved Stokes at every step, prodding the young man, wanting Preston to see that he was a lawman from the first word on.

"Got a customer for you, Sheriff," he said, pushing Stokes into the small office. "Found this fool boy in my hotel room. Do you know him?"

"Oh, damn," Sample said seeing Jim Stokes, blood dripping from head wounds. "That's Ben Stokes' son, James." He wiped his forehead, stood up and looked into Stokes' eyes. "What were you doing? Don't you know this is a U.S. Marshal? Damn, boy, your father is going to have a fit over this."

"Ain't none of my father's business. Get Mr. Miller over here. He'll have your hide for this, mister marshal," and he spit at Chance. Chance threw a single left hook into Stokes's jaw and the big man crumpled to the floor.

"Lock this little pecker head tight, Sheriff. And don't let him out under any circumstances. He is being held by a federal law officer. Do you understand?"

"I do Marshal. I do."

"What time does Miller usually hit the bank? I want to be there."

Before Sample could answer there was the sound of heavy boots coming down the board sidewalk outside the sheriff's office. The door flew open and Preston Miller and one other man came through. "What the hell do you think you're doing, Sample? What happened to your head, Stokes? I better get some answers damn quick here," and he turned to glare, first at Sample, then at Chance.

"You want answers? I got answers," Chance said, softly, but with a definite threat. "Do you want to do the introductions, Sheriff?"

Sheriff Sample found himself in exactly the position he did not want to be in. "Yes, I will," he stammered. "Mr. Miller, this is U.S. Marshal Jacob Chance. Marshal, meet Preston Miller, owner of the Preston Bank."

"Who's the other jerk?"

Sample cringed when Chance called the man a jerk, but continued. "Marshal, this is Clarence Toby, one of Mr. Miller's associates."

"This is one of the men that Miller hires to

intimidate the business community? I see," Chance continued. "Then, since Stokes here is dressed as the employees at the Bucket of Good Hope, I can assume that he too helps Miller maintain control of the valley?" Sample shrunk from the questions and started to slump into his chair.

"Well, sheriff, while Miller and Toby and I have a little conversation, why don't you take Stokes back and make him comfortable in one of your nice cells." He glared at Stokes, took a quick step toward him, and Stokes backed off enough for the sheriff to take him by the elbow and walk him toward the cell block.

"Hold on now," Miller all but shouted. "You can't put Stokes in jail. Who do you think you are? This is my town, Chance. You don't have any authority here. You let him go Sample. Let him go, now." Miller's face was red, beads of perspiration were on his forehead, and the anger flowed from his system.

"Lock him up, Sheriff. Now, Miller, you listen to me very carefully. My name is Jacob Chance, Deputy U.S. Marshal for this territory. Since there is no legitimate law officer in this valley, I am taking over the duties until an election for sheriff can be held. As of this moment, Peter Sample is now my deputy, and will have the authority of the government of the United States, as I have." He looked at Toby, then at Miller, then back at Toby.

"Miller, this is not your town or your valley, it is a community within the Territory of Nevada, and federal and territorial law will prevail. The U.S. Attorney for the western jurisdiction has sent me here to clear up problems dealing with land law. I will see you in your office tomorrow morning, and I will expect nothing but full compliance with my requests. Anything less will subject you to possible arrest."

He looked over as Sample returned from the jail area, smiled ever so slightly. Miller looked like he might collapse or have a stroke, or pull a gun and shoot Marshal Chance. "Good night, Miller. Take Toby and go home. I want no interference with what my job calls for."

Chance looked over at Sample again. "I remember you saying something about having some good coffee around here. Let's have a cup, shall we?" He moved to pull a chair out from the desk when Clarence Toby made a move for his weapon. Chance's gun appeared in an instant and Toby froze. "Slip that piece of iron real slow, Toby, real slow, and put it on the desk. You're within half a second of death right now."

Toby's fingers slowly grasped the pistol butt and he pulled the revolver out of its holster, took one step toward the desk and laid it down. "Sheriff, looks like you have another customer. Lock this fool up, but not in the same cell with Stokes." He looked over at the banker, at the same time picking up Toby's pistol. "Any tricks from you, Miller? No? Good, I'll be in your office in the morning. Go home."

Chance and Sample had their coffee, talked for another hour or so, and Chance walked back to the hotel. The manager had already set him up in a new room, one with a complete door. "Thank you. Sorry about kicking in the other one, but it comes with my job, I'm afraid. Young Mr. Stokes will be happy to pay you for that door," he said, smiling.

Settled in his new room, he jammed a chair under the door knob, sat on the edge of the bed and took several pages of notes to himself. "Looks like this will be a tough little job, making this community right again." He sat still for a couple of minutes, remembering what Pappy had taught him. *He used to be a regular philosopher when we were out in the fields. The old mules pulling a plow or mower would seem to get him started.* A long smile came across the lawman's face and he wished he had either a cold beer or a cup of boiling camp coffee. He found himself talking to himself, out loud.

"That man taught me that it wasn't wrong for a man to fight, but the question of why to fight had to be answered before your first fist flew or you drew a knife or gun. That question called for you to be honest with yourself first, then make the decision. I came home pretty bloody one day, and I thought I would really get in trouble for fighting at school, and when old Pappy said, 'Let's go out to the barn, boy,' I knew I was gonna get it." That smile came slowly across his face again, and he got up, walked to the hotel room window and let his thoughts continue drifting.

The first thing Pappy asked was, "What got the fight started?" There was no willow switch, no belt off his trousers, just a valid question. When I told him that Bud Spreckles had punched Judy Torrance in the face, he smiled, looked long and hard at my bloody face and bruised jaw, and asked, "Did you whup the little bastard?" I knew I had made the right decision, and I was being honest. I loved that old man.

After writing notes to himself, he penned a long letter to his boss in San Francisco, and made it ready for the next outbound stage. Thoughts of the banker and saloon keeper were flashing through his mind. *How does one become such a degenerate, and in particular, living in country like this? It must have something to do with how one was brought up, to be ruthless, have no regard for any other human being.*

It would be interesting to know how Miller was raised. He's a blow-hard, he's a determined criminal, and most important for me to remember, he is dangerous. He was almost to the point of actually getting into bed, and he had another thought. *Is Miller working with or for this so-called colonel, George Dickson? If one name comes up, it seems the other does as well.* It had been a long day, his head now firmly on a pillow, a blanket wrapped around him, and sleep came fast for the marshal.

Chapter Four

It was a fitful sleep that night, and Chance was up early again, well before the sun, well before the café opened. A cold splash of water got him fully awake and he walked to the livery to saddle Mr. Morgan for another round of making sure he knew his way around the town and the immediate surroundings. "At some point," he was muttering, "I have to find Sarah Jackson as well. Without her, I wouldn't even be here." He noticed that two men just happened to walk onto the porch of the Bucket of Good Hope as he trotted out of town.

"Well good," he thought, "that will get back to Miller and Dickson right away." He moved along the river for about a half mile, then across and onto the plain to the east. "That's pure snow melt, old son," he murmured to the horse as they made their way across the river. "For ranches and farms in this country, that water is pure gold. I wonder if that fool banker thinks he owns the river too?" There was no smile when that thought popped out of his mouth, and he again thought about how this land grab would affect so many people.

The ground was rolling with little valleys, each seemingly filled with rabbits and quail, each ending at the Good Hope River. He found he could move from the north end of town to the south through that open country and not actually be seen. "Must be the way the hills dip and fold, and all those willow trees along the river." For more than ten years Chance has been dealing with those who didn't much believe in laws and rules, in respect for other's property or right to live, and knowing how and when to remain out of sight had saved his life more than once.

He found a ford and crossed back onto the west bank of the river, and came across a trail that led south out of town. He followed that for about a mile or so, then turned more west and started north again, trying to keep the town in sight and himself out of sight. It was a full two hours before he got back into town, just in time to join Sheriff Sample for breakfast.

"What a sunrise that was, eh Mr. Morgan, sir? No camp fire, but we can forego that once in a while, particularly when we have a warm bed in a clean hotel." He shook his head a little, then continued his dissertation with his horse. "No, as nice as that bed was, it isn't the same as a bedroll plastered across some tall grass or boughs from a tree."

After putting Mr. Morgan back in his stall and saying good morning to Jerrod Stockton, he walked to the café. "Well, now, if Miller and Dickson thought I was riding out of town, they know now I wasn't. After last night, it might be interesting to see what will happen around here today." He carried his rifle in the crook of his arm, his revolver always right at hand, and walked down the street with the air of a man not afraid of anything.

Sample was already at the café waiting for him when he arrived. "Good morning, all," he said to those in the restaurant, pulling out his chair. "Sheriff. I hope your two inmates had a good night's sleep. You might want to tell the young Stokes boy that the hotel will be sending him a bill for the door I destroyed," he said with an eye wrinkling grin.

"I think Toby's jaw might be broken, Marshal, but other than that, they are still alive and angry as hell. No one has ever stood up to Miller before, and they sure as hell didn't see it coming." Sample was sitting up, straight in his chair, with a warm smile on his face. "Thank you," he said, out of the blue. Chance took a few seconds for it to sink in, then just smiled and nodded.

"There's a lot more to come, Sample, but I understand, and as I said last night, I'll do what I can to keep things from exploding around here."

"Cookie wants to buy you a steak for breakfast,

Marshal. That okay with you?" the waitress asked, giving Chance a full face smile. She was at least ten years older than the marshal, wore far too much makeup for this time of the morning, and, he noticed, a wedding band as well.

"The law says I have to pay for everything," he lied, "but tell him thank you for the offer. I would like some chunks of side meat fried up with potatoes and onions, though, if he could stir that up for me." His smile was genuine, and the lady all but squealed as she danced into the kitchen with the order.

Chance glanced out of the side of his eye at the sheriff who was cackling at what he just saw. "That's enough, now," Chance said, trying to scowl. "I'm going to have to cancel our meeting with Miller for this morning. After last night I know I have to have more information from some of the people around here. The way you put it yesterday, the town's people aren't going to be forthcoming out of fear, so I'm going to take a ride out to some more of the ranches.

"Yesterday's visit with Ben Stokes and our talk last night makes me wonder just how far this fool has gone. According to Major Randall, he's my boss, there aren't any deeds filed on any property in this valley, except the homestead deed by the Jackson woman. A man that would do all that would probably not stop there, and that's what I need to find out."

Breakfast was served and the two men plowed in, talking as they ate. "I've heard rumors of Miller and Dickson demanding kickbacks from cattle sales from some of the smaller operators, but nothing that I could specifically tell. Just rumors," the sheriff said.

"How about water? Can't run spreads like I've been seeing without water, and that river is one fine source."

"Don't know about any kind of water deals."

"It would be a natural. Stokes didn't say anything, neither did Cotton Phelps," Chance said. "Devious gangsters like Miller and Dickson wouldn't pass up an opportunity like that. Unless of course, they haven't thought of it yet. No," he said, "they would have thought of that." His plate well cleaned, the marshal made his move to leave.

"Take some food to the prisoners, then tell Miller I'll see him either later today or early tomorrow morning. I'm heading out." He shook hands with the sheriff, nodded a smile to the waitress, gathered up his rifle, and headed out the door.

***

Again, the Bucket of Good Hope Saloon had eyes on Chance as he rode out of town, this time going south. He nodded to a couple of shop keepers getting ready to open their stores and was surprised when not one of them returned the gesture. "These people are seriously frightened," he said, touching the big stud with his spurs as he neared the outskirts of the village. Frightened people aren't much good in a fight, he was thinking, and wondering just what might be in store for them when the dust finally settles.

Fights over property rights could get ugly fast, and in a community like Preston, where there hadn't been a law presence, only angry bankers and make-believe colonels, people will be hurt physically and mentally and economically. These thoughts were plowing through Chance's head as he traveled through miles of lush pasture, seeing ranch after ranch, all holding hundreds of head of fat cattle. "First time we've been on the south trail, Mr. Morgan. This is mighty nice country."

Rolling hills cascaded down from the towering peaks to the west, with tall grass and brush in profusion. With a light breeze blowing in the morning warmth, he could see the tops of the grasses waving as the grains did when he was growing up in Missouri. Many of the ranchers were bringing their herds in and milling cattle were spread as far as he could see.

Again, the thoughts of having a ranch, of giving up the badge, slipped into view. "Takes a lot of work to run one of these places," he mused. "Just about every rancher I've ever known was married and had a passel of kids. The old farm was like that, and I fought that every second of every day. Would a ranch be different?" He let the question hang in the air, wondered, only for a second or two, what it would be like to be married, to have a home. "A home? Since I left the farm, I've never had a home," and that thought bothered him.

"I've spent the last ten years either in camps or hotels since I joined the marshal service. Hell," his muttering continued, "even when I was that hick town sheriff I lived at the jail. I haven't had a home since I gave my share of the old farm to my sister. I must be getting old, Mr. Morgan. Thinking of having a home."

One ranch looked a little forlorn as he passed by on the well-used trail, and he turned in to meet the owners. The path leading to the ranch house wasn't well used, he noticed, and the fences around a five- or six-acre pasture alongside needed some serious mending. In some of the ranches he rode by the grasses were high and lush, and in some, like this one, the grasses seemed weak, almost dried out. A grizzled old man and thin old woman were standing on the porch of a well-built but also well-used home as Chance rode up.

"Morning," he said, waiting for an invitation to step off the horse.

"If you're from that bastard at the bank, you can turn right around and vamoose off this here ranch, mister." Chance saw a man behind the door holding what looked like a double-barreled shotgun.

"Not from the bank, mister." He slowly pulled his serape aside to show that big shiny badge. "Name's Jacob Chance, U.S. Marshal. But I do want to talk to you about that banker."

"Step down off that horse of yours, nice and slow, and we'll talk. From a distance, now, don't be coming up on the porch."

"Wouldn't do that," Chance replied, tying off the stud. "You there, behind the door, I mean no harm." He looked at the old man and woman again. He could see fear written deep in lines and wrinkles, but also a fierceness that said they were willing to protect what little they had. "This is the same fear I saw in the faces of the people in town," he was saying to himself. "These people are willing to fight for what they have, but I wonder if they would be willing to back my play. That's where a marshal can get himself in trouble, hoping for backing and then not getting it." He put a warm smile on his face, kept both hands in the open as he made his purpose for being there known.

"I'm here investigating what appears to be some criminal activity being perpetrated by Preston Miller and George Dickson. Can we talk?"

The whole scene softened as Chance said that, the man behind the door, spitting image of the man on the porch, minus about fifty years, came out, and the old man invited Chance onto the porch, and asked him to sit in one of the many chairs on that wide veranda. "Marshal, eh? Don't think I've ever met one before. Well, howdy, Marshal, I'm Eb Kiefer, this is my wife Adelaide, and my son Bruce."

"Pleased to meet you all," Chance said. "Mind if we talk about your ranch and the banker? I noticed you don't hold him in very high regard."

"He's doing everything he can to run us off, Marshal. Everything. First, he increased our mortgage payment, which is killing us, and then that whiskey-sucking bar owner Dickson cut off our water. We'll be forced to give up this place very soon. Can't raise pasture grass and food without water, and can't get our cattle to market cuz that bastard has told all the cowboys that work for him not to hire on here for the fall drive down. We're gonna pull out soon, just leave everything, I guess."

Chance was thinking he had never seen such a sad face on an old man ever before, not in Missouri, not in the badlands, never anywhere. "What did you mean, exactly, when you said that Dickson cut off your water?"

"Well, you see, the way those bastards work is like this," the old man drawled out. His wife interrupted before he could continue.

"Would you like a cup of coffee, Marshal? It will only take a few minutes to get it going."

"That would be very nice, Mrs. Kiefer, very nice indeed." She limped off the porch into the house, getting a little help from her son.

"Broke her leg this spring and it never did set right," the old man said, watching her go in. "Well, as I was saying, Miller owns the land and we bought that from him with a ten-year mortgage, and Dickson owns the water, and we lease a specific amount from him with monthly payments. We need the water for our own use, but we also put up a lot of hay for winter use." He sat back in the old cane chair, rubbing the stubble on his chin, a most angry look across his old wrinkled face. He spat a wad of juice out into the dust and continued.

"First, that bastard at the bank doubled our mortgage payments, and when we found it hard to make the water payments, Dickson cut off our supply. We're out of business, Marshal."

This was the first that Chance had heard of the water problems in the valley. No one else had mentioned that Dickson was saying he owned all the water in the Good Hope River. He was almost mumbling to himself about Stokes not saying anything, about Jerrod Stockton not saying anything. And, he remembered, nothing about water was mentioned in the letter from Sarah Jackson.

"Tell me about this water deal that you have with George Dickson. I'm most interested, sir."

"Well, here's what I know," and again he made himself comfortable in the old chair, ran his hand through the few scraggles of hair left on his head, and spat another load of juice into the dust. "Dickson cut several irrigation ditches that lead out of the higher end of the river and feed the ranches up and down the valley that need irrigation. Some ranchers dug their own wells and don't use the ditches, but Dickson has tried to charge a small amount for drawing water from the wells. The big profitable ranchers won't pay it.

"He says that Utah granted him all the water rights in the valley, and along with the deeds that Miller owns, they own the valley. I wasn't able to dig any wells for irrigation, so we connected to one of his ditches. It worked well for the first few years, but then all the prices started getting so high, and they wouldn't let us get behind." He teared up at that point, pulled a horrible old rag out and wiped his face and blew his nose.

"When I got behind in my ranch payment, that bastard Toby came out with another man and beat the hell out of Bruce. His right hand was damaged to the point he can't hardly use it now. I don't know for sure why you're here, Marshal, but I hope it has something to do with all this."

"It surely does, Mr. Kiefer. It surely does." He sat quietly for a few moments, putting everything together in his mind. He was about to say something when Adelaide came out onto the porch, holding a tray full of cups and a large pot of boiling coffee. "Ah," he said, "Perfect timing, Mrs. Kiefer. That smells delicious." She was followed by Bruce, who held a platter of sugar-coated doughnuts. "You know, folks, I may not leave knowing this is all here." General laughter eased the tension of the previous discussion, and cups were passed along with the sweets.

"From everything I've heard in the last few days, this banker Miller and saloon keeper Dickson are breaking many laws, Kiefer. I hadn't even heard about the water rights problem until just now. I'm going to be putting those two men under arrest very soon, but it's important for you to know, this valley is going to get very dangerous in the next few days and weeks.

"I strongly recommend that you keep that scattergun of yours handy, Bruce, and Eb, it sure wouldn't hurt to strap on an old piece of iron yourself. It's going to take some doing, but property rights, water rights, land ownership and money problems are not going to get cleared up for a while. If you have access to that irrigation ditch, open it up, Mr. Kiefer, and use what water you need. Mr. Dickson does not own the water in this valley, in fact, I doubt very much if he owns anything, including that gaudy saloon of his."

The conversation went back and forth for another hour, the coffee pot was emptied, and nary a doughnut was in sight as Jacob Chance rode out from the Kiefer ranch. "It's always the good people that take it in the pants when the criminals are out and about," he said to Mr. Morgan as they made their way back to town. Lingering thoughts of having a home, of freshly fried doughnuts, even of having a wife danced through his mind. "A beautiful valley like this in complete turmoil. A ranch? Maybe many years down the road, but this is the kind of work I'm cut out for."

He could see the ditches that were cut for irrigation as he traversed back and forth across the river. "There aren't any of these ditches on the north side. I'm sure I would have seen them. Maybe Ben Stokes or maybe the blacksmith can bring me up to speed on this." As soon as he said the Stokes name, thoughts of Jennifer flashed through his mind.

"Hold it up right there, Mr. Marshal, sir," he said right out loud, as if he was talking to someone. "She's a beautiful young lady and I'm sure she wouldn't even consider dancing with me more or less anything else, and besides, you damn fool, you've got too much work to do around here without thinking about getting all messed up with some pretty lady." The thoughts of Jennifer kept getting mixed up with land fraud and water rights and ranching and gunfights for the next couple of hours riding back to town.

***

Sheriff Sample's stomach was roiling, he could taste bile as he made his way from the office to the Preston Bank. Ever since breakfast with Marshal Chance his only thoughts were of this meeting with Preston Miller. Miller has berated him at every chance, despite the fact it was Miller that appointed him sheriff. Sample was aware of just how weak a man he is, knew he might cave depending on what Miller said or did, and knew he would not be able to look himself in the eye ever again if he failed the marshal. On weak and wobbly knees he entered the bank not too long after it opened.

"I'm sorry sheriff, but Mr. Miller hasn't arrived yet. Is there something I can help you with?" The clerk behind the teller's counter almost smiled, and Sample's anger rose up, for the first time in years.

"You tell Miller that Marshal Chance will be in to see him later today or early tomorrow. You wouldn't happen to know where that fat gentleman might be, would you?" and he too had a slight smile on his face.

"Not here, is all I can tell you," the clerk snapped back, and Sample caught him glancing at Miller's private office door. He walked over and opened the door with a jerk, finding Miller and Dickson inside.

"Morning, gentlemen," he said, stepping into the office, leaving the door wide open. "Glad to find the two of you together. Marshal Chance had to see some people out of town this morning and wanted me to let you know we wouldn't make our meeting." He found his knees almost shaking with fear, but also found a strength he didn't know he even had.

"The marshal wanted me to tell you, Mr. Miller, that he would see you either later today or early tomorrow morning."

"Get the hell out of this bank, Sample. I order you, right now, to take that badge off, to let your prisoners go free, and move your stuff out of the jail. You're fired." He was talking at the top of his voice, so loud it could have been heard on the street outside.

"I'm afraid you can't fire me, Mr. Miller. The office of sheriff doesn't exist in the first place, just a position you created, but Marshal Chance deputized me, and I'm operating in the capacity of a Deputy U.S. Marshal. The prisoners are federal prisoners and will remain in custody until a territorial judge arrives in Preston, which could be within a week or two."

The thoughts going through his mind were jumbled at best, relief that he said all that, fear that he might be shot at any moment, and a great desire to get the hell out of that office and that bank. Miller was as red in the face as he had ever seen, but it was Dickson who spoke up.

"You are no more a deputy marshal than I am, Sample. You listen to me, now," and he stood up, that huge moustache bristling like a bramble bush in a wind storm. "This is private property, although we call it a town, named it for Mr. Miller's grandfather, but it is private property. Mr. Miller and I own everything in this valley, Sample, so get that straight.

"You march your butt back to that jail, let those men out, leave your badge on the desk, and clear out of this valley. If you're not gone in two hours, I'll shoot you myself," and he used his big hand to give a hard push to Sample's shoulder. "Get out, now," he bellowed, shoving the sheriff again.

"You'll regret this," Sample said, hightailing it out of the bank. He walked slowly down the street, wishing that Marshal Chance was walking with him. He knew that because of his association with Miller and Dickson that he didn't have a friend in town, that right at the moment he was as alone as any man might find himself. He made his way down the street to the jail, locked the door and closed the storm shutters on the single front window.

He stoked up the fire in the old pot belly stove, put together another pot of coffee, and sat down at his desk to wait for it to brew. He pulled the cleaning kit from the bottom drawer of his desk, and took his revolver out, unloaded it, and started cleaning the weapon. "I better make sure every gun I have here is clean, loaded, and ready to use. I have been a fool all these years, but that Marshal is giving me a chance and I'm not going to let him down, or any of these people in this valley."

It was three hours later that a knock on the door brought Sample up out of his chair, rifle in hand. "Sample. You in there?" It was Chance.

"Hang on, Marshal. I have the door locked," and he opened it up, still holding the rifle.

"Some trouble while I was gone?" He walked over and poured a cup of very hot, very strong coffee. "Whew," he said. "This has hair. What happened?"

Sample spent the next hour telling Chance about the meeting with Miller and Dickson, and Chance told about the meeting with the Kiefer's. "Looks like the two of us learned a lot today, eh Mr. Sample? Good, that will make it a little easier to continue our work. We'll meet with Miller in the morning. That way the two of them can stew in their anger and frustration all night."

"See you in the morning, Sample," Chance said, walking out. He went down to the stables to see Jerrod Stockton. "I'm going to need a lot of help, Jerrod. This problem is much bigger than I thought. I have help coming,

68

but it will be a day or two. I'm sure there are people in the valley and in town that are fed up with Miller and company and I need to talk with them. And it will be dangerous. I'm meeting with Miller in the morning. He and Dickson have already threatened the life of Sheriff Sample. Can you arrange for a few good men to meet with me, here, about noon tomorrow?"

"I think that's a very good idea. I have a few that are not fed up, they are angry as hell and haven't known what to do about it. Yeah, I'll have your back-up here."

Chance whapped him across a massive shoulder. "Thanks, smithy. I'll see you then. Have a good night, I'm off to the hotel and a nice long sleep on a soft mattress."

Chapter Five

Following the clash with Sample, Dickson left Miller and headed back to the Bucket of Good Hope Saloon. He called several of the local men at the saloon over, most of whom did not look like local ranch hands. "I don't care where you go to find them, but I want some hired guns in this town within the next few days. Federal marshal or no federal marshal, I'm not going to let that man take this little prize away from me." He motioned for one of the men to talk with him for just a moment.

"You remember my old partner from Salt Lake? Good, go get him and bring him back. We're going to need his good guns. Hurry, don't take no from him. Take some money and get moving."

It dawned on one of the men standing there that Dickson and Miller must be partners in their land schemes. Hank Adams had spent most of the day before talking with Jenny Stokes about putting together a crew to bring her cattle down from summer range, and had also discussed how her father felt about the way Preston Miller had been selling and then foreclosing on land that he might not actually own. Adams was big, standing close to six feet tall and weighing in at about two hundred pounds. On holidays, when boxing matches are held, Adams was a sure bet to win. He was not aware of the meeting between Stokes and the marshal.

"You really think that's a good idea, Colonel? Bringing in hired guns to fight a federal marshal? That marshal's gonna have a lot of friends around here, and he's probably already got some back up coming in."

"Don't you question me, Adams. Why don't you just go on home, get the hell out of here. If you're too afraid to stand up for Preston Miller, just get the hell out." That quick temper flared, Adams' fist balled up, he stood as tall as he could, and was about to knock the colonel on his back when he felt the barrel of a pistol pressed into the back of his neck.

The other men around Colonel George pulled their guns and Adams backed away slowly. The only joke ever told about Hank Adams in Preston had to do with his pistol. Seems he bought an old Army cap and ball pistol, mostly rusted iron, and it only fired once in a while. Those at the bar knew they would not have to face Adams in a gun fight, and forced the man to leave. On the way out of town, he spotted Jerrod Stockton outside the livery.

"There's some serious trouble brewing, Stockton. There's a U.S. Marshal in town talking about putting Preston Miller out of business, it seems that Col. Dickson might be Miller's partner, and he's sending for some hired guns.

"I also heard that this marshal has arrested Toby and young Jim Stokes. This is serious, Stockton, damn serious."

"Come in for a cup of coffee, Hank. We need to talk." Stockton took the lead rope from the big man and held his horse while he dismounted. "Marshal got into town yesterday and already has things riled up pretty good." They walked into the livery and found chairs inside the office, near a pot belly stove red with warmth. "You can feel the fall coming on, already. Ranchers gonna be busy getting the herds down out of the hills, and some may find out they don't own the land they're ranchin'."

"I don't know much about law, Stockton, but if I buy a piece of ground from a bank, I sure would believe that I own that piece of ground."

"That's just about the whole problem, Hank. You've seen how the bank has sold and resold land over and over, and you know that Preston Miller has said hundreds of times that he has deeds to that land he's been a-sellin', but nobody else has ever seen those deeds. Now that I think of it, I don't think anyone has ever paid off a mortgage, so probably nobody has ever seen a deed." He sat back in his chair, poured another cup of coffee, and wondered out loud, "I don't know if my lease here for this livery and stables is legal, but I pay it every month.

"You've seen how he throwed Sarah Jackson off her place. She has a paper from the government says that's her land. Cain't two people own the same piece of ground, Hank. Marshal's name is Chance, Jacob Chance, and he wants to meet with some of us in the morning. You up to that? Might get nasty if Col. George is sending out for guns."

Hank Adams stood up to his full height, warmed his hands in front of the stove, poured another cup of boiling coffee, and gave the question a full reading in his mind. "I don't own any land. You know I wanted to get a ranch, but just didn't have any money, but Sarah told me about this idea called homestead. If what Miller and Dickson are doing is wrong, I would sure like to help Sarah out. What time is that marshal gonna be here?"

"He's meeting with Miller when the bank opens, then coming here. Probably be here before noon. Cotton says he'll be here. Miller hired him to run Sarah's ranch, but he figures he's still working for her." There was a gentle chuckle from the blacksmith as he said that, and the two men clinked their coffee cups in agreement. The blacksmith rubbed his chin, closed his eyes for just a moment.

"This is a beautiful little valley, Hank. Soon as I saw it I knew I wanted to live here. A fine river flowing through it, right here in the middle of the high desert. We have an Eden." His brow was furrowed and he continued, deep in his thoughts. "Tall grass scraping the belly of your horse when you ride through the meadows, deer and antelope everywhere, and always there's some fool gotta mess it up. That marshal is gonna need a lot of help, Hank, and I'm throwing in with him."

"Jennie Stokes wants me to ride with her crew to bring their herd down, but I think when I tell her what's happening, she and the old man will want to be here. She told me that Ben Stokes is having second thoughts about whether or not he actually owns his ranch."

"Marshal was at the Stokes ranch yesterday, Hank, so Jenny knows all about it now, and Phelps was there, too."

"I'll be here in the morning, then. I'm glad Cotton Phelps is in on this. He's a good man." The two shook hands, Hank Adams stepped into the stirrups and trotted out of town, toward the Stokes ranch. He didn't see the two men in the willows alongside the river as he left.

"Looks like Adams and Stockton are up to something, Pete. Let's get back to the saloon and tell Col. George about this. Miller's paying good money to the men that will ride for him. Let's make sure they know we're on their side."

***

Dickson and Miller were up late, sharing a bottle of fine bourbon brought in from San Francisco, discussing how to fend off the federal marshal. They were in the upstairs offices at the Bucket of Good Hope Saloon, a suite of rooms paneled in fine walnut with hanging tapestries, elegant oil lamps hanging and sitting on desks and tables. The carpeting was thick and nicely patterned, and in the corner, a large fire burned warm and friendly in a rock fireplace. Colonel George believed in the good life, and was planning to spend the rest of his life in this kind of opulence.

"He's just one man, Miller, take it easy. I sent for some help, we'll have five or six well-armed men in town to back us within a day or two. Don't get yourself upset like this. Hell, one man, badge or no badge, can't stand up to five or six men. Take it easy, Preston."

"Take it easy, my ass. You take it easy." Preston

73

Miller had sipped his share of the fine liquor, had beads of perspiration across his brow, and was showing the signs often seen in a man deathly afraid. "I saw him whip that pistol out and stop Toby in his fastest stride. That man is dangerous, George, and I mean dangerous." He poured another bit of bourbon in his glass, his hands shaking so that he spilled some of it. The banker was not a fighter, he was the type of man who hired people to fight for him, or he shot his man in the back. He was mean, selfish, and as arrogant as the colonel, but was terrified of having to be in a physical fight.

"He said he would come to the bank in the morning and he wants to see those deeds we got from Salt Lake City."

"You mean, the deeds we say we got?" the colonel laughed. "Hell, Preston, just tell him he'll have to go to Salt Lake to see them. See? No problem. Just don't lose yourself. Stand up to him like I would. You have claimed that land, it's ours, and no federal marshal is going to take it away. Stand up to him, tell him the deeds are on record in Salt Lake, and for him to get the hell out of Preston." He was giving orders as if he was still in a military unit of some kind, and Miller, always fearful of those with obvious power, gave in.

"You're probably right, George. That's what I'll do. You really bringing gunmen into town? Is that a good idea?"

Dickson allowed the conversation to come to an end and ushered Miller out of the offices. "Just tell the man to get out of town, Preston. Now, go home and get some sleep."

Dickson went back into the inner office, poured another shot of bourbon in his glass and walked over to the fireplace. "Coming fall early this year, it feels like," he mused, sipping the good whisky.

"Excuse me, Colonel George. Two men just came

in and want to see you. They didn't want to tell me why."

"I'll be down in a minute. Do you know them?"

"No. I've seen them around town, but I don't know who they are." Dickson nodded okay, finished his drink, warmed his hands one more time, and followed his man down into the saloon.

It was a busy saloon he walked into, with live music from a couple of people on stage--one playing a banjo, the other a piano--cocktail girls, the colonel's choice of description, were dancing with some of the customers, others just cozying up with some, the gambling tables were full, and men lined the long bar. Most of those in the busy bar were buckaroos from some of the surrounding ranches. This was, after all, payday weekend. The bartender pointed out the two men who had asked to see Dickson.

"What can I do for you two?" he said, motioning the bartender to keep an eye on what was going on. "I don't think I know you."

"We've been in town for a few days, Colonel George, looking to hire out on a ranch, or something." The man talking, the one called Pete, was shuffling his feet, wringing his hands, and about as nervous as a cat. Dickson was about to say something when Pete continued. "Anyway, we saw something tonight you might be interested in."

"All right, go on. Nobody's gonna shoot you," he snarled. "What did you see?"

"We was at the Stokes ranch earlier today, looking to sign on for their fall drive, and met a big man named Adams, Hank Adams. Well, tonight, we was gonna set up camp along the river, just out of town, and saw this Adams feller talkin' with the blacksmith. They was talkin' about settin' up a meetin' in the morning. Said somethin' about a marshal gonna be there.

"Well, we thought you might want to know that," and all the nervous energy of that cat was at the surface, the feet shuffling, the twitch in the eyes, the worried smile of a man scared out of his wits.

"Why don't you two gentlemen have a cold beer on me," and Dickson motioned for the bartender to pour two. "I'm glad you came to me with that. Did you happen to hear what time this meeting might be?"

"The blacksmith said sometime before noon, I think. Isn't that right, Sonny?" Sonny nodded, and gulped down half his beer.

"Well, thank you gentlemen, thank you." He started to walk off, then turned to say, "By the way, did you sign on for the Stokes roundup?"

"Yes sir, Miss Stokes said for us to be there two days from now, and the roundup will begin. I guess we got lucky with our timing." Some of the nervousness had been washed away with the cold beer.

"Have another beer on me, gentlemen, and I wonder if I could ask a large favor of you. You will be paid generously if you will do something for me." Both men nodded in the affirmative immediately. "Good. Go to that meeting tomorrow at the livery stables, don't tell anyone that I sent you, and tell me all about it afterward. Can you do that?"

"Yes. Yes, sir," both said, almost together. "We'll be there, Colonel, yes sir, we'll be there." Dickson had another two draughts poured for them and walked down to the other end of the bar, motioning for the bartender.

"Round up Jake and Cozy for me, Cappy. I have a small job that needs to be done by large men tonight. And, keep an eye on those two, don't let them get drunk and don't let them start talking to people in here."

"Toby and Jim Stokes are both in jail, Colonel. You sure you want Jake and Cozy? They been in a lot of trouble lately."

"Damn, I forgot about that. No, I can trust Jake and Cozy, and send them up to the office. Right away." He lit a cigar and headed up the stairs, putting together plans for tomorrow, maybe even for this evening.

Chapter Six

B ells were screaming out "Fire! Fire!" Men were heard running, women, and children were crying, and as Marshal Chance came out of a sound sleep, he could see the flames and smoke billowing up from the end of the main street. "Oh, my God," he said out loud, "that's the livery." He was in his shirt and pants, boots pulled up, and out the door in minutes, heading up the street at a full run. Stockton was lying on the ground, bleeding profusely from gashes splayed across his head, a couple of town ladies tending to him when Chance got there. The blacksmith had blood all over him, his head wounds open to the bone, his eyes already turning purple, his lips split, and it looked like maybe a tooth or two might be missing.

"Jerrod, what happened? Are you alright? Come on, man, what happened?" It was a pretty good sprint up the length of the town's main street, but Chance wasn't even breathing hard.

"Two men, Marshal. Two men broke into my room and were beating the hell out of me with ax handles, and then threw a couple of lanterns into the hay. I tried to get the horses out, but the smoke and the beating, and I guess I passed out. Are the horses okay?"

Chance knew at once the horses were not okay, and as he looked about he saw the sky in the east just turning toward morning. "That's the way cowards do it," he thought to himself. "Wait until your victim is as sound asleep as he will ever be, and break in."

He rocked back on his heels, breathing in the horrible aroma of burning horse flesh, and mumbled to himself, "This has to be the opening shot of my little war." Stockton was dazed, trying to get up, people swarmed the area in their vain attempt to get the fire out, but with a dried wooden building, tons of hay and grain, they were losing their battle. In the midst of chaos and evil, the sun was making its attempt at the glory of being there.

Chance looked around at the crowd, trying to see if he could pick out men who might seem overly interested in what was going on. "It's an old trick," he muttered to himself, "for the people responsible to want to see just how much damage they have caused." He saw men and women roused out of their sleep, and he saw a few drunks who managed to find their way out of the saloons, and back in the willows, near the river, he saw two men watching the proceedings. To himself, Marshal Chance said, "I know what you look like and I will find you and we'll have a little chat, soon."

He worked his way as close as he could to the entrance to what was now just a hulk of burned-out building, thinking, "I rode into this beautiful little valley just a couple of days ago and thought what a wonderful place it would be to put down roots. How many of these people," and he took another long look at the crowd, slowly making their way back to homes and businesses, "came here with that same thought?" His eyes had a glow, crinkled lids half closed, and the anger of what he saw and felt was obvious in the set of his mouth, the jut of his jaw, and the twitching of a right hand lightly fingering a large caliber pistol sitting at his waist.

"It takes an ugly and evil mind to even contemplate doing something like this, and then hire someone to do it because you're a coward. You won't like it if I find you," and his thoughts were ugly as well.

One of the women tending to the smithy started crying, sobbing that only two horses got out alive. Stockton tried to get up, and passed out from the effort. Chance worked his way through the men who were still fighting the fire, and knew he could not get inside to free any of the horses that might still be alive. He could hear the horrible sounds of a screaming horse, dying in the fire and smoke.

He went back to the smithy who was just coming to, his heart aching for the horses, his mind deciding just what kind of terror he would create for whoever is responsible.

"Did you recognize the men, Stockton?" He knew he would not get the answer he wanted, but he had to ask. "This has been a hell of a day, so far. Can you give me anything to go on?"

"Neither one of them said anything, Chance. Not a word, just whupped those ax handles at me, and then threw the lanterns." He was sitting up and lifted a hand in Chance's direction. "Help me up, Chance, I got to help with that fire."

Chance helped him to his feet, but wouldn't let him go. "The place is gone, Stockton, you can't do any good here. Can you tell me what those two men looked like? How were they dressed? How big were they?" Chance was starting to get irritated, but knew that Stockton's injuries were slowing him down. He knew most men would not be able to withstand those heavy blows from ax handles and it was only the size and condition of the livery stable owner that saved his life.

"They weren't cowboys, Marshal. Maybe pretty big, but not from one of the ranches around here. They had their bandannas across their faces, wore big hats pulled down low. I don't know if I would recognize them if I saw them again. I could smell whisky on their breath, and both of them wore gun belts, not like the cowboys do, you know, up high so they can ride, but down on their hips, kind of."

"That's a big help, smithy. You got someplace to go to get some sleep? You and I have a big job to do."

"I'll get a room at the hotel. All those horses, gone. My old mule. God, Marshal, I hope that stud of yours got out. Damn, I'm sorry, Marshal. All those horses, gone." Tears were running down the huge man's cheeks mixing with blood and mud, his head was bowed as low as it could get, and sobs wracked his body. The blacksmith known as

Jerrod Stockton was a horseman of the highest order and has just lost a small herd of horses. He wasn't crying because he lost his business, he was crying for the loss of those horses. "We'll get those bastards, Chance. We'll get them."

***

The sun was up and shining by the time the large blacksmith headed for the hotel, and Chance took a look over toward the willows. He saw the shadows of two men through the thicket and headed in that direction. He heard the horses trot out of the thicket toward the road that led out of town, but kept walking to where the men had been. "Well now, look at this," he said, finding the remains of where the men had camped. "At least I know what they look like. I don't think they are the ones that whipped Jerrod, but I bet they saw who did. And, I bet they will be willing to tell me," he said, walking back onto the main street.

Chance went back to the hotel and was alone in his room, pacing, stomping, trying to put some kind of order to what was likely to become one of the longest days of his life. From the time he left his little camp high in the surrounding mountains to right now, he had had maybe four hours sleep.

"This little community is completely out of sorts with the rest of the world. This is anarchy. A banker and a saloon keeper think they own everything and everyone, and seem to be getting away with it." He tried to lie down for a quick rest, but his mind wouldn't stop working. "I've hunted down men who have killed for the thrill of killing, I've hunted down men who rob, steal, murder, and I've been responsible for many criminals either finding their permanent home in a cemetery or prison, but I haven't run into this level of blatant depravity in all my career." He paced for another couple of minutes, continued his muttering, reminding himself, "These men are more dangerous than most I've dealt with."

He knew he had to get out of the room, had to do something, and the thought of possibly losing his horse was more than he wanted to think of. "These men are cowards. Won't stand up for themselves, even though what they stand for is evil, no, no, they have to go out and pay someone to do their level of filth. I feel sorry for them right now, because I know what I'm going to do to them."

It was with just a wisp of a smile that he strapped on his big revolver, threw his serape on, grabbed his rifle and stormed out of the hotel. "I hope that big stud got out. Horses, even as big as they are, are still prey animals, and will run from a butterfly. Terror will make them run right into the trouble sometimes." People were still milling around the burned-out stables when he arrived, and moved out of his way when he went into the charred mess.

The first thing he found was his saddle and bridle, burned to a crisp, and only tatters of his saddle blanket showing. "Mr. Morgan may have escaped, eh?" Other stalls were filled with dead animals, mules, horses, even Stockton's milk cow, dead. Marshal Chance walked out the back end of the large barn, into a double row of corrals, some with terrified animals, some empty. At the far end of the alley-way stood a large black Morgan stallion, pawing the ground, ears laid back, eyes showing as much terror as ever seen on a horse.

Chance advanced on the horse slowly, one foot at a time, knowing the horse could panic and bolt at any second. "Easy now, big boy," he all but whispered, and started humming an old song that he often sang around the camp fires he and Mr. Morgan had shared the last few years. "Take it easy, now. Everything's going to be fine." It took several minutes to get close enough to touch the animal. "That's a good boy," he said, stroking the stud's neck, letting the horse smell his hands, his breath, mess with his sombrero, as he liked to do, and Chance had the horse calmed and under control.

"Let's see if we can find you a nice stall, big boy," and he led the horse to the last stall in the line, the one farthest from the still smoldering barn. He took his kerchief off, soaked it in the water trough, and started wiping down Mr. Morgan. "Got yourself singed some, eh pard? Let's see what we can do about that." He spent another hour washing soot and singed hair from his horse, not even noticing that it was mid-morning, that people were moving about through the wreckage of the blacksmith shop and barn.

"You been up all night, Marshal?" It was the sheriff standing at the corral fence. "I know those two men are bastards but I never thought it would come to this. Banker Miller and that Colonel Dickson have gone too far this time." He was a dejected man, standing amid the ruins of the conflagration, wearing a badge that meant nothing to anyone in the town.

"Smithy said two men did it, whipped him with ax handles, then burned him out. There are probably twenty animals dead in there, Sample. Jerrod Stockton is alive only because he's so damn big and strong, and you're talking to the angriest, meanest son of a bitch that ever wore a U.S. Marshal's badge. I hope you're up to it Sample, because I'm going to take this town apart, starting in about one minute."

He finished cleaning and caring for his horse, looked around the outside of the barn and found some fairly fresh hay and threw it to the few animals that were still alive, picked up his rifle and started out through the barn. "You coming, sheriff?"

Sample had a hard time keeping up with Chance's long stride, and the two walked down the middle of the main street in Preston, Nevada Territory. The two marched into the café and ordered breakfast, "with lots of coffee, please."

"You seemed awfully sure of yourself, Sheriff,

naming Miller and Dickson as being responsible. I would think, too, that they are, but why are you so sure?" Jacob Chance had years of dealing with criminals and criminal activity, and his gut told him the sheriff was right, but there was no evidence that would stand up to a court proceeding. "Thugs hired to intimidate me by way of burning out, almost killing a man who has publicly declared that he is siding with me. I need your thoughts right now, Sample. You know these men."

Sample put his fork down, took a long draught of hot coffee and tried to put his thoughts in order. "I'm embarrassed to wear this badge at the same table as you with yours, Marshal, but I can tell you about Preston Miller." He scrunched himself down into his chair, harrumphed a time or two, and began. "His grandfather, on his mother's side, came to this valley on his way to California during the gold rush period, maybe even a year or two before the big discovery. He was moneyed, had ranching in his blood, and when he found this valley, the river, he called it paradise and never left.

"The territory belonged to Mexico at the time, but they didn't care, and Preston didn't either. He just settled in, took what he wanted, raised some fine cattle, and a daughter that became Preston Miller's mother. Miller doesn't have deeds to this land, it's what his grandfather took, and now, the egotistical fool thinks he owns everything in sight." There were perspiration beads glowing on the sheriff's forehead, his mouth was dry, and he knew he was going to be in the fight of his life.

"That's the kind of information I need, Sample. I'll do what I can to keep you out of the line of fire, but with Stockton out of the fight now, I can't guarantee anything. You go back to your office, don't let those two galoots out, and I'm going to go to the bank for a little discussion with our friend Miller." He called back over his shoulder, "Better find some men to clean up that mess at the stables.

That'll get mighty ripe very soon."

The sheriff ordered two breakfasts for the men in jail as Chance walked out of the café. The street was quiet, only a few men out, some getting ready to open their shops and stores, others looking at the remains of the blacksmith shop and barn. Chance, his serape thrown over his shoulder, the big revolver gleaming in the morning sun, again walked down the middle of the street, daring anyone to make a move on him.

As he neared the bank, Jerrod Stockton came out onto the street to greet him, carrying a shotgun and wearing a revolver at his waist. "You should be in bed, Stockton. I just had the sheriff find some men to work on taking care of the dead animals, and put the place in some kind of order, but you're not in any condition to be out on the street. Go take care of yourself, I'm going to need you soon, and I want you well and strong." Chance said that with the hint of a smile, but there was no smile on Jerrod Stockton's face.

"You need me right now, Marshal. I hurt like hell, but not half as much as some others I know, or hope to know. Where you go, I go, until somebody is in chains or dead." The big man had lumps on his head, bad lacerations all over his head, and was walking with a decided limp. He was also carrying that double-barreled shotgun and nursing an anger that was growing like weeds in the sunshine.

Chapter Seven

"Are you sure, Hank?" Big Ben Stokes was having his morning coffee on the front porch of his main ranch house, daughter Jennifer in a chair opposite. Hank Adams had walked over from the bunk house when he saw Stokes on the porch. "Hired guns? Hank, is it possible you heard wrong?"

"No, sir, Ben. Col. George sent several of his men out to find outlaws that would come to Preston and kill the marshal." He stopped long enough to take the coffee offered him by Jennifer. "Thanks. I told Jerrod what I heard, and that's when he told me about the marshal coming into town. He said you met him, is that right?"

"He was here. Miller has gone too far this time." Hank Adams and Jennifer Stokes watched as Ben Stokes's body shook in a rare show of emotion. He often showed public anger, but this was an inner rage, coupled with the fear of losing what he had spent years building. He caught himself and settled deeper into the large chair.

"You know, Jenny Girl, we are just as guilty as that miserable banker. All of us, you, me, Hank, Cotton Phelps, even the blacksmith. We have let that bastard get away with all this scheming and land stealing. He has been running this valley as a dictator runs a nation, and we've just gone along, happy in our innocence." Looking closely one would see the arms of the chair bending to the strength of the man. The tremendous amount of inner tension all at once visibly released.

"I'm going into town." He got up suddenly, put his cup down, and looked around the ranch area. "I'm not going to lose this place Jenny, but I am going to help put that fool banker and his Col. George on ice for a long time.

"I want you to get the crew organized but don't head up into the high country until I get back. Hank, I want you to go find Cotton Phelps and then join me in town.

That marshal is going to need some back up, and we're going to give it to him.

"How dare they think they can run this valley with hired guns? Get my side arm and rifle Jenny while I saddle up." He almost jumped off the porch in his hurry to get to the corral and find his horse with Hank Adams matching him stride for stride.

"Jerrod said the marshal wanted him to get some men together and meet at the livery stables later this morning. Cotton already said he would be there, so I'll ride in with you, Ben." Stokes nodded his okay, and both men looked up to see two men ride into the barn and corral area. "Those two were hired by Jennifer yesterday, Ben, and I think they might also be associated in some way with Col. George. I know I don't trust them."

Ben Stokes had his anger building, pressure in the steam unit getting pretty hot, and he didn't like what Adams just told him. "What do you two want here?" he said more than loud enough for them to hear.

"Miss Stokes hired us yesterday, Mr. Stokes, but we wanted to tell her that we can't start until tomorrow. Something very important has come up, and we have to stay in town for another day." *Whimpering* and *liar* were the first two words Ben Stokes thought as the smaller of the men started to dismount.

Stokes's mind was on fire as he looked at the two men and knew that they probably worked for Miller and Dickson, and were here to spy on what was going on at the valley's largest spread. He pointed at the one who did the talking.

"Get your skinny butt back on that horse, mister. You don't work here, never have worked here, and never will work here. You slither like that foul snake you are back to your Col. George and Preston Miller, and next time I see you, I might just shoot you dead. Now, get off this ranch right now." As he was talking, Adams drew his revolver, cocked it, and let it casually aim at the man. They left at a high lope in a cloud of dust, Ben Stokes shaking his fist at them and laughing at the same time.

"Won't see them for a while, Ben," Adams said, breaking into a big laugh as well. Jennifer brought arms and ammunition as the two saddled up for the ride into town.

***

Chance and Jerrod Stockton strode down the street to the bank, Chance with his rifle in the crook of his arm and Stockton holding that mean-looking shotgun. "Just what gauge is that thing, Stockton? Looks like you could bring an elephant down with it."

For the first time in many hours Jerrod Stockton got a smile on his big face. "It's only a ten gauge, Jacob, built like a punt gun the commercial boys use to splatter ducks and geese all over a pond. Don't know about an elephant, but I'm hoping it will splatter a colonel I know."

"Keep the wolves from gunning me down from behind, Stockton, while I scare the pants off our banker friend." He stopped suddenly, and turned to the smithy. "Are you positive that you are up to this? This is not the time to play hero."

"I'm hurtin' everywhere there is to hurt, Chance, but I'm in plenty good enough shape to back your play. I've got more than half a dozen men coming into town to meet with you in a couple of hours, so give Miller hell in there, and I'll keep things in order out here."

"This is what trust is, Mr. Stockton, thank you," and Chance walked into the bank and told the cashier that he had an appointment with banker Miller. The teller, about as nervous as a cat on the wrong side of the dog's fence, said that Mr. Miller had sent word that he wouldn't be in today.

"Let me tell you how this works," Marshal Chance said, leaning his rifle against the highly polished wood of the cashier's cage. My name is Jacob Chance, U.S. Deputy

Marshal for Nevada Territory, and I'm here investigating some possible land fraud. You are interfering with my job, and that, kind sir, is a federal offence. Which of those two doors is Miller's office, and if you screw with me, you'll be in jail in five minutes or less."

Under weight, under height, under threat, the little man in the striped shirt and green eye shade pointed at the door on the right. Chance nodded, picked up his rifle, and walked into the office to find Miller sitting behind his desk. "You're not welcome here, Marshal. This is private property, and you are not welcome." Miller's eyes glazed over, his hands were shaking and the banker tried to hide that by moving them from the desk to his lap. "I own this building, every building in this town, every lot, every street, every business. I'm telling you now, leave Preston. You're not welcome."

Miller had been sitting at his desk since just after the fire started in the livery stables, and in his heart he knew that Colonel Dickson, his partner, was responsible, which in turn made him an accomplice. He remembered his grandfather telling him all of the stories of finding this beautiful little valley, of building his ranch and letting a town of sorts grow up around the home ranch.

"We settled this valley, Pres," he would say, rocking in an old cane chair, chomping on a cigar, and holding, then sipping from a glass of whiskey, "and there will come a time when you might have to defend our right to be here. It was open land, free for the taking, and I did. Yes, sir, Preston, I did, and soon it will all be yours. Defend it, defend it, keep it for all time."

Miller looked up in the middle of these thoughts and found U.S. Marshal Jacob Chance standing in his office door. "Get out. Get out of my town. This is my town and you have no right to be here." He had never spoken to anyone like that before. He had never been this afraid of anyone like this before. He was about to collapse, like he did the first time he got into a fist fight, took a blow to the nose, and cried for three days, alone in his room.

Chance walked over to the big oak desk, settled into a chair opposite Miller, stood his rifle up leaning on the desk and just watched as the banker slowly came apart. It was a full thirty seconds before he said anything. "Glad you got that out of your system, Mr. Miller. Now, we can talk," and again let things go quiet. Miller wouldn't look at him, his hands still shaking, even in his lap, his lips quivered, and he was as red as a fine sunrise just before a storm.

Looking a man in the eye is something that comes natural to those who don't commit criminal acts, but for a man like Miller, his entire life has been one lie compounded by the next, one foul deed following and following. When committing himself to a lie, it was generally through intimidation of someone already intimidated. A banker could easily threaten a man indebted to him... Jacob Chance was not that man.

"You've told a lot of people that you own this land, that you have deeds to it from Utah Territory, and if that's the case I probably won't give you too much more trouble. If you will simply show me those deeds, then I'll take up my other problems with the good Colonel Dickson.

"There are laws, Mr. Miller, even for people that think they own something. Laws that protect both the owner, and the person attempting to purchase. If you do own this entire valley, and I don't believe you own a single acre of it, simply show me those deeds."

Miller reached inside his coat, Chance stiffened and slipped his revolver out of the holster, and the banker pulled a handkerchief out and blew his nose, wiped his eyes, and wanted a solid belt of whiskey in the worst way. Chance slipped the forty-five back in its leather, sighed gently, and said, "Now, Mr. Miller. Let's see those deeds."

Miller coughed, eyes roaming around the room, never resting on Jacob Chance, remembered what George

Dickson had told him. He sat a little straighter in his wing back chair, wanted to look this marshal in the eye, but couldn't. "I don't have the deeds here, Marshal. They are on file in Salt Lake City. If you want to see them, you'll have to go to Salt Lake." *There*, he thought, *I did it.*

"We have a little problem with that, Miller. My boss is the U.S. Attorney for these western territories, and he tells me there are no recorded land deeds on record in Utah Territory for this valley, and since this is now Nevada Territory, I know for a fact there are no recorded land deeds for this valley on record in Carson City. You're a fraud, sir." He settled back in his chair, glared at the banker, then stood suddenly and slammed his fist on the desk top, howling, "And a *liar*." He said later he was sure Miller almost wet his pants.

Chance was still having a difficult time understanding how one person could ride into a valley like the Golden Valley and simply say, "This is mine." Even one totally uneducated knew that land was transferred to claimants, and the idea of riding in, claiming the entire miles-long valley, then building a town, erecting a bank, and selling off parcels of that land, never recording a deed anywhere, wasn't something that one comes upon very often.

"Now, if you'll stand up, it's time to take a nice stroll down to the jail, and have a good long rest while I try to clean up this mess you've made." He couldn't imagine how long a job like that might take. "You'll be talking to dozens of federal prosecutors, federal land agents, and federal prison guards for many years, Miller. Now, on your feet."

Before Miller had a chance to say or do anything, there was a commotion, including swearing by more than one person, and breaking furniture in the front of the bank. Chance grabbed his rifle, motioned Miller to sit back down, and started toward the office door.

Two more loud thumps were heard from the front of the bank, and Jerrod Stockton yelled, "Where are you, Chance?"

Chance opened the door saying, "Right here," and found Stockton standing over two large men, both with revolvers still in their holsters and both bloody and out of the fight. "Take their weapons, smithy, and bring them into the office here." He looked over at the clerk, standing in a corner, terrified as he had never been, and said, "Lock that front door and if you let anyone in, I'll shoot you first." Smiling broadly to Stockton, he ushered the three into the office.

He looked over at Miller, cowering behind his desk. "You better come up with some answers here, Mr. Miller." He made sure Stockton had control of the two gunmen, and looked over to Miller. "You own nothing here. Even those that have paid you off, thinking they now own their plots, don't. Not one single parcel of land in this valley has ever been recorded by any lawful agency."

Chance backed up just a bit, understanding that Miller was fully aware of the seriousness of the situation. "So, Mr. Stockton, sir," and still holding his rifle at the ready, said, "just who are our visitors?"

"I don't know these two, Marshal," Stockton said, slamming the first one down into a chair. "Don't think I've ever seen either one before."

"Any chance you met them last night?"

"They are the right size, but I don't think so." When Stockton pushed the second man into one of the chairs in the office, the man's jacket came open revealing a brocade vest underneath.

Chance looked first at Miller, then at Stockton. "So, it looks like Colonel George, has a couple of ruffians on the payroll. Damn, Jerrod, these charges just get piled so high Miller and Dickson won't ever get out of prison." He strode over to where the banker was slumped in his chair and slapped him across the side of the head. "Did you really think you could pull this kind of a caper off against the federal government? Well, let's see if we can hustle these fools off to the jail, Jerrod. Here's how we'll do it," and he laid out his plan for moving the two thugs and Miller off to Sample's jail.

***

Big Ben Stokes and Hank Adams rode out of the Stokes' pasture onto the trail leading into town after chasing the two yahoos off. "Those two are trouble, Hank. I think we'll be seeing more of them. Did Jerrod say what this marshal might have planned?" The ride in would take more than an hour, so they just walked their horses, then trotted for a while, and then returned to a walk. Lots of miles could be covered doing it that way.

"He sent a letter off to his boss in San Francisco asking for help, and with Dickson planning to bring hired guns into town, he's sure going to need that. Miller is a crafty old bastard, but Dickson, he's downright mean. Miller will cheat you out of whatever it is he wants, but Dickson, that man will kill you to get it. This marshal is all by himself in this fight, and Stockton says he is asking for help from those that believe in law and order and justice." He looked over at his riding partner, smiled, and said, "I guess that's us, Ben," the two smiling as the long ride continued.

The conversation turned to the situation with the land owners, leasers, and those looking to become indebted to Miller and his bank. "I'm worried about the legality of what I've been paying for all these years," Stokes said. "If it turns out that Miller doesn't have those deeds he always talks about, and if he sold me land he didn't own, what happens to me and Jenny and Jim now?" This was the first time the full impact of the question had been fully voiced by Stokes, and he knew in his heart the ranch and everything he had been building all these years was in serious jeopardy.

"It was this combination of events," he said to Hank Adams, "that brought all this out in the open. First, Utah Territory becomes Western Utah Territory, then that becomes Nevada Territory, and then the government comes along with their Homestead Act, and this beautiful little valley has no owners. None."

"Well, Ben, there might be one. Sarah Jackson has actually filed her claim with the government under the Homestead Act. She might be the only legal land owner in the valley."

From about a mile out, following along the Good Hope River, they could smell the horrible aroma of burned flesh, and saw smoke coming from where the livery stable should have been standing. "It looks like we might be too late, Hank," Stokes said, pushing his big stud into a solid lope. "Looks like our war has started without us."

The scene got worse the closer the two got to town, and it was gruesome when they arrived. Several men with wagons and teams were sifting through the still-smoldering barn, dragging dead horses, mules, and a cow out, trying to get them loaded on the wagons. Stokes and Adams tied off their mounts in front of the hotel in time to see Jerrod Stockton walk into the bank carrying a shotgun. "I hope that doesn't mean what it looks like, Hank. Is he going to do something really bad? Damn, we better find out what the hell is going on."

There were town people milling around, in the middle of the main street, on the board sidewalks, even looking out of second story windows. "It looks like it's been one hell of a morning around here," Hank Adams muttered. "We need to see what Stockton is doing at the bank carrying that old double-barrel monster of his."

***

Jerrod Stockton, showing all the bruises, scrapes, and bumps from his beating walked out of the bank, shotgun held high, escorting one of the men who had tried to break in. "Come on, jerk, down the street to the jail, and one misstep, you are one dead son of a bitch," and he prodded the man with the mean end of his scatter gun. Because of the ruckus earlier, the livery being burned to the ground, and the bank being closed, the sight of the town's blacksmith holding a man at the end of a shotgun and marching him down the street toward the jail drew many pairs of eyes.

"One of your friends tries to help you, and you die first. Just so you know, I'll only shoot you with one barrel so I can use the other on your friend. But, of course, you'll still be dead first." Stockton caught sight of Stokes and Adams as he marched his prisoner down the main street.

"Sure glad you two are here. Come on, walk with me, and keep your eyes wide open. As the marshal said a minute ago, this town is about to blow up." He used as few words as possible to bring Stokes and Adams up to date, about the livery, about the banker not having any deeds, about these two jaspers looking to kill the marshal, and now about trying to get everyone from the bank to the jail without anyone getting shot.

"Looks like we got here just in time, Hank," Stokes commented, checking to make sure his rifle had one in the chamber and his revolver was ready to be pulled at a moment's notice. Adams was doing the same thing. It ended up being almost a parade as many of the locals joined in, some giving Stockton plenty of encouragement, others just being typical looky-looks.

"Here you go, Sheriff. Marshal Chance said to lock this jasper up tight as hell and don't let him talk to anyone. Gotta go back for more. I'll get you some help down here in a bit." Hank Adams said he would be glad to stay and back up any play that might take place at the jail.

"That'll be fine Hank," Sheriff Sample said. "I now have three men in here, and you are telling me that all three work for Dickson? He sure as hell won't like that."

At the bank, Chance had the other hired assassin take his jacket off. "That's a vest like those worn by the people hired by Dickson. You work for that dude? I really hope so, because while I plan to make the rest of your life hell, I'll make his worse. Answer me," and he poked the man hard in the belly with the barrel of his rifle. "I don't mess with fools, jerks, or idiots," he said, slamming the rifle barrel across the man's head. "Give me an answer while you can."

"I work for Toby. He give me the vest. I don't know no Dickson." Chance stood stock still for a few seconds, pulled the hammer back on the rifle and very slowly brought the big piece to his shoulder. The man in the vest turned white, was shaking all over, Miller howled not to do it, and Chance lifted the barrel just an inch or two and fired one round over the man's head. The muzzle blast alone put burn marks on the man's face and knocked him back into the chair. Miller was screaming, the fear of the devil himself crawling up and down his spine.

"Like I said, I don't mess with fools," and jacked another round into the chamber of the big gun. "Oh, now look what you've done. You pissed all over the banker's nice carpet. You're getting that chair stained. You are just an idiot," and he laughed, and again, slowly brought the rifle up to his shoulder.

"All right. All right, I work for Colonel George. God, man, don't shoot."

Chance took the hammer off set, reached over with his free hand and slapped the dude as hard as the man had ever been slapped. "You got some sense, now boy. What were you supposed to do here? What did this fine upstanding citizen, Colonel George, have in mind for your little employment offer?" He pulled a chair over and sat facing the outlaw, his rifle cradled for a quick shot if it was necessary.

"Miller, you might want to listen to this, because when I'm through with this boy, you're next. Don't be pissing in your own office, now, Mr. Banker." He looked back at the dude, smiled at him actually, and asked his name. When the man didn't answer, Chance's finger tightened just a bit on the rifle.

"Willoughby, Frank Willoughby. God man, don't shoot," and he rubbed some of the burn spots on his face. "Me and old Tom got into town last night and Colonel Dickson offered us money and work if we took care of you. He didn't say you was a marshal or nothing. He said you and that big guy was gonna rob the bank, and we would be helping the town."

Chance was laughing so hard he had to stand up and walk around the office about three times before he could speak. "Well, son, in a way you are helping the town right now," and there was more laughter, more animation as he continued walking around the office. About that time the clerk brought Jerrod Stockton back into the banker's chamber.

"What the hell's all the laughter?" he said, looking from one to the other of the three men inside. "What'd I miss?" Then he remembered his guest. "Look who I found."

"Ben Stokes. I am glad to see you. Has Jerrod brought you up to date with what has been going on around here the last couple of days?"

"He has at that, Marshal. Hank Adams rode in with me and he's down at the jail with Sample. I met these two jerks at my ranch early this morning, before Hank and I rode into town. They must have beat us by just enough time to get our fine blacksmith all riled up," and he was smiling at Stockton as he said that. "This giant is ready to take on the whole rebel army this morning."

"He should be," Chance answered. "A couple of guys beat the hell out of him last night, then burned the

97

stables to the ground. Yeah, you don't want to get on Stockton's bad side today." He looked back at the man in the chair, rubbed his chin for just a minute.

"You were in the willows early this morning watching the livery burn. I thought you were familiar. So even after I fire a round over your head, even after you piss your pants, you're still willing to lie. You bastard, you know who beat the hell out of Mr. Stockton. Tell me now, you might live to see the jail," and he raised the rifle again, cocked the hammer back, and took long steady aim.

The man was crying, actually sobbing. Banker Miller was terrified at what he knew was about to happen, and both Stockton and Stokes were wondering whether the marshal would actually shoot an unarmed man. "I don't know their names. I'm not lying, I don't know their names."

Chance lowered the rifle and smiled at the man. "See? Telling the truth doesn't hurt anywhere near as much as lying. Are those two men still in town or did they run off like cowards? Give me a straight answer," and he paused for just a moment, "or else."

"Colonel George sent them away on some kind of job. I don't know where they are right now. That's the truth."

Chance looked over at Stockton and Ben Stokes. "Looks like the Dickson fool is taking over the operation." He looked at Miller. "You're out of job, Mr. Banker, sir. Your partner is running the program, so we'll just scoot you down to the jail and then I think I'll have a talk with this so-called colonel.

Chapter Eight

Two men came riding into Preston from the south, their horses lathered with white foam, their mouths and noses spitting more, the men filthy from trail dust and their own way of living. With no regard for their horses or for the people who might be on the street, they slid the ponies to a stop in front of the Good Hope Saloon, bailed off while the horses were still sliding, and dashed into the drinking parlor. The bartender simply pointed up the stairs when the two slammed their way through the main doors, and bounded up the stairs and into Colonel George Dickson's private office.

"Got good news, Colonel George," the larger of the two men said. "Looks like we'll have three or four of those Brady boys coming into town later today. We rode all night, found that bunch, told them what you said to tell them, and they aren't too far behind us." He was still panting like an out-of-shape bull rider just got throwed, and plopped down in one of the office chairs. His partner was already sitting, his lungs sucking every ounce of air they could find.

"That is good news, boys. There was a terrible accident after you left last night. Seems some ruffians showed up in town, men with a need to settle an old argument with Jerrod Stockton. Beat him mercilessly and then burned the stables and blacksmith shop." There was just the slightest hint of a smile as he said that and the two men exchanged knowing glances. "I don't know whether Mr. Stockton is going to make it or not, but it would be a good thing for you boys to walk about our fine little town, and see what you can find out." There was a most disagreeable look on Dickson's face as he said that and the two men started to stand up, understanding fully what the colonel meant.

"We had our horses lined out before we stopped at

the livery, so we were well out of town before the fire alarms were being hollered about. Doubt anyone saw us, Colonel George. Anything else you want, or just to walk around town?"

"Stop for something to get your throats cleared on the way out. No more than one shot of whiskey, now, don't want to slow your thinking, now, do we," he said, handing each man two twenty dollar gold pieces, more than they would make in two months on one of the ranches. "That was good work, boys. Good work indeed."

He waited for the door to close before he broke out in a full and gratifying smile. "Come busting into my town and mess with my way of life, Mr. U.S. Marshal, and you'll find enough trouble to send you to other, very hot, places, indeed." He poured himself a snifter of fine brandy, lit a cheroot, and sat at his walnut desk, satisfied that he had things under full Colonel Dickson control. "If I helped wrest California from the Mexicans I can sure as hell hold on to Preston."

***

The Brady boys, as they were known, were two brothers, Wayne, who was about twenty–three, and his older brother, twenty-five year old William, and their cousins, nineteen year old Amos and twenty-one year old Silas, and a meaner family bunch wasn't known in southwestern Nevada Territory. Each carried a ten thousand dollar bounty along on the trail, with the side note, *dead or alive*. Their trade mark had generally been other peoples' cattle, horses, or money, and often not leaving witnesses.

"Sounds like a pretty easy little chore," Wayne said, tying off his bedroll to the back of the saddle. "One lousy marshal to knock off and intimidate the rest of the townsfolk, and this Colonel George jerk is gonna pay us a thousand dollars. That's two fifty each, and now we find out the town has a bank as well.

"Might's well take it while we're there, eh boys?"

and the laughter rang out as they all mounted up for the fifty mile ride to Preston, Nevada Territory. They had a small ranch deep in the Panamint Mountains of south-eastern California, had raised all kinds of hell in Las Vegas Springs, a Mormon community in an area that might have been in Nevada Territory or maybe Arizona Territory, had been a part of Mexico not too long ago, and had been home for about a week before Dickson's men had found them. Whoever might have owned or worked that ranch they called theirs wasn't known.

For starters, the Brady boys had taken control of all criminal activity in the northern Mojave Desert, the Owens Valley, and had been known to rob the few miners who could be found in what was called Death Valley.

They were going to ride at a gentle trot/walk/trot pace, spend the night camped just outside Preston, and go into town the next day. "One marshal? This sure as hell should be about the easiest money we've ever made, boys. Wonder what kind of a man this Colonel George is?" and Wayne shook his head about it all.

"Think with just one marshal to worry about, he could do the job hisself," cousin Silas said. "Remember when we was up in Austin and the sheriff and his two real brave deputies took off for the hills when we rode into town? That bank had lots of gold and silver in its vaults."

"Yeah," said Wayne, "more than we could carry out. Sure hated to leave all them gold coins, but just couldn't get 'em in the saddle bags." Laughter among the Brady boys rang through the desert territory as they continued north. "Shoulda brought a damn buck board for that job."

***

"You two take this jackass down to the jail, and keep your eyes open. We've made a pretty big play this morning, and that Dickson bastard is gonna get his play going soon. I'm going to see if I can make Mr. Banker the fraud here piss his pants," and he looked over at Miller, smiling a big friendly *howdy pard* smile. "Here's a little advice, you two, that was given to me when I joined the marshal business.

"Don't take any crap from anyone and shoot to kill. I can't make it any more plain than that. Dickson is a dangerous man, has enough money that he hires lots of people to do his dirty work, and some of them are liable to be out on the street right now, looking for you two. Be careful as hell but don't take any crap and shoot to kill." Stokes and Stockton looked at each other, knowing the other would be a fine partner in this mess.

"Before I head out, Marshal," Stokes said, a long hard worried look across his face, "when you win this fight, what will that mean to those of us that are working land that may not belong to us?"

"It's going to be long time before all of that can be worked out, I'm afraid, Ben." He sat down on the edge of Miller's desk, giving the question plenty of time to settle in. "I'm afraid there will probably be years of court battles, of deals and dealing among lawyers and government agents, that money and property and families will be sundered by whatever comes about." He knew that wasn't a good enough answer, that people would be hurt, that land would be lost, that families would be destroyed.

"This kind of situation is the worst most families can think about. You strike me as the kind of man that is as honest as the day, and I don't have to tell you this, but if you have kept all the records of all the payments to this greedy jerk," and he nodded toward Miller, "all the letters and notes that refer to your deals, you may come out in fair shape." He stood up, walked around behind the desk, and glared at Miller.

"You boys better head out. Get them to jail, then head back here. It's close to time when we were going to have our meeting with your friends, Jerrod, so if you see any, bring them here to the bank." He got one of the Jacob Chance grins across his face. "Looks like I have new offices. This is now a federal office building," and he took a swipe at Miller, almost in jest, laughing at his comment.

Stockton whupped his prisoner across the side of the head, saying, "Get up jerk. Going-to-jail time for you." He and Stokes ushered the man out the door, had the clerk open the main door, and stepped onto the wooden boardwalk. "You lock that door tight and don't let anyone but me back in," he said, fingering the hammers on his shotgun. Chance turned his attention to Banker Miller.

"Here's where we are, Mr. Miller, just you and me, alone in your office, your clerk out front unable to hear a word we say. Feel confident that I'm not going to kill you. That just wouldn't be right," and he smiled down at the fat little banker. "You have destroyed the lives of many people in this valley because you are a cynical, selfish, criminal bastard, and I am here to try to salvage some of the wreckage.

"I can't believe you just rode into this valley one day and said, 'Oh, my, I think I'll take all of this for me,' or is that exactly what you did?" Miller didn't say a word and Chance slapped him across his jowly face, hard enough to almost knock him out of his wing back chair. "Well?" the marshal said, cocking his fist for the next shot.

Miller's mind went back to when he came to this valley, meeting his grandfather for the first time, sitting at his grandfather's side on the veranda porch of a large ranch house, looking out over the entire valley. "All this, Preston, is mine. I came here, saw this beauty, this potential, and staked it out. Someday, never forget this, it will all be yours." What he didn't tell Miller or anyone else is that he never registered his claim anywhere, Mexico, Utah, anywhere. The old man may have put up some posts somewhere, as claim monuments, but he never laid claim to the land in any legal manner. The old man had tried his hand at working the Rocky Mountains and rivers and valleys for beaver skins, tried to be a mountain man, but it wasn't in him.

Old man Preston was a predator in most men's eyes, a cheat at cards, a cheat in business, a foul-mouthed fool who would cheat even when he didn't need to. He was run out of those late beaver camps along the Green River, in Salt Lake, even along the Humboldt River, and wasn't welcome anywhere in the Missouri River waterway. He and an acquaintance, along with some pack mules, headed southwest out of Salt Lake and stumbled on this pristine valley, and it was believed the acquaintance didn't live to see the second sunrise. In his limited vision, all that was needed was to say he had staked his claim on the entire valley. In the 1840s men were independent to a fault, the law was what they made it, and for those with no personal boundaries, the land was open and free for the taking, regardless of who might say it wasn't.

When the old man died, Preston Miller became the owner, that ranch slowly evolved into the town Miller named Preston, and then another devious soul arrived on the scene. The banker's lip was quivering, he was almost sobbing he was so frightened, and he knew that it was George Dickson who had created the problem. It was Dickson who had come to the valley ten years ago or so with these grand plans for a town, for a bank, for a plan to sell off large parcels of the valley at high prices, and foreclose on mortgages at the least provocation. And Preston Miller thought at the time, "what a wonderful idea," and the two men were now wealthy as those mythical men in Virginia City's mines.

"It was Dickson, Marshal," was all Miller said, and Jacob Chance could almost believe him. "Dickson said since my grandfather said that he laid claim to the valley, that it would stand up in court. He put this whole plan together, and we have a signed partnership agreement."

Chance hadn't heard that before, that paperwork on this majestic conspiracy existed, and that could put Miller and Dickson in prison for many years, if nothing else did. He was about to gently cuff the man when gunshots rang out, close to the front of the bank.

"You move, you're dead," Chance said to Miller, sprinting to the front area of the bank, and seeing the front door shredded by heavy blasts from a shotgun. The clerk lay on the floor bleeding, whimpering, and Chance dove behind the cashier's cage as another volley of rounds came through the front of the bank. On his belly and looking around the base of the cage, Chance saw two men about to burst through the door with that menacing shotgun leveled for action. His rifle up and steady, he blasted two rounds through the door, heard some loud screaming, and stood up, firing twice more, then pulled the big forty-five. Two strides and he was at the door, yanked what was left of it off its hinges in time to find Stockton and Stokes coming up the street at a high lope and two men writhing on the ground suffering from bullet wounds.

Chance disarmed the two wounded gunmen and yelled at Ben Stokes to get in the bank and protect Miller. "Our war is underway," he muttered, helping Stockton get the two men up on the boardwalk. "The clerk was wounded, too, Jerrod. Bring him out here." He motioned at one of the bystanders who had already gathered about for a look at the marshal's handiwork. "Go get the doctor," he hollered at the man.

"Ain't no doctor in Preston," the man said, and that surprised the marshal.

"No doctor? What do you people do when you're sick or injured? Nearest town is more than fifty miles away, and across those mountains," and he jerked his head to the west. Jerrod brought the clerk out, and all he had were a few nicks from some splintered wood, no shotgun wounds. "What is this, smithy, no doctor?"

Jerrod Stockton stood up from making the clerk comfortable and said, "Well, Chance, since I take care of doctoring most of the animals around here, I also take care of doctoring most of the people. Of course they burned out my medical supplies," and he took a little pause before adding, "and my clinic," said with an ironic smile on his face. "I think the best bet is to take these people down to the jail. I can work on their wounds, and we can protect the prisoners from any more attacks."

"Yeah, I agree," Chance said and got a group of local men to help carry the three wounded down to the jail. Chance brought Stokes and Miller out, and put Miller in the middle of the group, and walked the bunch down to the jail, every gun at the ready. "This guy Dickson is behind the whole problem, Mr. Stockton, and it appears he will stop at nothing to keep his position."

He was looking at the two men he had shot and couldn't place either one. "I've only been in town a short time, Stockton, but I don't recognize these two. Have you seen them before?"

"They have been trouble for a couple of years, Chance. Work at odd jobs for Dickson and Miller, and I would be willing to bet they are the ones that attacked me and burned the stables. They make sure people pay their mortgages and rent on time, they are the collectors, and are as mean as any two men I've ever known."

"Hmmm," Chance said. "Don't seem to have much fight in 'em right now." He gave the two a terrible scowl, and spoke to Stockton and Stokes. "If anything erupts as we walk toward the jail, these two die first, but we want to save the life of Miller, if we can. We will need him to testify against Dickson, and then, it would be nice if they ended up in the same federal prison."

The entourage made it to the jail, and as they got the wounded hustled inside, Chance noted four men, rough, dirty, and ugly mean, riding down the street. "Don't look hard, Jerrod, but who are those men? Looks tell me they are hired to take me out."

"Them's the Brady boys, Marshal. I would think you're right, and four meaner men you won't meet in this territory. Each has big bounties wrapped around his neck, each has killed many more than one man."

"Dickson must have sent the word out for some reserves. Well, I did too, but it will be some time before my people get here." He closed the jail door as the four rode by, and each of the Brady boys was giving the marshal the evil eye, glaring at the man, almost calling him out with just a look. "Gonna be a fight," was all the big man muttered, pouring the first of many cups of boiling coffee.

***

Chance settled into one of the cane chairs in the jail office, remembering what the kinds of looks he just received from the Brady Boys had meant in the past. "I was down near Angel's Camp one time," he was thinking, "when I got looks like that from a gentleman who was standing at the end of the bar. He wouldn't let up, just kept glaring at me, and for the life of me, I couldn't place the fool." He took a couple of long drinks of that boiling coffee, and kept remembering bad times.

"After two stiff glasses of whiskey that fool came up the bar and challenged me. When he pulled his revolver he was drunk and ugly mean, and I put two slugs through his chest." There was sadness written across his broad face. "Bartender told me later that the man didn't have any idea who I was. He was angry at someone else and died for it." He finished off the cup of coffee, stood up and stretched some. "Those Brady Boys," he said to the group in the office, "are going to be big trouble. My job is to try to head off this kind of trouble, and if I can't, to end the problem any way possible. I don't want you men to try to take on these jerks. If they make a play, simply back me, but don't become a hero. Most heroes die and I don't want that to happen here." He walked to the coffee pot and filled his tin cup with another load of boiling tar.

***

"Yeah, we saw him comin' in. Doesn't look that mean and tough to me, eh boys." Wayne Brady and his boys were in Colonel Dickson's upstairs office, whiskey glasses in hand. "One marshal, you've got guns, hell, Colonel, you look fit enough to take him out. What you need us for? Now, don't get me wrong, we want what you gonna pay us, but why not do it yourself?"

He had been nursing that problem the whole time since they left the Panamints, and something didn't seem right, and he didn't know what. Wayne Brady had made it through the third grade before being asked not to return to school, couldn't read a word, but if it was money, he could count very well. "Do you have some kind of a plan, or do we just pick a fight with the gentleman and leave his worthless body in the dust and mud?"

Dickson smiled at the comments, sipped his own belt of good whiskey, and smiled at the four vulgar outlaws he had hired to protect his interests in Preston. "I have dispatched many men during my military career, gentlemen, but in my retirement, I find it more fitting to hire the job done." Self-satisfaction was written broadly across his ugly face, none of it understood by the Brady boys.

"As to a plan," he continued, "it is important that those trying to wipe me out be put to rest. I believe my men offered you one thousand dollars to end this quest by the marshal, but there are others now that also need to be gone. I'll give each man one hundred dollars for each of those others that are killed. I have a list here," and he handed a sheet of paper to Wayne Brady, "and I'll leave the details to you to work out. I want you to be very careful not to kill my partner, Preston Miller." Dickson knew that without Miller and his bank, none of what they had built would stand. Deeds could always be found in the strangest places.

The Brady Boys looked for room at the bar downstairs and found that many who stood there moved when they stepped up. A bottle and glasses were produced and the four got down to business. "Get everybody on this list, and the marshal, get paid by the colonel, then the bank, and we'll be on our way, boys," Wayne laughed, draining his first glass of the hot amber liquid. The four had every reason to believe they had stood up to stronger foes in the past, that this would be more of a hoot than a serious job. "Haven't been to a real turkey shoot in a long time," Amos Brady commented, downing a hefty shot of whiskey.

***

Dickson was pacing, shaking his head, and not smiling as he contemplated what was happening in his town. "That Jackson woman has to be behind this, and now Miller is in custody. He'll break with a simple slap to his fat jowls." He walked out of the office and called his floor boss upstairs. "I need every man on the payroll to be in town, Jack. Strip the ranches and move those men along with our dealers into the hotel. I want every room on the second and third floor of that hotel to have two men at the front windows. If that marshal or anyone with him moves, I want them dead.

"The Brady gang will be out on the street, so don't shoot them, but right now it looks like most of the men who have declared themselves to be with that marshal are at the jail. This has gone as far as it has because I didn't act soon enough, Jack, so make sure that bunch is dead. Every damn one of them." He returned behind his desk and poured himself a shot of bourbon.

"I have possession of every inch of property in this valley, Jack, and every man that stands with me on this will get a parcel. Stokes will lose that ranch of his when he's dead, and we'll break it up into pieces for you men that stand with me and Preston Miller. You make sure every man on my payroll understands that." He was smiling as another thought came to mind.

"Have a couple of the boys pay a visit to that Sarah Jackson, will you?"

"I will colonel. I heard that Cotton Phelps has been helping her out."

"We'll take care of that bastard Phelps as well. But make sure she is paid a nice visit by a couple of our boys. Get moving now and get as many men as you can inside that hotel."

Floor boss Jack Hastings hadn't gotten two steps out when Dickson called him back. "I think you might be right, Jack. The Jackson woman needs to be eliminated. Okay, here's a new plan, and I want you to see to it that it is carried out. Use some of the men from the ranches on this. Kill Jackson and her daughter, then lie to Jennifer Stokes about her father being in town and needing help.

"Yeah, that's good. I like this kind of thinking. Bring that Stokes girl into town, and we'll use her as a hostage. Yeah, get on that right now, Jack," and a satisfied smile returned to his ugly face.

Chapter Nine

Chance had his prisoners locked up, Stockton was trying to work on those who were wounded, and Chance called Stokes and the sheriff to join him for a cup of coffee. "Ben, this is going to be nasty as hell for the next couple of days. I don't expect any of my people in town for another couple days at the least, and from what I've seen, Dickson has a pretty good bunch of guns waiting to end this problem." Stockton came back into the front office about that time.

"One of those two is gonna die, Marshal. I can't fix a bullet to the gut like he took. The clerk and the other fella will be okay if I can get some iodine or alcohol and some bandages. I'll go over to the apothecary and pick some stuff up," and he moved toward the door.

"Not so fast, Mr. Stockton. From now on, nobody walks out of this building alone. We go in twos or threes, never alone." He put his cup down and reached for his rifle, which he had reloaded when they arrived. "Ben, your son Jim is in one of the cells back there. This would be a good time for you to have a man-to-man with the boy. He's on his way to big-time criminal charges and I don't think he recognizes the problem. He can still make things right for himself."

"Thank you, Marshal," Stokes said, recognizing the offer just made by Chance. "The boy's a hot-head," and with just the hint of humor, said, "like his father before him." Stokes took his cup of coffee and a cup for his son and walked toward the cell area in the back of the building. "If you need me, Sheriff, yell loud and strong."

"Chance, I would like to go with you and Jerrod when you take your swing through town." Hank Adams was holding an empty coffee mug and chewing on an unlit cheroot, almost itching for a fight. "There's too many things that have happened over these last few years, so many of us have just let them happen, and I'm pretty embarrassed by it all. Sarah Jackson was the final insult, and none of us stood up to these people, that is, not until you got here.

"I know most of these people here in town, Marshal, and while they may not be ready to pull a gun on these criminals, they also won't help them. With Jerrod and me walking with you, they will understand this is their fight as well."

"You should not feel embarrassed or ashamed, Hank. We have all let it happen," Jerrod Stockton piped in, looking like the bad end of a train wreck and itching for a fight. "We've seen men beat and watched property taken, and now, because little Sarah Jackson called for help, not from us, but from the government, we have a chance to do what's right."

Chance had the start of a smile listening to Stockton and Adams. "This town is going to be a better place because of men like you," he said. "It takes leadership to bring a town together, something I learned a long time ago. The phrase 'follow me' works a lot better than 'do this.'" Stockton held that big shotgun at the ready. "Grab one of Sample's rifles there, Hank, and let's see what we can find in this old town. Come on then, let's go get those supplies. Do you need anything, Sample?"

"No," he said, and then, with worry written all over his face, he continued. "Are we setting up for a siege here?"

"The thought occurred to me," Chance replied, "but I don't think we need to do that. These gentlemen and I are going to take a walk around town, talk to as many of the people that live and work here as possible, and try to keep a lid on things until my people are able to get here. If a big old fire fight develops, innocent people are going to get hurt, and I'm going to try to stay away from that." With his battered old hat in place and his serape set just so, Jacob

Chance, U.S. Marshal, opened the door to the jail and with Jerrod Stockton and Hank Adams right behind him, both toting big guns, walked out onto the streets of Preston, Nevada Territory.

***

"Son, you got yourself one big wildcat by the tail right now. Here, have some hot coffee and let's talk for a bit." Ben Stokes was looking into a pair of very sad eyes on the one hand, and an angry young man on the other. "I'm not going to preach anything at you, Jim, but I want you to understand the seriousness of the situation." The question lurked in the back of Stokes's mind, *Will he understand?*

So many times during his growing-up years, this boy, one Jim Stokes, did stupid things just because of misplaced anger, or a lack of thinking and reason. Ben Stokes hoped he would be able to get his son lined out, maybe keep him out of prison.

"You assaulted a federal marshal, Jim, not just another saloon drunk, and I just watched him shoot two of Dickson's men, one of whom is about to die. This isn't a game, and you are in trouble." He paused for what seemed like a long minute, his son taking a sip of hot coffee, and not looking at him.

"Marshal Chance has indicated that if you help out here, he might make it a little easier on you. Miller and Dickson do not have deeds to any of the property in this valley, they have been stealing everyone's money for years, including mine, and everyone's property rights are at risk right now. We're talking about a valley that is miles long filled with prosperous ranches, all possibly lost because of these two men. Do you understand what I'm saying?"

Young Jim Stokes, filled with anger about something he didn't understand, embarrassed by his actions, and now, young but an adult, catching hell from his father. He continued to stare into that coffee mug, would not raise his eyes to face his father, and also would not answer the question.

"Jim, don't be a fool. Right this minute is the most important time in your life. Nothing before right this instant means anything, and right now, the rest of your life depends on what you do or say. Grow up, damn it." Stokes' temper came to the surface, and he continued. "Be a man for the first time in your life. Stand up for something that means something to you, to your family, to the people in this screwed-up town." If the two hadn't been separated by steel bars, he might have reached out and punched his own son, or given him a good shaking.

Jim Stokes shirked away from his angry father, sat down on the edge of the jail house cot, and cupped his head in his hands, letting the coffee mug fall to the floor. Ben Stokes couldn't hear but could see that his son was crying, not great sobs, but muted sighs that were filled with grief. Finally, he looked up at his father, his face as sad as Ben Stokes had ever seen it. Tears filled his eyes, streamed down his cheeks, his nose was running, and he couldn't talk. The young man pulled his neckerchief off and blew his nose, wiped his eyes, and just stared at his father, softly crying his misery.

It was long minutes before he could say anything, and Ben was wise enough not to force the issue at this point. "Dickson and Miller have hired some professional outlaws to kill the marshal, along with Jerrod Stockton, Hank Adams, and myself. This may be the only time we will have to talk, and if things go wrong, this may be the last time that we will have together." Ben's temper had cooled, he was speaking quietly, in father to son fashion, with love and compassion, and what he said brought Jim to his feet, the crying jag over for the moment.

"Colonel George wouldn't do that," he said, then added, "Would he?"

"Have you ever heard of the Brady Boys, Jim?"

"Sure. Everybody knows about them. They're

here?"

"They're here to kill Marshal Chance and all the rest of us that are standing with him. Four bad men, four bad killers, in town right now, and if things go the way Marshal Chance wants them to go, you will be going to prison or be dead in the dust alongside the Brady Boys. It's time for you to make a decision on where your life is going. It's time for Jim Stokes to be that man I wanted for a son."

All of the years he had built that big ranch, raising a son and a daughter, knowing deep in his heart that his son was not growing up to be a man of honor, was able to shirk his responsibilities at any moment, that his daughter Jenny was the stronger of the two. "Now," he thought to himself, "I'm looking into the eyes of a criminal, my son, and I don't know if I can save him." If one could compare the eyes of the two men it would be difficult to tell which was the sadder.

The two men stood on opposite sides of the iron bars, one tall and husky, graying hair and just a stubble of beard, the other, almost citified in his brocade vest, white shirt, and string tie, one with fierce eyes penetrating the other's sad but defiant eyes. The younger Stokes broke first. "The colonel said that I was doing the right thing, trying to chase the marshal out of town. He said that Mr. Miller would be pleased with my work, that I would have a place in his company. It still doesn't seem right for that man to ride into town and tell people they don't own the land they have been paying for."

"What's right in this matter, Jim, is simply this. Neither Miller nor Dickson owned the land they were selling and then foreclosing on. They are the criminals in this matter and they have made a criminal out of you. Now, they have brought men into town to kill in order to protect what they stole in the first place. Get that through your head, damn it, Miller and Dickson are criminals of the highest damned order." Again, that Stokes' temper was coming to the surface and young Jim was having a hard time keeping his in check as well.

"Don't yell at me like that. I want to do the right thing, I really do, and I thought I was. Let me alone for a while, please Dad. Please. Let me alone for a while and let me think this through. I want to do the right thing," and he was ready to burst into tears again. Ben reached through the bars and tousled the boy's hair.

"I'll be back as soon as I can," he said, doing his best to smile at the boy. "I know you'll do the right thing." He stood there for another minute, just looking at what he thought was the saddest moment in his life; seeing his son in jail for assaulting a federal marshal. Finally, he turned and walked back to the front of the sheriff's office.

Sample was standing at the open door of the jail watching Marshal Chance, Jerrod Stockton, and Hank Adams cross the dusty street toward the Crystal Saloon. "Looks like those boys picked up a bit of a thirst," he joked as Ben Stokes joined him in the doorway.

"We've never gotten along very well, Sample," Stokes said, "But if the marshal is willing to work with you, then I want you to know that I am too. This is going to be one hell of a fight, I'm thinking, and all of our backs are gonna need someone standing close."

"You're right Ben, you're right. I've been an old fool working for Miller and Dickson, and I know I'm not the man Chance is, or you, or Hank, but I want to do the right thing, at least once in my life. I've always taken the easy way out, but I can't do that this time. I'll cover your back, Ben, don't doubt that."

The two men shook hands, forced smiles toward each other, and watched their three companions head into the Crystal Saloon.

***

"I thought you were going into Preston this morning, Cotton, but thank you for bringing some of our stuff over. It's really true, then, isn't it? There really is a U.S. Marshal come to Golden Valley and put Miller in jail. That why you were supposed to go to town? To help?" Sarah Jackson started talking as soon as she saw Cotton Phelps ride up trailing a mule carrying some of her belongings. Jennifer Stokes had come by the day before to make sure she and Georgia were okay, and knew that Phelps was supposed to be at a meeting in the morning.

"Jerrod said this marshal wants to talk to some of us. It's an ugly mess, Sarah, an ugly mess. I'm keeping your place the way you want it, but Dickson and that fool Toby want to make some serious changes. I don't know how long I can hold out against those two."

Cotton Phelps had worked cattle and been a ranch hand just about from the day he was born on his grandfather's ranch along the Arkansas border with Texas. His hands were gnarled from thirty years of rope work, thirty years of doctoring cattle, thirty years of hot branding irons, and yet, Sarah Jackson knew how soft and tender this large man could be. She had seen him hover over her daughter Georgia when the little girl got scraped, cut, or bruised, and seen this man brought almost to tears when she was thrown off her property.

Phelps moved west when it became obvious that a war between the states was going to happen, when militias were formed in southern states and men were conscripted to fight for the south despite their personal opinions on the issues. His grandfather--Phelps lost his father in an accident when he was just a boy, and his mother became a weak and unknown figure in his life-- told him, "Go, leave this country, go west, get away from this war that is about to blow up."

Before he could leave, armed militias forced the issue by confiscating the ranch, all the cattle and livestock, and demanding the old man, the young man, and the almost-mad woman to leave. On the way across Texas in a miserable old wagon, with a couple of saddle horses and a mule, Phelps's mother died from falling out of the wagon while it was moving, and then two weeks later his grandfather was killed by renegade Mescaleros.

At fifteen years old, Cotton Phelps became a man, brought that wagon and all the family possessions across Texas, Colorado, Utah, and found Golden Valley by accident. "Ran into some fellers at Las Vegas Springs one night telling me about this beautiful valley. Turned out to be Dickson agents selling land. I wasn't buying, but they said there was work aplenty for a good cattle and horse man. Three days later, here I was, and I ain't leaving.

"Dickson is the biggest bastard and most dangerous man I ever met, and when I found Sarah Jackson, I vowed to end that man's existence." As he rode into Sarah's camp he was remembering all of that, and trying his best not to remember just how much he felt for that beautiful lady.

He had told the story to Sarah Jackson, but no one else in Nevada Territory was aware of his background. Sarah had said many times to Jerrod Stockton, to Jennifer Stokes, even to Hank Adams that she had deep feelings for Cotton Phelps, but not the kind of love that would lead to marriage. It was Jennifer Stokes who told her father at the dinner table one night, "I think Sarah is kidding herself. She loves that man."

Sarah listened as Cotton Phelps talked while unloading the mule, found she was having a hard time understanding what he was saying. "Cotton, please be careful in town. I've lost a husband, I've lost two ranches now, and I don't want to lose you." Tears were welling, her voice was cracking, and the big strong cowboy put down a package of something, slipped an arm around Sarah's waist.

He drew her in close, she willingly put her arms around his heavy, strong shoulders, and felt more comfortable and safe than she had in years. "Won't do nothing stupid, boss lady." He kissed her on top of the head, continuing, "What I am going to do is put a stop to all this stealing land. I am as sure as I can be that what Dickson and Miller did is illegal. That is your ranch, with a deed from the government." He gave her a gentle squeeze, and then continued.

"And now, Dickson wants to combine your place with that run-down wretch of a place that Toby has. I doubt a single marshal can do anything, but I'm going into town and at least listen. I'll swing by later, pick up the old mule and let you know what I hear." He walked the mule over to a hitching rack that Sarah had put up and continued undoing the ropes holding the packs in place.

"Jennifer Stokes said her dad and Hank Adams were going into Preston this morning, also. You be careful, Cotton Phelps, you're the one man in this ugly valley that I trust, so don't get yourself killed or hurt." Her eyes gave her away faster than her words, and Phelps knew then that someday the two would be a couple. She was standing near the tent she called home now, looking down into the dust, brushing some of it first this way then the other with the toe of her boot. Her heart knew, her mind knew, only her stubborn attitude was fighting, and now, she knew that Cotton Phelps knew as well.

The big cowboy put his arms around her shoulders again, gave a strong hug, smiled down into her long sad face, and promised to be careful. "Jerrod said they wanted to meet sometime around noon, so I'm already late." He wanted to bend down and give her a long warm kiss, knew he couldn't do that, and squeezed her shoulders one more time, let go, and walked to his horse. "Be back in a little while," he said, mounting his cow pony. "Be careful unpacking. Your chickens are laying well and I have some eggs in there for my favorite two girls." He waved and rode off toward Preston.

Thoughts of his grandfather, the old ranch with the

large herd of cattle, belly deep in Arkansas and Texas grass, worked their way through his mind. "This valley is kind of like that place, not as humid, and sometimes we get a real winter here," he was thinking. "I can see us with a nice herd of cattle, raise some fine horses too," and he quit thinking when the idea of having children crept into his thoughts.

"Come on, caballo, let's get to town," and he spurred the horse into a nice lope, smiling like a ten year old with fresh fish on the end of a line.

***

"Heard all the guns earlier," the old barkeep said as Marshal Chance, Stockton, and Adams came through the saloon doors, armed to the teeth. "Glad to see you're all right." He started pouring three cold beers, and continued talking. "Did I see the Brady Boys ride into town? There's a bunch of bad guys I don't want to see in this bar. They come for you, Marshal?"

"'Fraid so, old man, but they won't get me." He quaffed half a pint of beer, laughed gently and said, "And won't like it if they try." The two old men were still sitting at the end of the bar, watching everything that was happening. "We're just walking around town letting people know that there might be some bad trouble, but that we aren't the bad guys.

"So you know, Preston Miller is in jail, and as soon as I can, I'll get a process started that will hopefully settle all these questions about land ownership."

One of the old guys at the end of the bar whapped his glass hard on the heavy oak bar and gave a long "Whooee." Then it got quiet as everyone understood the war had been declared.

"Those Brady Boys hired by Dickson?" The barkeep had a worried look on his face. "They tore up a town south of here a while back. Dickson might have bit one big hunk of trouble off the end of that cheroot he chews on. He might pay them to kill you, but he won't have enough money to pay them to end it then. Hope you're as tough as you look, Marshal."

Jerrod Stockton laughed at the comment. "He's a hell of a lot tougher than he looks. Shot two men this morning, broke old Raccoon Toby's jaw last night, and had a plate full of horseshoes for breakfast. He's one tough marshal." Jerrod laughed through the whole speech and everyone at the bar was laughing when he got through.

Jacob Chance smiled but didn't join in the laughter. "We had all better be tough enough to eat them nails Jerrod uses on his shoes, I think, if we're going to live through this mess. You men hear anything you think I might need to know, get a message over to the jail. And, by the way, Pete Sample is on our side, he's not Preston Miller's sheriff anymore."

The three men downed their beers and headed back out onto the streets of Preston, looking to go business to business and be seen and heard. Four other men were walking out of the Bucket of Good Hope Saloon at that same time, also looking to wander about the streets of Preston. And, one other man was seen riding into town, gaping at the ruins of the livery stable. The lone rider spotted Jerrod Stockton along with Hank Adams and Marshal Chance, and rode toward them. Stockton saw the four on the wooden walkway turn, and one of the Brady Boys started to draw his revolver.

At the top of his lungs, the bear of a blacksmith yelled, "Take cover, Cotton," and raised his shotgun and fired, despite the tremendous distance between him and the Brady's. Chance had his rifle to his shoulder and jacked two rounds. One killed Silas Brady instantly, and the other slammed through the leg of Wayne Brady, taking him out of the fight for the moment.

It was Amos Brady who had pulled his iron first, and the bullet nicked Cotton Phelps' left elbow as he dove from his horse. He had iron out before hitting the ground and actually got a shot off as he rolled through the dust, ending up behind a water trough. Chance and Adams found refuge behind a wagon, and Stockton wedged himself between two buildings. "Cotton, can you hear me?" Stockton yelled across the street.

"I'm right here, Jerrod. What the hell is going on?"

"Them's the Brady Boys, and I'm with the Marshal. It's just us, Cotton, so make your moves carefully." He looked over at Chance, smiling like a little boy with new candy. "I got something here will make them boys think before shooting at us again," he said, breaking open the double barrels. He pulled the remaining shot shell out and put two different shells in. "These are my deer loads, Chance, watch this."

He leveled the scatter gun and aimed it at the water barrel that William Brady was hiding behind. One barrel at a time, fired about two seconds apart, and that water barrel exploded. With a loud "Whoee," Hank Adams fired two quick shots from his rifle, and William Brady was out of the fight. Amos Brady, running and dodging, made his way to the Bucket of Good Hope, a fusillade of lead not touching him, and dove through the doors. There was no return fire from him or from Wayne Brady, but several guns opened up from the second floor windows in the hotel. None of the shots found their marks.

"Looks like Colonel George has more back up than we knew," Chance said to Adams. "Stay down low, and we'll have to work on those fools one at a time. Don't waste any of your ammunition. Jerrod, can you see Cotton Phelps?"

"He's behind that water trough in front of the hotel. I don't think the men in the rooms upstairs know he's there." Stockton had put two more of his big deer slugs in the shotgun and was aiming at one of the hotel windows. Chance saw the shadow as well, and saw the man slammed back into the room when Stockton fired. "Got twenty or more deer with this puppy, Chance. Now, I've got my man."

Chance watched as Phelps crouched to move into the hotel, and was prepared to give as much cover fire as might be needed. "Cover that man," he said, and he, Adams, and Stockton sent a volley of rounds into the various windows of the hotel. That was followed by some loud screaming inside as many there were hit. The return fire was scattered, but it was there and Chance and company sent more rounds into the old wooden building. Walls of the hotel were thin, and rifle bullets went right through.

Chance took that moment to make a charge across the street and was surprised as another large volley of shots echoed up and down the main street of Preston. He dove behind the water trough where Phelps had been, and saw more than a dozen men with rifles, pistols, and shotguns lined up from the Crystal bar to just behind where he and Adams had been holed up.

"We got your back, Marshal," one of the old timers who spent most of his days at the end of the Crystal Saloon bar hollered across the wide street. "We got your back," and there was another round of shots fired into the hotel, this time with no return fire.

Chance crawled over to where he thought Wayne Brady should be and found the man, sprawled on his face in the dirt, dead. "Looks like that bullet to the leg took out a blood vessel." He then made a dash, with no fire coming his way, into the hotel to join Cotton Phelps. "Nice to meet you, Cotton. I've heard good things about you."

"Likewise, Marshal. Damn nice to meet you."

"Let's see if we can't get that bleeding stopped. Good thing that round missed your bone, there."

Another volley of shots from the Crystal Saloon boys and Adams and Stockton made the long run across the street and joined Chance and Phelps. "We need to clear this building and then get back to the jail. I don't know how many men that fool Dickson might have, but we know for a fact that, with Phelps here with us, and the two at the jail, there are six against them."

Stockton corrected the marshal. "Looks more like twenty to me, Chance. Looky there," and he pointed as the men from the Crystal saloon, now led by Sheriff Sample and Ben Stokes were spread out and almost marching toward the hotel. Chance almost smiled at the sight, and continued working on Cotton Phelps.

It seemed the entire town was armed and ready to march on Colonel Dickson and the Bucket of Good Hope Saloon. Chance got them out of the street as fast as he could, reminding them, in the strongest language possible, that Dickson still had a lot of fire power and this wasn't the time to die in a foolish and maybe vain act.

"What we're going to do," he said when he got things quieted down, "is take this hotel apart, one floor at a time, one room at a time. There were a lot of armed men shooting at us from this building and I don't believe for a minute they are all dead." He created little three-man groups, each led by one of his original team--Sample, Adams, Stokes, Stockton, Phelps, and himself--and gave them their marching orders.

"There are armed and dangerous killers in this hotel, gentlemen, and you better believe that or you won't live through the hour. Now, Jerrod, you and Stokes take your men and clean out the third floor. Adams and Sample, take your team and clear out the second floor, and I'll have my people with you guys. The rest of you, clear out this main floor." He reloaded his weapon, as did the rest when they saw what he was doing. Some people just simply need to be led.

"If you find people alive, don't kill them unless you have to. Bring them down here to the lobby and don't take any foolish chances. This fight isn't over by any stretch of thinking. We could be days away from help, so don't do anything stupid. Let's go," and the groups started their search for survivors and killers. Chance left the two old guys who held long-term leases on the end stools at the Crystal Saloon to defend the lobby until others could join them.

"You two need to understand that Dickson still has many men, and he could charge this hotel. Keep out of sight and keep a sharp look out for any trouble that might be coming. Shoot to kill, gentlemen," he said and bounded up the stairs to join his group.

Chapter Ten

The message was marked urgent, highest priority, and Major Randall, U.S. Attorney for the western division and Chance's boss in San Francisco, read it for the third time. "Looks like that letter we got from that woman in Nevada Territory was more than accurate." He had called his Deputy U.S. Attorney, Ira Stone, into the office. "Chance needs help, he says here, and needs it as soon as possible. Put together a couple of men, and you get to Preston in the territory as fast as you can ride." He had a sheaf of papers in a leather case, and handed it to Stone.

"It looks like a banker is claiming land in the Golden Valley, we discussed this last week, Ira, I'm sure you remember," and Ira nodded yes, he certainly did remember, "and has foreclosed on property that falls under the 1862 Homestead Act. According to this report from Chance, they have hired guns coming to back up their criminal actions."

"I'll bring Bettencourt and Martinez, travel light and fast, and should be able to get there in just a few days, maybe four, maybe five. No nice easy way to get to that valley from here. It's on the east side of the White Mountains, and they're on the east side of the Sierra Nevada. It'll be a rough ride, Major, but we'll give Jacob the backup he needs."

The two men shook hands, Stone had the case file and with a strong look on his rugged face left to make plans. Over the years there had been a few foolish men-- when considering Ira Stone only from the fact he was an attorney wearing a fine suit of clothes--who didn't realize what a scrapper he was. Before law school, before becoming Deputy U.S. Attorney, Stone rode cattle trails out of Missouri and Texas, and had been on the winning side in many a saloon brawl. Broad in the beam and hard as a rock, Stone had held his own in many battles. When he was appointed as a Deputy Attorney General, he became one of the few in the department who also carried the badge of a U.S. Marshal.

"I served with some of the finest men I've ever known, and being a member of this service is something I will always be proud of. No, I'm not willing to give that up," he told the major when the appointment was made. Wearing the two badges gave him broad jurisdictional powers.

The Department of Justice was formed by President Washington in 1789, and the U.S. Marshal Service was created as part of the department. Ira Stone was the ideal man to come to the rescue of Jacob Chance. He and Chance had ridden together on more than one case, in particular, Stone remembered, when they were sent to protect federal District Judge Manuel Cortez in Monterey, five years ago.

Like so many in California, family heritage could be from Spain, Mexico, or somewhere back east, and many in the government had relations who had been living in the Golden State for generations before it became a part of the United States. "Cortez was an outspoken supporter of the constitution, and he had a number of vicious criminals from California's past out to get him. "I and Marshal Chance had a hard go protecting that man," Stone was quoted by the *Alta Californian* in a lengthy newspaper report.

It took less than half an hour for Stone to find Bettencourt and Martinez and make them aware of what was going to happen. "This is going to be a fight between U.S. Marshals and hired gunslingers, gentlemen, and we have to get to Golden Valley as fast as possible. Old Jake Chance is up to his belt buckle in trouble and needs us yesterday."

Stone picked two of the best to ride with him. Marshal Gregory Bettencourt had been in the Texas division before the war started, worked with and against some of the fiercest Mexican and Indian gangs known.

Bettencourt stood about five foot ten, weighed about one sixty, and had been known to take on two drunk Indians with knives and put them in irons without so much as suffering a scratch.

"Bettencourt is one of the toughest marshals in the service," Stone told Major Randall. "I'd never feel anything but safe having him on a mission. I've seen him clear a saloon just by coming through the doors. And his partner, Marshal Stan Martinez, could whup a grizzly bear if he put his mind to it. Meanest Apache I've ever met. I've always been grateful that he's on our side," and he said that with just the hint of a smile.

Stone too had a reputation that dates back some ten years or so in the service. He was attached to a cavalry division that patrolled sections of the emigrant trail through the plains after gold was discovered in California and the great migration began, then began work as a sheriff in some tough cattle and railroad towns when great herds of beef moved into the north from Texas and Missouri, joining the Marshal Service some five years ago.

***

"It's going to be a long, hard ride, boys," he said as the three of them stood in the corrals kept by the Marshal's Service. "Good horses, two strong mountain pack mules, rifles, shotguns, revolvers, ammunition, food and blankets, and we can leave," he said. "Chance is in trouble and we're already late for the fight." They were packed, saddled, and mounted within the hour, half a dozen stable hands jumping to the chore, and Major Randall was there to see them off.

"Our best bet, once we're on the trail, is to saddle up and be off before sunrise and ride until after sunset. I've had dried meats packed into the saddle bags, so most of the time we'll doing our chewin' as we ride." All three were good trail riders with thousands of miles in the saddle. Stone continued, "We'll cross the Sierra Nevada first, then head south to the Owens Valley and cross the White

Mountains. If we have to, we'll conscript some good mountain horses in the Owens Valley. We'll have good water the whole way."

Randall had been working himself into a rage from the moment he received the urgent message from Jacob Chance. "I sent him to investigate a possible violation of the Homestead Act of 1862, and he walked into a range war, Mr. Stone. Chance has already been attacked once, and now he will be facing hired killers.

"I want those bastards in Preston dead or in jail, Mr. Stone, and that is an order."

"Yes, Sir, Major. I'll see to it," and the three rode out of the San Francisco corrals for a steamer that would take them to Sacramento, where they would head for the Sierra Nevada the following morning. The voyage through the delta and part way up the Sacramento River took many hours, and they rode into the night out of Sacramento toward the towering Sierra.

"This will be a cold camp boys, but we'll have a good first meal before leaving out tomorrow," and they unpacked, picketed their animals, crawled into bedrolls and were snoring softly within minutes. Ira Stone was the last to finally drift off, his mind blazing with the problems he might be facing on this assignment. "This country is so big, it takes so long to get from one place to another, I just hope we can make it to Preston in time." He wouldn't allow himself to imagine what the end result would be if they were late.

First meal found them in the foothills leading to the massive granite peaks of the Sierra Nevada. The foothills, gentle, rolling hills, each considerably higher than the previous, covered in oak, massive fields of California poppies, just as golden as the metal the state was named after, other hardwoods, abundant grasses, and clear blue skies. These foothills didn't tell the truth, often hiding what was just ahead.

The Sierra Nevada range was high, rugged, and those that could remember emigrant disasters like the Donner party knew it was very dangerous. Stone took the Carson Pass route, well-traveled since the days of the discovery of silver in Virginia City, and made good time. Hangtown behind them, they made each hour count, climbing higher until Bettencourt remarked he thought he could touch the top of the sky.

Resupplying in the Nevada Territory capital of Carson City, the troop then traveled south through the lush agricultural Carson Valley, went across the pine nut range and followed the Walker River south, arriving at Mono Lake.

"This will be the final push gentlemen," Stone said on a cold early fall morning. "We'll drop down to the Owens Valley, then through a high pass over the White Mountains and down into Golden Valley."

The men were in excellent physical condition, but a forced ride like this would take it out of just about anyone, and Stone and his deputies were trail worn at best. Cold camping each evening but starting the day with a large hot meal and stuffing pockets with hard tack for mid-day seemed to be working, and the tactic's worth would be tested going over the Whites.

First, they had to work their way down out of those high mountains and into the Owens' Valley, seeing the massive granite of the White Mountains for the first time. With the Sierra Nevada on their right and the Whites on their left, Stone said later that they almost felt trapped. The group of dedicated lawmen topped out at about ten thousand feet on their trek, and gazed down into the valley below. They still had at least a full day's journey, maybe more, in front of them.

***

Chance found five men with serious wounds and four more dead when they cleared the hotel rooms. He called Cotton Phelps to help him. "How many of these men do you recognize, Phelps?"

"Looks to me like the Colonel cleared out his saloon, Marshal. Most of these men work the gambling tables or the bar. A couple of them are ranch hands from some of the ranches that Dickson and Miller have foreclosed on and work themselves." Phelps stopped for a moment, thinking almost out loud.

"It looks like he is pulling all of his employees in, Marshal. There's probably at least seven or eight more, and they either are on their way to town or are holed up at the saloon."

Chance walked over to one of the wounded men, one that looked more like a working cowboy than a hired killer or gambler. The man cringed when the marshal kneeled down next to him. "You're already hurt," he said, smiling just a bit. "All I want are some answers. Why are you backing that fool Dickson with your life? And are you fully aware that I'm a U.S. Marshal?"

The wounded cowboy choked up on that last question. "A Marshal? Colonel George said you were hired by the Jackson woman to put him out of business. He promised all of us some ranch land if we would protect him." His eyes were as wide as a wounded man's eyes can get, thinking about what had just happened. "He said that Mr. Stokes and Hank Adams worked for you and Miss Jackson, and the Stokes' ranch would be broken up and split between those of us that helped him."

"Hank, Cotton, did you hear most of that?" Chance asked, looking around the hotel lobby filled with men toting rifles and shotguns, and men spread out about the floor, some dead, some bleeding their last, and most moaning.

"I sure did, Marshal," Cotton Phelps answered. "That's the kind of slimy game Dickson plays." He took a deep breath. "Sarah is in trouble, right now. I'll bet he has men on the way to her camp, right now. Marshal, I got to get the hell out of here," and he started for the front door.

"No, no, no," Chance yelled, jumping up. "Not alone." He looked around the room. "Is there some way two or three of you could get out of here, get some horses, and not be seen by those in the saloon? If you move out onto that street, those guns at the saloon will cut you to pieces."

Hank Adams grabbed a man, owner of the feed and supply store, and stood with Chance and Phelps. "There sure is, Chance. Out the back door, and Randy here keeps five good horses behind his store."

"Sure does," Jerrod Stockton piped up. "Too damn cheap to keep them at my stables." He changed his smart Alec attitude, and said, "And a good thing for that, right now."

"Okay, then, Cotton, Hank, and Randy, get out to Jackson's as fast as you can. Don't take any stupid chances with these fools. They think I'm a hired killer and they have become hired killers. Get her back here safe and sound."

"We need to get over to Stokes' place too," Adams continued. "Jennifer is there with just the camp staff. The buckaroos have probably already moved up to the first line camp. We were scheduled to start the fall drive down in the next couple of days."

"Okay, here's a better idea," Chance said. "You three get the Jackson woman and take her to the Stokes Ranch and hole up there with whoever is there. You'll probably be safer there than here." Randy Beuller led the three out the back, across two lots and into his carriage house behind the store. They were saddled, across the river, and out of town within ten minutes.

***

Chance was shaken by what the wounded man told him. "Jerrod, is Dickson that much of a bastard, that he

132

would steal Ben Stokes' ranch and split it up between a bunch of men he hired to kill me?"

"I would not put it past him, Marshal. He is evil from the first word. Look what he did to me and my stables. Look what he and Miller did to Sarah Jackson. That's why you're here. Sarah had enough courage to ask for help."

"This makes our job a little more difficult. I wonder how many people in town have been told that I'm a hired killer out to wipe out Dickson and Miller? We need to end this as quickly as possible before many innocent people end up dead.

"Jerrod, I want you to take charge of this little army we have here. I'm going to take Ben Stokes and go down to the jail and have a talk with Preston Miller." He knew there were days' worth of trouble in front of them, and if he could learn something from Miller about Dickson, he might have the edge he would need.

"Is there any food here in the hotel, or close by?" he asked, remembering that the café where he ate and met Sample for the first time was down the street a ways, and on the other side. "Can't get to the café. We'd be picked off like jack rabbits."

"I'll scare up what I can, Chance. I can get some from the café by dodging down the street so that I'm out of range, then doubling back. There's a little alleyway that can get some of us from here to there without being seen. Don't worry, Chance, I'll take care of these guys," and he smiled, stuck his huge hand out, and shook with the Marshal.

"Ben, let's you and I get down to the jail. Stay as close to the walls of these buildings as possible, and we better move fast."

"Thank you for sending those men to the ranch, Marshal. If that bastard lays a hand on Jenny, I will rip his guts out with my bare hands."

"I have a lot of confidence in Hank Adams, and

now that I've met him, Cotton Phelps, so I'm sure your daughter will be safe. From what I've heard, she's a spit fire, and I guess Sarah Jackson is too." He didn't bother to mention that he would certainly like to get to know Jenny Stokes a lot better. Thoughts of a ranch were still dimpling around in his head.

Stokes had to laugh at that, knowing full well its truth. "Whatever man ends up falling for either Jenny or Sarah better be more than up for that challenge." Chance was thinking about that kind of challenge, and found that he liked the idea very much.

It was a good four hundred feet from the hotel, down the street, and then across that broad and dusty street to the jail. "I sure hope Major Randall got my letter," he said, as much to himself as to Stokes as they worked their way down the street.

"If he did, and if he could get some men underway, they could be here sometime in the next two or three days. When we get to the jail, and before we talk with Miller, I have an idea I want to go over with you." And the two found themselves across from the jail, and ready for the sprint. "From the Bucket of Good Hope Saloon to here is one long shot, but a man with a good rifle could make the shot, so stay low and go fast, Ben," and the two jumped out like rabbits.

Five shots rang out and none made their mark as the two blasted their way into the jail. "Dickson was primed and ready for us, Marshal. How the hell many men does he have working for him?"

"Miller can tell us that, but first, let's have a cup of that boiling coffee and talk for just a bit." Known in the Marshal Service as one who could think from a critical point of view, Chance was probably well into tomorrow in his ideas on how to stop this problem the town was facing.

"Dickson's fire power may exceed ours, Ben, but those that are holed up at that hotel right now will be fighting for a cause, a very personal cause, just as you are, and because of that they will be hard to beat down. I'm thinking that Dickson will try to make a big attack once the sun goes down, either tonight or tomorrow night."

"That's logical, but that hotel is vulnerable, as we proved, with bullets flying right through those flimsy walls."

"That's exactly right, Ben. Now, here's my plan. I'm going to head back to the hotel and leave you here. I'm going to spread those men all over town and have them stay put, not move at all. That way, the only people that might be seen moving around town will be Dickson men."

Stokes picked up on that right away. "That would put ten or more guns facing the street from many angles. I like that."

"Good. I'm going back to the hotel. Sample, you and Ben give me some cover fire when I take off. I'll send some men back to give you strength here. Dickson will want Miller out of jail. Don't let that bastard get hurt back there." Stokes and Sample let fly with round after round into the Bucket of Good Hope Saloon as Chance made the dash across the street safely.

"Could be a long night, Sheriff," is all Stokes said, reloading his rifle.

Chapter Eleven

The three men were out of town in minutes, following along the Good Hope River, hidden from view by the heavy stands of willows. They stayed on the river's edge for about a mile, then moved up out of the breaks and onto the main trail north. "That foul aroma from Jerrod's burnt-out old stables will be with us for a long time, I think," Cotton Phelps said as they worked their way through the willows. "Most honest man I've ever met, and look what that bastard Dickson did to him."

The men were quiet for a few minutes when Hank Adams spurred his horse just a bit. "That marshal is one tough man, but I sure wouldn't want to get on the wrong side of old Stockton right now. I'm thinking that Dickson has had plans for some time on what to do if he and Miller were ever challenged on their land deals here. First, Stockton gets the hell beat out of him and his stables are burned to the ground, then the Brady Boys show up, and then the hotel is all at once filled with guns." He looked at the other two with lots of worry showing on his weathered face.

"Let's get Sarah and Georgia first, and I think quickly, and then head to the Stokes Ranch," Hank said as the men put their horses into a miles-eating trot. "For the life of me, I can't understand how I let that bastard Dickson get away with this all these years." He wiped sweat and dust from his face, scowling mad with as much anger toward himself as toward Dickson and Miller.

"They made it sound like it was right, Hank. They sweet talked some of the time, and they brought heavy and hard arguments when they were challenged." Cotton Phelps had fear written across his mug, knowing how much Dickson and Miller hated Sarah Jackson.

Phelps' mind was reeling with what he felt were the possibilities--losing Sarah, saving Sarah--either of which didn't answer his biggest fear. *Am I man enough to marry that beautiful woman, raise her daughter, build a successful ranch, have children of my own?* He had been mulling those same questions for weeks, months actually, and now was forced to face reality. *I've known how much I love that woman for a long time, and I'm still worried about myself.* He knew, but was afraid of the answer.

It was when Toby and three other men arrived at the Jackson place to evict her that Phelps realized his true feelings for her. He helped her pack, made sure nothing was broken, helped set her camp up and promised that he would take care of her ranch until she got it back. After he had settled her in, she had handed him an envelope.

"Get this in the mail, Cotton, as fast as you can. I own that ranch, have the papers to prove it, and this letter will get me the help I need." He had looked at it carefully. It was addressed to the U.S. Attorney, San Francisco, and his heart fell. He hadn't believed there would be any help coming.

Randall Beuller hadn't said much since they lit out, and was quiet even now. To himself, he was remembering how it had been when his lease on the store came into question. He finally had to open up to Adams and Phelps. "My little Cathy-Ann was threatened by Miller when I got behind in my lease payments. We had been married only two years, lost our baby, and the costs of her sickness and making the final arrangements for Terrence were more than we made in the store." Tears were welling, making mud across his face as they streamed from his eyes.

"We worked so hard to get away from the war, spent every dime we had just to get across the plains. Wanted to go to Oregon, but ran out of money in Salt Lake City and got sweet talked by one of Dickson's people there. 'Come to Golden Valley' that man said, 'and you can build that store you were talking about, and the bank will let you in with an easy mortgage payment.' He made it sound like paradise, until I got in a financial bind.

"Miller came in one morning and suggested that terrible things seemed to happen to wives and daughters when mortgages weren't met. I exploded, I have never been that angry, and when I moved to knock the crap out of that banker, Clarence Toby grabbed an ax handle and beat the crap out of me. Miller just stood there and watched, Cathy-Ann screaming and crying, finally fainting onto the floor. Only then did Toby stop hitting me, and he and Miller walked out of the store, breaking the large front window on the way out.

"That's why, when I saw all the men gathering outside the Crystal Saloon with their rifles and shotguns, I joined in." He got very quiet, as did the two others, and the miles slipped by quickly. Each of the three men had his story, each of them knew they would fight to the end with Marshal Chance. As they got closer to where Sarah Jackson had her little camp, they could see dust in the area.

"Let's go, men. Sarah's got a problem. Come on, King, let's go," and Cotton Phelps spurred his big ranch horse into a full gallop, Adams and Beuller right with him. "That's not wind-kicked dust, that's being kicked up by animals," he hollered, giving the brute full rein.

They were about a hundred yards from the camp and could see two men on horseback riding in circles around Sarah's tent, and shooting pistols into the air. Cotton Phelps heart was pounding as he rode toward the camp. He pulled his revolver and took a shot from way too far out, but did catch the attention of the two marauders. "I'm gonna kill you bastards," he was screaming, near enough now to get off a telling shot.

Shooting from the back of a horse at a full gallop was hard enough, actually hitting something with that shot was almost out of the question, but Phelps could only see Sarah in danger, and knew he had to do something. The two outlaws saw the three coming, and turned to run. A stray bullet from Cotton Phelps hit one of the horses in a hind quarter, knocking the horse to the ground and crushing its rider. The other man was run down by Hank Adams, beat bloody, and brought back to the camp.

Phelps didn't wait for his horse to come to a full stop, was out of the saddle and running as fast as his legs could carry him to the tent. "Sarah," he cried, "Sarah! Where are you?" The tent was empty. He came back out and hollered loud and long, "Sarah! Sarah, it's Cotton. Where are you?"

A muffled cry came up from the willows, and the three men ran to the area, leaving their prisoner on the ground, bleeding. "Sarah, cry again, I can't see you," Phelps yelled. Again, just a muffled cry, and the men spotted little Georgia, covered in mud, whimpering from what looked like a beating with willow branches. "Whichever bastard did this is one dead man," Phelps said, pulling Georgia to her feet, wrapping his arms around her, hoisting her up. "Where's Sarah? Where's your mama?" he asked, holding her as tight as he could.

"I don't know," she whimpered. "They whipped me and threw me into the mud. Mama!" she cried, "Mama ..." and seemed to pass out, go limp in Cotton's arms.

As Cotton yelled, "Spread out, we've got to find her," they heard a horse's hoof beats running off, and they ran from the willows in time to see their prisoner on Stan Beuller's horse, racing through the pasture land toward the trail that led to Preston.

"I knew I should have shot him," Adams said, watching the man disappear in a cloud of dust. "Well, he's gone, let's find Sarah. We know there were two here for sure, one's dead the other gone, so Sarah should be somewhere close.

"Cotton, you tend to Georgia, and Randy and I will search," and he headed back into the willow stands, Beuller right behind him. "Go that way," he said, pointing, "and I'll look up this way. Dickson is one dead man right now, he just doesn't know it."

The search continued for at least half an hour, spreading further and further from the camp site. Phelps had Georgia tucked into her little bed inside the tent, had doctored her horrible whip lacerations, and went outside to join in the search. The first thing he spotted was the mule he had brought over with Sarah's belongings. It lay in a great pool of blood staining the dust, two or three gunshot wounds visible. He could taste the bile boiling from the anger, fearing the worst for Sarah.

"Over here, Hank! Over here," Beuller hollered from more than a hundred yards away. "I found her boot prints. Come on, I think I see her."

Phelps and Adams ran to the store owner and saw the prints from a small boot. "She's limping," Phelps said, and started following at a dog trot, where a man could cover lots of ground in a hurry. He broke out of the willows, into ground covered in high grass with just a few stands of brush to break it up. "Here she is!" he yelled, running now to where she lay, one leg twisted badly. "Broken leg, and she was able to get this far away," he said to himself, kneeling down and gently lifting her into his arms.

They made it back to the tent and Phelps began the nasty job of cutting off her boots and cutting away her canvas pants in order to tend to her broken leg. For so many men and women on the frontier, basic skills like splinting a leg or stopping the heavy flow of blood were learned and used often. "Cut me a nice straight willow branch, will you, Hank?" he asked as he tried to be gentle setting the leg. "She's lucky this wasn't up on her thigh. She'll be fine, I think. One strong lady." He leaned down and gently kissed her on the forehead. As he sat up he found Sarah Jackson's eyes brimming with tears, looking right at him.

"I think I love you, Sarah," he blurted, turning crimson as he said it, wrapping his arms around her and holding her close. Hank walked in with two stout lengths of willow and understood immediately what he was seeing.

"Here you go, lover boy," and he handed the branches to Phelps. "I'll just step outside the tent now, and discuss matters with Randy."

***

"Here's the problem as I see it," Randy said, when Adams and Phelps joined him after the doctoring was done. "We now have five people and two horses, and we have lost one of the men we tried to capture, the other one is dead. That man is going to head back to the colonel in a high gallop, and we don't have the resources to fight a large group of people."

All hands were in agreement with that, and it was several minutes of kicking dust before anything was said. Phelps was the first with an idea. "We need to make Sarah and little Georgia as safe as possible. That bastard Dickson wants her dead. Remember, she's the reason Marshal Chance is even here. If we put Sarah and Georgia on one horse, and Randy, you and I walk her to the Stokes Ranch, Hank can ride ahead and bring some cowboys back with him for protection."

It only took a couple of minutes for the plan to be accepted, and much longer to get Sarah Jackson and her daughter Georgia onto a horse. Hank had lit out right away for the ranch. "We need to go cross country, Randy, not use the main trail. Let's cross the river up ahead there, and then use the natural terrain to hide us from the trail. We're really vulnerable right now."

Sarah was in great pain, her leg ached, her head ached, her whole body ached, and trying to sit on the horse made it worse. "Don't let the horse trot, Cotton, please. I hurt everywhere." Georgia was hanging on tight, as tough a little ten-year-old as ever seen on the frontier. They made their way across the river and up the bank on the other side. "Those men were there to kill me, Cotton."

"I know," he answered, leading the horse through the willows and out onto the valley floor and through pasture grass, far from the main trail. "It will take us about two hours to reach the Stokes Ranch, so bear down. I'll die before I let anyone ever hurt you again. I shouldn't have left you this morning."

"You did the right thing, Cotton. The right thing."

For the next hour and a half the little group walked through tall grass, skirted some bluffs, and kept a watch for riders that might be coming from Preston along the main trail. It was dust from the other direction they saw. "Sure hope that's Hank and the Stokes' crew."

When the riders could be seen on the trail, about a mile from where they were, Cotton fired his pistol in the air, was spotted on the hill side, and was joined in minutes by Hank Adams, Jennifer Stokes, and two cowboys, each trailing horses for Cotton and Randy.

"That fool Dickson sent two riders to tell Jennifer that her father had been hurt and that she needed to come into town with them. I got there just as they were getting her horse saddled.

"When I showed up, one of them pulled a gun and I killed him dead. Jennifer didn't hesitate, just jerked her rifle from the saddle and shot the other one. That was very close, because if she had gone with them, she would have been a hostage. Let's get back to the ranch as quick as we can."

***

Jennifer made Sarah and Georgia comfortable in big beds with large pillows of soft goose down and blankets hand stitched. "You two stay warm and comfy, no moving around and no arguments. I'm in charge now." She smiled, smoothing Georgia's hair down, holding her hand, and murmuring the things that women murmur to each other.

Georgia had never had much opportunity to scowl, Sarah was thinking, looking across the room at her daughter, but she had a strong, almost mean look on her face. "Mommy, please don't let Cotton go away again. I want to go home."

"I do too, honey," and she smiled for the first time in many hours, "and, honey, I'm not letting Cotton leave, ever again." Georgia closed her eyes, her face softened, and she was asleep that fast.

"Thank you, Jenny. We'll be fine. Ask Cotton to come in, will you?" Jenny smiled back and walked out the bedroom door, thinking what a lucky woman Sarah was right then.

"That lady in there wants to see you, Mr. Phelps, sir, and you be nice to her," and the smile told Cotton everything he wanted to know. "Hank," she said, almost as if talking about a conspiracy, "did you know what has been going between those two?" and everyone got a good laugh at Cotton's expense. He was again beet red going through the door to see Sarah Jackson.

"Come out on the porch, Jenny, we have to talk," Hank said, holding the door open for her. "We have to get more guns back into town to support Chance, but we can't just ride off and leave Sarah, Georgia and you."

"I already took care of part of that, Hank," she said. "I sent old Jesus up to the line camp to bring the crew down. When they get here, that will give you five more guns, plus the two men who are already here. I'll keep Jesus here, he's a crack shot with that rifle of his. I am too, and Sarah will be able to shoot, so we will be able to take care of ourselves here.

"It makes it much easier to protect yourself when you know you're in danger. I would have ridden back into town with those men, and daddy would have been in more danger than even I was. Why do people do these things to each other? Why isn't my brother helping the marshal and daddy? Hank, I know the danger. I don't have any answers, but I know that we will be safe here."

Hank and Beuller started to argue and the Stokes' temper came into play. "No, damn it, Hank, it's more important to destroy Dickson and Miller than to worry about me and Sarah. We're just as tough as you boys and don't ever forget that." Her eyes were blazing, chin jutted out just like old Ben's, and little fists knotted up, resting on slim hips.

"Better not think of fighting that little tiger cat, Hank. She'll whip your skinny butt in a minute." Beuller was chuckling softly, pretending to duck away from Jennifer Stokes. "We'll take off as soon as your line crew gets here, Jenny."

al

Chapter Twelve

Ben Stokes was in the back of the jail, coffee mugs in hand. "Jim, you're out of time, son. Dickson has hired guns trying to kill me and everyone in the family, everyone in the town that has backed the marshal. No more little boy crap, no more tears, no more nothing but being a man. You either help, and I mean right now, or you rot in jail with your criminal friends." He set the boy's coffee cup on one of the cross pieces in the cell, not handing it to Jim, stepped back a step or two, and took a swallow of his own.

Ben Stokes had eyes that could burrow into a man when he was angry, and at the moment they were cutting his son into little pieces. "Hank Adams and Cotton Phelps are on their way to our ranch right now to protect Jennifer, and you're sitting in jail. We are in a long fight that might lead to us losing the ranch we have spent years building, and you're sitting in jail.

"I've been shot at three or four times so far today, and you're sitting in jail because you're protecting the very people doing all this. Help now, or it's goodbye." He pulled up a wooden chair and sat down, his whole body slumped, his mind reeling with questions: *What if he won't grow up, what if he really doesn't care about his family, what if I lose him?* Questions that only Jim Stokes could answer.

"Mr. Dickson wouldn't hurt Jenny. He's not a criminal."

"Then it's goodbye, son," and Ben Stokes got up and walked out the door, a beaten man, but one with hatred and anger continuing its climb. He slammed his coffee mug onto the sheriff's desk, slammed it again just to prove the point, and paced around the small office for several minutes.

"I've lost him, Sample," was all he said, slamming that mug one more time, then filling it with boiling coffee.

145

"Trade this for a shot of whiskey in a heartbeat, and I know that would not do me one bit of good right now." He paced around the office like a bear looking for a fight. "What does Dickson have that would make a young man give up his family, give up the ranch he helped build as he was growing up?

"I've never been this angry, ever. I don't know who I hate the most right now, Dickson or my son, and that's a horrible thing to say."

Sample was standing at the open door of the office, in the shade of the building. "Looks like movement, Ben. Grab your rifle. Don't know if they're ours or theirs, so better get ready." He closed the door and set the wooden bar across it. "If we don't recognize the voice when they knock, just shoot right through that door."

They heard gun shots and running boots and the sheriff raised the bar and opened the door. "Figured they'd be friends if they was getting shot at," he grinned as four big men burst into the office, bullets bouncing off the side of the building. "Good thing they can't see the doorway from that saloon."

Jerrod Stockton, his big shotgun gripped tight, led the four in, puffing from the run. "Chance has a plan," he huffed, plopping into the sheriff's chair. "Damn, if this keeps up I'm gonna be one skinny little blacksmith," he snickered, trying to catch his breath. "He wants three or four of us here in the jail to protect the prisoners, three or four more to be at the Crystal Saloon, and then the rest spread about the town, in the hotel, and in some of the shops."

He continued huffing, Stokes gave him a mug of coffee, and he settled down some. "We tried to figure out how many men Dickson might have, and it looks like quite a few. He pulled in some of his men from the outlying ranches, a few more have been seen coming into town, and he thinks they might wait until dark to hit." His breathing back to normal, the huge man settled a bit deeper into the chair.

"He thinks they will try to hit the jail and get Miller out, then take out the rest of us. If we're all over town, they'll have a hard time of it. Anything moves, shoot it. That's the plan, get in one place and stay there. That way, anything moving will be one of them, and we won't be shooting each other."

Stokes, smiling a bit and rubbing his chin, went back to pacing, and finally said, "So, it will be the six of us here, a bunch at the Crystal, a bunch at the hotel, and some scattered about up and down the street. I'm glad he went with that plan. It sounded real good when he outlined it." He looked around the room, most nodding agreement. "What's the matter, Sample? You don't agree?"

"Most of the people in town are like me, Ben. We've been intimidated and whipped into submission by those bastards for so long, I'm afraid some won't be able to fight back. I'm so embarrassed by what I've done, I know I will fight, but some, I don't know, Ben. I don't know."

"I'm looking forward to whipping the crap out of Dickson," Stockton said. "At first, I wanted to shoot him in the head, but right now, as sore as I am, as beat up as I am, I want to take ax handles to that fool. Many ax handles." He whipped his huge arms back and forth, scattering some of the men who found themselves too close to the giant, bringing grins from everyone else.

"If we have Jerrod Stockton on our side, we have to win," Stokes added to the light air moving through the group. "What Chance said, though, is very true, and Jerrod, you just backed it up. Those of us that live here have something very real to fight for. Those fighting for Dickson are just hired hands, not protecting their very lives and future. Sample, I've not seen one, but is there a back door to this building?"

"Not a door, but there is a small window. I think a

man could squeeze through. We'll need to guard that. The only other way in or out is the front door here, and that window next to it. We can close the wooden storm shutters from the inside, and they do bolt."

"Good. We'll need to break up into groups to cover all the hours, and we'll need food. How will we get that?"

"On its way, Ben," Stockton said. "After the food gets here, no more movement from any of us, or any of the others. Jacob said everyone should be ready for an assault by the time the sun goes down."

Stokes was still standing in the middle of the room, rubbing his chin, the anger was evident, and one could almost see a thought process moving across his brow. "I think they'll hit closer to midnight. It's been one hell of a day, all of us are exhausted. Many will run out of energy well before midnight. We need to be on our toes, but I bet they won't hit until after midnight."

There was general agreement as the six men broke into groups of three, with one man from each group at the back window and the other two in the front. Those not assigned, rested or slept for the later shift. "This is a good thing," Stokes was saying, as much to himself as to the others. "We are working together, as a group, as members, residents of this town, probably for the first time since any of us got here. That's what makes a community, people working together for the betterment of all.

"We've lived in Preston, but Preston hasn't been a community, until just now. It's been a place, a place owned and operated by someone else. No, Sample, I think you'll find just about everyone willing to work for something they can call their own, a community."

It got quiet as each man was left to his own thoughts, worries, and maybe even future plans. "I'm going to take the first shift at the back window," Jerrod Stockton said, filling his coffee mug once more, cradling that shotgun, and smiling an angry smile. "I sure hope somebody sticks their ugly head through."

***

"If we can keep up this pace for the rest of the day, we should be in Preston tomorrow, maybe even early tomorrow. Let's ride well into the darkness, gentlemen, make another cold camp, and get started early." Stone had no trouble urging Bettencourt and Martinez along. Jacob Chance was in trouble, and they knew their job. "I don't know what kind of a nest of crap Chance has found himself in, but we need to be there and get him out of it. That man can find trouble when he's not even looking for it."

"Do you remember that mess he got us into in Green River a couple of years ago?" Heads nodded and Stan Martinez continued. "Just a simple bank robbery, the note said, and Major Randal sent us off to help with whatever might happen during the trial. Trial? Hell, we walked into a nest of thieves and killers."

"Chance broke up one of the largest gangs of robbers and killers in the west, and his note just asked for help during the trial. He had five men in jail and then all their friends and neighbors came to help. We had an open war for almost two weeks when we got there," Stone answered. "This might not be any different, I'm thinking," and again, the nodding of heads.

The entire marshal service knew that Jacob Chance was usually given the tough assignments, but a land law dispute rarely evolved into what Major Randal had described. Bettencourt put it into words for the group as they topped out on the White Mountain pass they were following. "The major must know more than he was telling us, Sloan. A land law dispute and we are going to be facing hired guns?"

"That's exactly what Chance's letter said. I read it, Greg," Sloan answered back. "A woman filed for homestead and some banker had her removed from the ranch at gunpoint, saying he owned the property.

According to the major, no deed has ever been filed on the land. It looks like the banker, probably with help somewhere, has been selling land all over the valley, but doesn't own a wee drop of it."

"Nice, if you can get away with it," Bettencourt said. "Nice trees and fresh water about a mile down the hill, Sloan. Looks like a good place to bed down. Sure is cold at night up this high. Doesn't feel like early fall, it feels like early winter to me," he said as they rode toward a small spring-fed creek.

"Snow will be twenty feet deep up here in January and February, and that's what makes that valley down there so special. Water all spring, summer, and fall. I bet the cattle are so fat they waddle like ducks." Sloan took a deep breath of the chilled fall air, thinking about what they would face down there in the valley. "That's why that banker is hedging his bet with hired guns. Well, Jacob has some hired guns on our way, eh, boys?"

They piled rocks in a big circle, piled dead wood inside the circle, then put their bed rolls around the perimeter, lit the fire, and settled in for the night. "Let's work on moving out about first light. We got enough food for a light meal before we move?"

"We got a few pieces of side meat left, and some hard tack, and that's about it. Used the last of the coffee this morning, and no more beans either. We'll be eating light tomorrow, so, if I remember my training, a hungry soldier fights harder." Hard laughter, some twigs, and a few stones were aimed at Martinez following that comment, and trail-tired sleep wasn't far behind.

***

"Look at that sunrise, will you? My God, no wonder people live in this country. I could see something like this for the rest of my life." High in the western mountains, often one could see for hundreds of miles, the ranges off in the distance slightly lower, and defined as wave after wave of blues and purples, enhanced by a setting or rising sun. One could see purples, yellows, reds, blues, every color in the spectrum, dancing through air so thin and cold, it hurt to breathe deep.

"Let's go out of our way to describe these days we're having to Major Randal when we get back, eh boys?" Sloan knew the major would feign anger, but deep in his heart, would have given just about anything to be with them.

"I fought with the major in New Mexico during the war," Martinez said, "and as much as he would love this crisp air, these beautiful mountains, and all this scenery, what he would like best would be riding with us to fight with Jacob Chance one more time. Major Randal was my commanding officer, and I would fight with that gentleman anytime, anywhere."

The three, shaking their heads in agreement, with cups of cold water and chunks of hard tack downed, horses and mules made ready, mounted and headed off down the long trail from more than ten thousand feet in the White Mountains to maybe four thousand feet in Preston, Nevada Territory. "Still seems strange to me that the town of Preston, all the ranches up and down that beautiful valley, and not one single deed recorded in either Salt Lake City, when this was Utah Territory, or Carson City when the change was made. Before the war, this was Mexico, but the Mexicans didn't come this far north, so they don't have any deeds on record, either. We got our work cut out, boys," Sloan continued, leading the group off.

"I wonder why there aren't any Indians in the valley?" Martinez said. "This would be someplace my people would have wanted to live. Plenty of water, probably plenty of game, looks like lots of wood would be available. No mention of Indians at all, Sloan?"

"Not one word, Stan. Not one word. This valley is surrounded by the White Mountains to the west and barren desert north, east, and south. It's been a paradise lost, I think."

The trail twisted and turned, back and forth, mile after mile, horses and mules balking at the effort of walking downhill. Into swales, up little hills, then back down a long steep section, thick with tall pines in some places, scrub brush in others, not really being able to discern whether they were actually getting close to that valley down there. Distances in the high country could be deceiving, moving in and out of timber, up and down through the swales, made it even more so.

"Looks like a pretty nice river running through that valley, Sloan," Martinez said. "I understand why someone would want to settle in. Shame that banker fool didn't do it legally. Must have been in these parts since it was Utah Territory. Would have been pretty simple to file a claim with the folks in Salt Lake."

"That's what's wrong with criminals, Stan. If they could think, they wouldn't be criminals. We're gonna be coming into Preston a bit late, I'm afraid. This is a long trail off that mountain. When we hit the valley floor, let's park ourselves along that river for a few and make sure we are ready for war. We don't know what we'll be riding into when we hit Preston."

With crystal clear cold air, judging distance off the side of a mountain could be very difficult, and Sloan was misjudging by a considerable amount. By late afternoon, they knew it would be late night before they got to Preston. "We better just make it to that river, sleep till just before sunrise, and make the final push into town. This has been one hard forced ride, boys. We need to be rested if we're going to be facing hired guns in that town."

"If that water is as clear as it looks, there will be fish, and as thick as those willows are, there will be rabbits, so we will eat tonight," Martinez said, and the other two agreed immediately. "Roasted rabbit, put a trout on a willow limb and hang it over the fire, and we'll sleep with a smile."

***

Cotton Phelps, Hank Adams, Randy Beuller, and five cowboys left out of the Stokes Ranch late in the afternoon for the ride into Preston. Not a word was said, but it became more than obvious that Hank Adams was the boss, and every man knew he was the right one to lead them into the war going on in town. "If we just ride into town we're liable to take shots from both sides. Until we know where Marshal Chance and that bunch are holed up, we're gonna have to be damn careful.

"Just because they were at the hotel when we left doesn't mean they are still there. Any arguments about waiting until we know where they are?" No one argued, most just nodded that Adams' idea was the right one, and they continued their trot toward town.

They moved along the trail, then slipped into the deep willows, and used the river as a shield when they got close enough to town to smell the still-smoldering remains of Jerrod Stockton's livery. "Chance had everyone at the hotel when we left, but he could have moved since then. It's going to be dark very soon," Adams said as they neared the livery. "Let's stay along the river here and see if we can see something. We know Dickson will shoot at us on sight, but we don't know where Chance is."

Cotton Phelps slipped off his big ranch horse and tied it off. "Let's spread out some but stay close enough to see each other when it gets dark. If we spot the marshal or someone we know, let's make contact without showing ourselves." Agreement reached, the men all dismounted and tied off, moving along the river bank, hidden by the willows. "Might be a long night," Phelps added.

The sky offered one of the late-summer-early-fall sunsets that took hours to unfold, with billowing clouds doing their ballet through the color wheel, nesting birds coming home in droves, and the air chilling quickly once it got dark. Eight men ready to kill, not ready to be killed, spread along many yards of the Good Hope River, maybe twenty men with the same thoughts spread among various stores, buildings, and hiding places in the town itself, and Dickson was standing at the rail at the top of the stairs in his saloon, giving orders as if he really was a colonel.

"This town has been turned against Mr. Miller and myself by a vicious criminal posing as a U.S. Marshal, and I have one thousand dollars in my pocket right now for the man who kills him. The blacksmith is responsible for this problem, and I have another thousand dollars for the man that kills him. I have land, cattle, and money for the man or men that free Preston Miller from that jail.

"This town belongs to Preston Miller and me, and no damned criminal is going to take it away from me. You men will be rewarded generously for doing this job. Now, let's go to work. The sun is down, let's move from building to building and kill every son of a bitch that stands with that man."

Chance and Stockton and the men with them could hear the cheers from the saloon when Dickson finished his pep talk, and the men along the river, deep in the willows were close enough to actually hear Dickson talking. "Looks like it's starting," Chance said to his group about the same time Adams said, "They'll be coming now." Everyone took that minute to check, one more time, the weapons they had with them. Made sure, once again, they had pockets full of ammunition, even, for the tenth time, made sure of the keenness of the blade on the knives. All had about the same thought, that they were doing the right thing--for themselves, for the law, and mostly, for Sarah Jackson.

The danger that existed was more than just Dickson and his hired guns, it was the fact that Chance didn't know Hank Adams and his crew were on hand, and neither Chance nor Adams knew that Stone, Bettencourt, and

Martinez were just a few miles downriver. The chances of those on the side of law and order shooting each other was very real. "Spread out into a single line in the willows, and when those fools come out of that saloon, shoot them dead," Adams said, moving closer to the edge of the willows, squirming through the tall grass to the edge of the river bank. The rest followed.

***

"Don't hesitate, men," Chance said. "They'll be coming out those doors soon. If you have a shot, take it. None of this wounding stuff, shoot to kill, because you have to know that's what they'll be doing." He was crouched in behind a wall and a water barrel just at the corner wall of the hotel, and had three others near him.

Ben Stokes and Peter Sample were looking out the doorway of the jail, two rifles aimed at the Bucket of Good Hope Saloon. "Won't be long now," Sample murmured.

Four men were spread along the front windows of the hotel, worrying about their businesses, their wives and children, and themselves, knowing all hell was about to break loose. Daniel Cook, a fine carpenter, showing the strains of the situation by talking to himself, said, "If I live through this, I won't be getting' drunk on the weekends ever again." That brought some hearty laughter from the others.

"Don't make those kinds of promises, Danny my lad. Here they come."

Chapter Thirteen

Dickson had sent Jeb Ralston out the back doors of the saloon earlier with instructions to get into the jail and free all the prisoners. He told him about the rear window and Ralston said he thought he was thin enough to scramble through it. "From the front of the jail you can't see that window," Dickson said, "and the cells are lined up along a corridor. That old fool Sample will cry like a baby, but I want you to make sure he's dead and Mr. Miller is safe. You better take someone with you to back your play."

Ralston took a rifle and his side arm when he left, and had one other revolver with him, for Preston Miller, and motioned for one of the cowboys, Dirk Johnson, to join him. They followed the river south, staying in the willows, then crossed over to the west side of the town and worked their way back to the jail.

It was getting dark as they dodged through the buildings and scrub brush, and slipped into the jail's back yard. "Kinda looks like a ghost town," Johnson muttered. "They ain't nobody out on the streets. Feels kinda spooky, like riding around a herd late at night. I used to whistle just to keep myself from bein' scairt."

"Shut up. That's the jail there. I'm gonna crawl through that window, and if anybody pokes a head out, shoot 'em. I'll have to help that fat-ass banker through that window, if he'll even fit. Now, be quiet."

The window, smaller than a standard window, meant to supply a small amount of daylight into the cell area, was about five feet off the ground, and Ralston edged up to it.

Stockton had not lit a lamp in the back area, and as the night crept on, it was even darker inside than outside. Ralston slowly tried to get a view of the inside and couldn't. He knew that the window swung open instead of moving up and down, and he worked it carefully to get it open.

Stockton heard the scratching, brought the shotgun slowly to his shoulder, both hammers cocked and ready, and waited to see who might try to come through. Jim Stokes and Preston Miller heard the scratching as well. As the window slowly swung open, Stokes hollered a warning and Stockton let fly with both barrels, almost knocking the huge blacksmith back into the wall from the recoil.

The massive blasts blew out the entire window frame and splashed Ralston's face and head all over the ground for about twenty feet. Stockton swung the long gun around, loaded it fast, and took long aim at Jim Stokes. "You little fool, that man was here to kill your father." Ben Stokes and Peter Sample crashed into the cell area in time to see Stockton lower the shotgun. "That little bastard tried to warn him," was all Stockton said, and walked over to look at all the damage he had done.

Johnson saw Ralston's head explode, saw great chunks of the wall blasted out of the building, and took off. The only one left who knew he had been with Ralston at the jail was himself, "and I sure as hell ain't telling nobody." He was never seen again along the Good Hope River.

"Looks like I stopped the first man, but we have a real problem now. No one's gonna have to crawl through a window to get in here." After some lengthy discussion, some of which involved the possible shooting of Jim Stokes, it was agreed that the prisoners would have to be put in the same cell, farthest from the large hole in the wall, and there would have to be two men guarding that hole, one on each side.

Ben Stokes and Peter Sample stayed in the back and Jerrod went up front. "It's best this way, Ben. I'm pretty damn angry at that kid of yours, and he's safer if I'm not back here right now." Stockton was remembering how young Stokes was as a kid, wanting to know how this was done, how horse shoes were made, how nails were made, how hinges for gates were made.

"Now that little bastard tried to get me killed, tried to help the people that are working to kill his own father. What's wrong with that boy, Ben? Give him to me for an hour and I'll teach him what it means to be a man." Anger, lost friendship, let down following a battle, all worked to make the big man even more dangerous than just his size.

"Get some coffee and guard that front door, Stockton. You deserve a little break about now." Ben Stokes gave him a strong hand shake, glared at his son, and joined Sample by the blown out window. "That's one mean shotgun, Jerrod." Miller, young Stokes, and Clarence Toby were locked up together, along with the survivor of the attempt on the bank.

"One of you make sound and I'll have Mr. Stockton back here with that cannon of his," Sample said, jingling the cell keys for emphasis.

The coffee was on the stove and the burly blacksmith found his hands shaking so bad he couldn't pour a cup. "I don't know if this is anger at the stupid Stokes kid or if it is coming from having to kill a man in cold blood." He tried to get himself calmed down when Stuart Payne stepped in and poured the coffee.

"Best if I help you, Jerrod," Payne said, "before you spill it all over the floor." The two men moved back to keep watch out the front door.

"Keeping this door open is a good idea, Stuart, but I think we better sit on either side instead of in front. You look south, I'll look north." From across the street, it looked like the jail was empty and the door was open. From one of the store fronts, however, it would have been an easy shot if one were standing in the doorway. "This way, it's almost an invite," Stockton said, smiling at the thought. "This Dickson's a wiley old bastard, eh? Knew that window was there, knew how to get it open. Just didn't plan on anyone being there except maybe Sheriff Sample.

"Of course, Marshal Chance is pretty wiley too. This is gonna be a long night, Stuart. A long day already."

***

"Did you hear that, Cotton? That sounded like old Jerrod Stockton's shotgun talking. Came from well down the street, near the jail I think. You think that's where Chance and all the others are holed up?" Hank Adams was hunkered down in the tall grass, just outside the line of willows. "We need to hook up with Chance as soon as possible. Damn, I wish I knew where he was."

"I didn't talk to Chance about his plans, but I think I know what I would do if this was my play." He motioned Beuller and the others to join him inside the line of willows. "Chance knows that Dickson has quite a few men, and he has Stockton, Sample, and Stokes along with half a dozen or so men from the town. If it was me, I would have spread my men around town and told them not to go out, but to shoot anything that is outside moving. That's how I would play it."

"That would work, Cotton," Adams said. "Those shotgun blasts would tell me that Dickson sent someone to the jail to break Miller out. I like what you just said, Cotton. Let's play the same game. Let's spread out, stay hidden, and shoot anything that moves. Unless of course, it's Chance or one of those men from town."

"I'd hate to shoot a friend," one of the cowboys from the Stokes Ranch said. "Let's make sure of our target. Some of those people with Dickson are cowboys from the outlying ranches. Damn."

There was silence for a couple of minutes while the comment sunk in. Cotton broke the spell. "You're right, but they are playing the hand that was dealt. If they are with Dickson, that means they are against Sarah Jackson, against Marshal Chance, and remember, against us. No, they would kill us on sight, we have to be ready to do the same."

General muttering, very quietly, but the men made their way back along the willows to take up positions. Adams was the first to say it out loud to Cotton. "This is almost like the war back east. Friend against friend, brother against brother. Old Ben Stokes seeing his son in jail because his son now wants him to lose his ranch, maybe even die.

"I'm glad I'm in this fight, Cotton, and I'm glad I'm on the right side. Even if we lose, I know I'm doing what's right."

The Good Hope River, like most of its kind, had been known to overflow its banks from time to time, particularly during spring thaw or from heavy mid-summer thunder storms high in the surrounding mountains. Makeshift dikes had been pushed into place over the years and were covered in thick willows and high weeds giving good cover to Adams and the rest of the group.

Staying low and on the river side of the dikes, they scattered up and down the river, still keeping in contact with the man nearest to them. "This looks good, Cotton. We can see just about the entire town along the main street and down the back sides of the buildings."

"I sure as hell hope I'm right, Hank. I sure do." It was as dark as any night would ever be as the group settled in. There was light coming from the Bucket of Good Hope Saloon, light coming from the Crystal Saloon, and light poured out of the open door of the jail. None of the store fronts, none of the homes, none of the buildings in Preston were lit. Along with the darkness was the quiet of the night.

The words from the cowboy echoed through everyone's mind as the darkness settled in. "I'd sure hate to shoot a friend."

One lonely coyote started singing on the south edge of the town waking many of the town dogs that all joined the chorus for a few minutes. An owl, sitting high in a cottonwood tree, keeping vigil for late night dinner, was hooting softly, and the Good Hope River gurgled and splashed its way through the quiet. If one didn't know the situation, one could enjoy an early fall night like this.

The men along the river watched as the lights were dimmed, one or two at a time in the Bucket of Good Hope. "Looks like Colonel George is about to start his play," Adams whispered. "Let's look sharp now."

***

"I'm sure I saw movement along the river, Marshal. I'm damn sure. Too dark to take a shot, but there are men behind the dikes and in the willows." The old man from the Crystal Saloon was pointing out the front window of the hotel toward the river.

"Dickson has enough men, that you could be right. Keep a sharp eye out." Chance had men at the windows upstairs in the hotel, and he and the old codger were in the lobby of the hotel downstairs. He could see that the door of the jail was open, but couldn't see in at all. "No movement down there since Stockton's shotgun spoke."

"That was one hell of a shotgun blast, Marshal. You suppose they are okay down there?"

"I think Mr. Stockton spoke very loud to someone. Dickson might have sent someone down there to break Miller out. Look sharp now, they're dimming the lights at the saloon. Dickson will be making his move very soon now."

As he spoke, two men emerged from the saloon, staying as close to the sides of the building as possible. They moved south about ten feet when two rifle shots rang out and the two men dropped, one trying to crawl back to the front doors of the saloon. One more shot rang out, and he too was dead. "Those shots came from the willows, Marshal."

"Good. Must be Hank Adams and Cotton Phelps." There was noise behind the hotel and Chance strode across the lobby toward the east side of the large building. "You keep watch out front, I'll be in the back." The hallway toward the back made a quick left then right turn and as Chance made that second turn the back door was splintered by heavy boots. He dove for the floor pulling his revolver out, putting five rounds through the door, holstered the weapon and fired three more from his rifle.

He stayed motionless for several minutes waiting to see if someone would still try to come through that door. When there was no movement at all from outside, he slowly got to his feet and inched forward. Two men lay dead in the debris of the hotel's back yard.

"The old man told me I'd find you back here. Looks like you took care of that action. I could see them from the window upstairs but couldn't get a shot. Would have had to lean out the window. Came down to tell you, just in time to hear all them shots. You hit or anything?"

"Thanks. No, not hit, just getting more and more angry at that fool Dickson. Go back upstairs and make sure someone is at your window, then bring someone downstairs to be with the old man out front, and then, rejoin me here. I think this will be our post for a while tonight." Chance was reloading his weapons as he spoke and ventured a glance outside. "These guys known to you?"

"That one there was with the Brady boys. I don't recognize the other. He ain't from around here." The storekeeper headed down the hallway and the marshal stepped out the door with the idea of grabbing the weapons from the dead men. A volley of shots immediately rang out, all missing their mark.

"We're in a fix now," Chance muttered to himself diving through the broken pieces of the busted up door. Most of the men were on the street side of the buildings up and down the main street in Preston, and it looked like Dickson had sent many men into the backs of the buildings along the river. "This is a pickle," he said again, squatting down in the hallway, out of sight from those outside. It was a good five minutes before Jose Alvarado made it back downstairs.

"I took a chance, Marshal, and had several men upstairs take the east side windows after hearing those shots. Hope that's okay."

"It's fine, Alvarado, it's very good." Chance was trying to remember how the hotel sat on the property, how it related to where the Bucket of Good Hope Saloon sat. "There should be a room or rooms to our south here. How do you get to them?" The storekeeper just shook his head.

"Keep a sharp eye out," Chance said, and slowly made his way down the hall, getting to his feet when he was far enough to feel somewhat safe. "Should be a doorway around here somewhere," he muttered, fumbling around in the dark. He was almost to the bend in the hallway when he found it. "Looks like a storeroom," he said to Alvarado. "No windows that I can see."

He moved back down the hallway to take up his position. "You been here long?" he asked the young Mexican.

"About two years. Maria and I came down from Virginia City when we heard that I could get a piece of property and open a store for very little money. I grew up in California on a Mission Ranch and always wanted to be free from that scene." He got silent for a couple of minutes, both men still watching out the broken door.

"Looks like I made the move from being a religious slave to being a banker's slave," he said, showing no humor. "Mr. Miller is mean, but Colonel Dickson is evil and dangerous. They get their money or you get bruises and broken bones." He patted the big revolver on his belt, "It feels good to stand up as a man again."

***

Chance smiled broadly at the comment and let his mind wander some, still watching the dark scene outside the doorway. "Such a beautiful little valley," he thought, "and so many people with dreams of a fine life. Ben Stokes and his ranch, Sarah Jackson and a new life, Jerrod Stockton building a fine livery and blacksmith shop. And selfish and deceitful people steal the dreams. Jose and Maria, coming from the mines in Virginia City to have their own business, lied to. I'm glad I'm here to help these people."

His thoughts went back for more than ten years in one direction, and to just a few days ago in another. "I don't know what it would be like to own a ranch like Stokes has, or if I could even do that kind of work. Was I kidding myself when I said it would be such a nice place to settle in?" Thoughts of Jennifer Stokes came into his mind, out of nowhere.

"My God, I don't even know the woman." He caught himself when he realized he almost said that out loud. "Where is this coming from? Quitting the service, marrying, owning property? Next I'll be thinking of raising a family." He laughed out loud, not to himself, put all those thoughts aside, and tried his best to concentrate on the open darkness on the other side of the broken door. "Maybe I'll go back to Missouri and be a row cropper," he said, again out loud. Jose Alvarado looked at him like he had gone mad or something.

"It's nothing," he said, just thinking out loud." He tried to get his mind back on the job. "When I was out front, we saw shots fired from the willows at men coming out of the Bucket of Good Hope. If Hank Adams and Cotton Phelps are back in town, they might just be ranged along the river dikes." He was talking to himself as much as to Jose Alvarado. "Cover me," he said, and on his belly, crawled up to the broken doorway.

"Phelps, you out there?" he yelled. No answer and he tried again. "Adams," he hollered, "you out there?" This time he got an answer, but it wasn't what he was looking for.

Two shots rang out and a voice said, "Sure we are. Come on out, let's talk," followed by some unseemly comments and guffaws.

"Sounds like at least three men back near the trees, Jose. Can't see them though." He was as close to the floor as he could get, trying to use the broken door jamb for protection, and fired his big revolver twice in the general direction of the voices. A volley or shots rang out, and using muzzle flash as a sight point, fired twice more. There was an answering scream of pain from one of the shots.

"Got one, anyway," he muttered, scrambling back into the hallway. "We're gonna need to be really sharp, Jose, really sharp."

Chapter Fourteen

"Stone! Stone, did you hear that? Gunshots coming from town. One loud blast woke me up, and now, several shots. Listen." Stan Martinez was out of his bedroll, trying to get his boots on. "We're closer to town than we thought. I don't think we're a mile out, Stone."

Ira Stone and Gregory Bettencourt were fighting off a deep trail-weary sleep, getting out of their bed rolls, fighting their boots and spurs, cussing and spitting. As they stirred, another volley of shots rang out. "They got a battle going on in that town, Ira. Sounds like old Jake knew what he was talking about one more time. Got any idea what time it might be?"

All three men started looking at the stars, shaking their heads, and finally Ira Stone got himself awake enough to pull his watch from a jacket pocket. "Looks to be about two o'clock in the morning," he laughed, looking at the other two. Then the anger showed and he entered a war mood.

"That's the best time to start a war, and it sounds like Chance has got one started. Let's pack up and move toward town, but damn careful boys. Except for Jake, we don't know anybody, and nobody knows us. We'll be targets from both sides, so slow and easy does it."

Camp was broke and packed on the mules, cold water was breakfast, horses saddled, and the three men started to mount. Bettencourt threw up a hand quickly. "Listen. Listen, can you hear horses?"

Out of the damp early morning air the three lawmen could hear several horses approaching on the trail, just yards from where they had bedded down. "Sounds like at least four coming hard, Stone. Maybe five." All three settled down on their haunches, hoping not to be seen, hoping their horses wouldn't be. Four riders galloped past the three, not seeing them at all.

"Wherever they're going, they are in one big hurry. Just a glimpse, but I didn't recognize anyone, especially Chance." Martinez swung into the saddle followed by the others. Laughing, he continued, "Looks like Chance is chasing the bad guys right out of town. Maybe our job's done, boys," and the bunch were laughing as they made their way onto the trail, headed toward town.

"How many fights like this you been in, Martinez?"

"Oh, hell, Stone, down in Texas it seems like we were fighting our way in or out of some town every week. Arizona was the worst, though. Every outlaw ever lived tried to be the king of Arizona."

"Yeah," Bettencourt piped in, "Arizona was bad, but California was bad, bad. The Spanish and Mexican land grantees had their lands stolen, and we were defending the people that did the stealing. Those days right after the Mexican war, when California became part of the United States, those were some wars over there."

All three men had tales to tell, and all three were riding with thoughts of a new war to fight. Martinez put the thoughts into words. "I think there's more to this than just some woman having her homestead taken. I think Chance is in a deep mud hole right now. Clearing up a homestead issue should not include hired guns and should not include open warfare at two O'clock in the morning." There was general agreement as the three rode down the trail.

The hulk of the old livery stable came slowly into view through the late night-early morning murk, and the stench grabbed their attention immediately. Three shots rang out, one round popping dust in front of Stone's horse. The three drove their horses and mules into the willows and went belly flat onto the ground. "Somebody doesn't like us," Martinez quipped, taking a long sight along the barrel of his rifle.

"Sounded like those shots came from that big

building over there on the left."

"That's a saloon, Stone. I can just make out the name in the dark. Bucket of Good Hope. Not very friendly, I'd say. I'm gonna get these animals back into the willows here, and then let's find out who the bad guys are." Stone gathered up reins and lead ropes and moved the animals back into the woods.

Martinez squirmed through the branches and weeds, easing himself on top of the low dike along the trailside. "One man in the shadows of the doorway, but I can't see his face or tell if it might be Chance." Just as he finished saying that, two rifle shots rang out about three hundred feet from Stone's left, and Martinez watched as the man in the saloon doorway was thrown back inside by the force of the two slugs.

"We got us a mess, right now, boys," Stone said, worming his way onto the dike. "Who are the good guys, who are the bad guys, and, where the hell is Chance?"

A volley of shots rang out from the other side of the large hotel building, followed a couple of minutes later by two more shots. "This is bad. Martinez, do you remember when we had to save that federal judge up north? The one that was kidnapped and held for ransom?"

"That was a fight. We damn near lost the man, lost two of our best deputies, and got you all shot up. Hell, yes, I remember. What are you thinking?"

"Chance had got into the gang, remember, and you and he had a secret signal of some kind to let him know you were close by. What was that signal?"

"Oh, hell, Stone. I forgot all about that. Our whistles back and forth. I know Chance would remember if he heard it. Let me try." Martinez cupped his hands near his mouth and gave a quaking whistle sound, not like any bird anyone might have heard, not like any other sound one might recognize. It fluttered and quaked and shrieked from those cupped hands for at least thirty seconds.

Martinez paused, then gave the whistle again, making it last even longer, going up and down the scale, actually sending goose bumps along Stone's back. "If he heard that, we'll know in a short time."

The whistle echoed through the quiet streets and alleys of Preston, everyone listening to the eerie sound, especially U.S. Marshal Jacob Chance in the hallway at the rear of the hotel.

"Watch that door," he said and stormed to the front of the hotel. Near one of the broken out windows, he cupped his hands and let fly a loud, quaking, thrilling rendition of Martinez's whistle. The old man from the Crystal Saloon was amazed. "All right," Chance said, waiting for the answer. "Those are U.S. Marshals out there, my friend, all the way from San Francisco, just to make sure you have your favorite stool at the end of the bar," and the smile broadened as Martinez gave the answering signal.

"Listen close, Martinez," Chance yelled down the empty street. "Somewhere to the east of where you are, there are at least two men in the willows that are friends. The bad guys are holed up in the saloon, slightly to your left, and along the back sides of some of these buildings. The good guys are in the buildings."

What he got back from Martinez was a full-fledged Apache war whoop bringing loud laughter from Chance. The old man just smiled and wondered what the hell just happened.

"Keep a close eye. I'm going back down the hallway to the back door."

***

"My leg hurts like hell, my ranch is gone, my little girl is hurt, and now, I find that I really do love Cotton Phelps, and he's gonna get hurt too. I want to go help him, Jenny, and all I can do is lie in this bed and feel sorry for myself." Sarah had slept for several hours after the men left for town, and darkness had set in over the Stokes Ranch and the big main house.

"He's a big tough cowboy, Sarah, the kind of man you need to be hitched up with, and he'll be back soon and carry you off to paradise." Laughter filled the little bedroom, waking Georgia from a long overdue nap. "Sorry, little one. Go back to sleep now, and we'll all have supper soon. My camp cookin' is some of the best in the valley, so get ready, girls."

Jennifer Stokes was in charge, and everyone knew it, including the hands still on the ranch, down from the line camps. "I've got a pot of stew going that will make a perfect ending for your horrible day. Sourdough biscuits to sop up the gravy. And, Georgia, we're gonna have peach cobbler to finish off tonight's supper."

Georgia gave a hearty yelp, one of the cowboys out front joined her, bringing grand smiles to both Jennifer and Sarah. "I want to sit out on the porch, Jenny. I think I can hobble out there," she said, trying to swing her broken leg out from under the pile of blankets on the bed.

"Easy girl, let me get one of the big guys to help you," and Jenny stepped out of the bedroom while Sarah and Georgia got into robes. Georgia had decided she didn't need any more sleep, if there might be grown-up talk to listen to.

Wes Mullins, almost six feet tall and about two hundred pounds, filled the doorway as Sarah stood up for the first time. "Whoa, Sarah, I gotcha," the big man said as Sarah Jackson almost toppled over. "You're not supposed to walk on broken legs, dear lady," he drawled, slipping an arm around her waist. "I'll make a fine crutch, just don't put any weight on that leg. You'll be fine," and they wrenched and bumped their way across the living room and out onto the large porch.

"Here, you go, Sarah. The big chair of honor," and Jenny helped her ease down into the chair usually occupied by Ben Stokes. "I've got hot coffee and sweet bread for us, and Georgia, how about a couple of sugar cookies? That'll tide us over 'till supper." She motioned for one of the men to help her bring it all out on the porch.

"I still don't understand about half of what seems to be happening around here," Sarah said, taking a sip of the hot coffee. "That Mr. Miller is really just as mean and, well, he is," she said, almost bringing smiles to some of those on the porch.

The night came on fast after they had supper, the cowboys spread themselves around the ranch to keep watch. It was the old camp cook who put a cap on the evening. "That Dickson, if he really is an old army man, knows the best time to strike is a couple of hours before sunrise, and that's when we're gonna have to be up and ready for anything."

"Not getting Sarah and Georgia, then not being able to trick me into town has probably got those old fools pretty much riled up," Jenny said. "I hope that marshal is as tough as he looks."

"What was he like, Jenny? I still haven't met him."

"He's big, kinda skinny. Needs some good ranch cookin', I think. Good looking," she said, and a quick little smile was caught by Sarah.

"Looks like you're thinking of being that person to provide those ranch meals? I saw that look in your eye."

"I don't think he's ever been dragged to the fire, but I'd put my brand on him. I think it was his eyes that got right to me. He looked all the way through me, like he could see into my soul." She felt shivers spread through her body as she said that, and that little smile returned. "We better get some sleep. Might be another very long day tomorrow."

***

Dickson was pacing back and forth in his upstairs office, trying to put the pieces together. His friend and longtime associate Will Cooke was sitting in one of the large wingback chairs, cheroot in one hand, glass of bourbon in the other. "George, I'm glad you called for me, but you waited just about too long. You got yourself in one hell of a hog wash, Colonel. You say all of this is because some woman filed homestead?"

"Damn that woman," Dickson muttered for the twentieth time. "I told Preston to shoot her, to run her out of the valley, but he's got soft. That's what it is, Miller has got soft, and now, I have to fight off a damn U.S. Marshal."

"Take it easy, George. We've done this before."

"Not with these stakes, Will. That big blast from down the street probably means that I have lost two good men, and that Miller and the others are still locked in that jail. You hear all that gunfire? I'm losing men by the handful." He was working hard to settle himself, to get that old military bearing back.

"Listen to me, Will. Preston got this valley when his grandpa kicked off, and I have now got one half of the valley property, one half of the town property, and I aced that idiot banker and own all the water in the valley. River and wells. Now, do you understand what I'm fighting for? Millions, Will. Millions." He couldn't help smiling when he said that, and the thought of all that money calmed him a bit.

"I brought most of the gold that I could get in the saddle bags from Salt Lake, and the horses are tied out behind the saloon. We're gonna have to make a run for it, George, and you know it. You can't win this fight, all you can do is prolong the end. You can win today's battle, but in the end, we're gonna have to run for it."

Will Cooke took a long sip of bourbon, puffed gently on the cigar, and stood up. "You sent those four men out to kidnap that Stokes woman. When they get back, this whole mess will end. You put big ropes on her, gag her soundly, march her out in the middle of the street, and this will end." Cooke was one of those criminals known in the tough mining and cattle towns as a shark.

He was excellent with cards and dice, making them do whatever it was he wanted them to do, but on top of that, he didn't have a weakness for giving anyone an even break. Cooke was wanted in several states and territories, under several names, and would do just about anything Dickson asked him to do.

"You should have called for me earlier, George. The Jackson woman and her screaming kid should have died. You sent the wrong men yesterday. Now, she's alive and you've lost more men. You should have simply taken the Stokes girl, not tried to entice her into town." He found himself pacing right along with Dickson. Both stopped suddenly.

"What the hell is that?" They ran out of the office and downstairs, joining several of Dickson's gunslingers near the open saloon doors. "There it is again," Cooke said. "That's not an animal or bird." It was quiet for another couple of minutes.

"It came from along the river, near the livery stables," one of the gunmen was saying, and was interrupted by another strange sound, this time coming from the hotel.

"Signals," Dickson howled. "They have people along the river." Then they heard Chance yelling to those in the willows. "Damn it, Cooke, they have people scattered all over town and now, it sounds like that marshal has help from out of town." More shots rang out from along the river when Chance stopped talking, bullets crashing into the door and window frames of the saloon.

"Let's talk, Cooke. Upstairs." Ignoring questions from their hired guns and others in the saloon, the two men hightailed it up the stairs and into the office.

"We have to prepare for the worst, George. This may not end well at all if that marshal has people coming in from California or Utah, and as you saw, has the townspeople on his side. You better prepare to get the hell out of Preston fast if this falls apart on us."

"No, Will. I own all this. I'm not giving it up to some damn fool marshal." He pulled the door open and walked back down the stairs, stopping about half way down. Every eye in the saloon was on Colonel George and Will Cooke. "I want you men to listen carefully now. Those men out there have some of the townspeople all riled up, and because of that, they are dangerous.

"These are not legitimate lawmen, they are criminals here to take what belongs to me and to Preston Miller. They are killers and our only defense is to kill first." A long and loud cheer went up from the gunmen scattered around the saloon. Dickson looked around and gave Cooke a big smile. "I need two men to sneak around behind that hotel and see if you can't get a really good fire going there. Then I need two teams of two or three men each to get as close to those willows as you can and set them on fire."

Men in the saloon were fighting and arguing with one another, vying for the opportunity to be on any one of those teams. Dickson pointed to various men and assigned them their positions. "Don't let me down. Remember, each of you has land, ranches, and position coming to you when we win this fight. I don't want to see any prisoners, is that clear?" and the cheers were loud and long.

Chapter Fifteen

"Shouldn't be any horses roaming around this pasture, Sheridan. Them has to be riders comin' on." The two cowboys were about two hundred yards from the main house, tucked in a stand of cottonwood trees just off the main trail from town. "They're too far away to see. Jump on your horse and alert the house, I'll do what I can here." The riders were walking their horses, so Sheridan had plenty of time to wake up the household, and the old camp cook, jack-of-all-trades cowboy, planned to stand his ground against whatever was coming up the trail.

"Sounds like maybe three, maybe four coming on," he muttered, pulling his rifle from its scabbard and kneeling behind the trunk of a big sturdy tree. As the riders approached, he jacked a round into the receiver, alerting the riders to his presence. "Hold it up right there, you men. This road is closed tonight."

Three shots rang out, none even coming close to the old guy, and when his rifle belched fire, two of the riders were thrown from their horses into the dirt and rocks. "I'll be damned," he said to himself, "there's four of the bastards." He fired three more times, then had to stop to reload. His last volley nicked one of the riders, and those two bailed off their horses, guns in hand, and started firing toward the old man's tree.

Between Sheridan's howling alert and all the gunfire, the house was up, armed, and ready for war. Sheridan and one of the cowboys turned and headed back to where the fight was going on while Jenny and a couple of the other cowboys prepared to defend the ranch house. Sarah Jackson hopped and hobbled out of the bedroom demanding that she be given a position and a rifle. "I brought all this on, the least I can do is fight, and you know I'm a crack shot with a rifle."

Jenny well knew that, and also knew she saw a tiger

about to roar. She pointed at one of the front windows, saying, "Here, take my brother's rifle and park yourself by that window." She gave everyone a grand Stokes' smile, saw Georgia coming out of the bedroom and chased her back in, and told her to stay put. Coming back into the living room, in a complete turmoil, she said, "Let's take some of these banditos out of the fight, shall we?"

The old man by the tree didn't have time to reload his rifle, so he pulled his revolver instead. Taking careful aim, he killed the man he had wounded earlier. "Give it up," he hollered at the one remaining. "You've got half a dozen Stokes' cowboys coming down on you right now, and I have you in my sights. Throw that rifle down, fool." Instead, the man brought the rifle to his shoulder and died with a bullet through his heart. The lure of free land offered by Colonel Dickson conquered thoughts of survival.

"Dumb bastard didn't have to die," the old man told the first of the riders to reach the scene. "Let's see if we know any of these jaspers. Yahoos, that's what they are. Yahoos." The others joined in, and the old man asked about Jenny and Sarah.

"They're fine. Itching for a fight, I think, so we'll have to be careful riding back to the house." They picked up rifles and pistols and tried to identify those on the ground.

"I don't know any of these men. Never seen 'em before," one of the cowboys said. "That Dickson and Miller must have hired a bunch of gunslingers. You did a fine job on them, Cookie. Maybe you ought to hire out, you think?" That brought more laughter, and they grabbed the loose horses, tied the bodies onto the saddles, and started back toward the main house.

"Let's get those bodies buried," Jenny said after the story had been told and retold, "and when it gets light, I think we need to get into town. Cookie, hook up the buckboard for Sarah and Georgia, and the rest of us will need to be heavily armed. I think if Dickson has enough men that he can afford to send four of them out here, Marshal Chance and my dad are going to need all the help they can get." Everyone agreed and got started on the jobs at hand.

"Cookie, I know you're a fine gunslinger," and laughter spread around the room, "but right now, we need one of your special ranch hand breakfasts. We ain't gonna fight this war on empty stomachs," and she sent him scuttling into the kitchen, leaving her with thoughts of Marshal Chance. What kind of man was he, besides being so damn good looking, brave, and . . . she had to stop.

"Keep this up," she muttered, "and I'll be doing something really stupid." She was smiling, more to herself than anything, still wondering *just what kind of a man is he?* She would be surprised to know that Jacob Chance had some of those same thoughts about her.

"I can fix you up in the wagon, Sarah, so you'll be comfortable, and Georgia can ride in the back with you. Keep that rifle and I'll have mine and a revolver. This is turning out to be a real war, Sarah. A real war."

***

"Hey, Marshal. Look at this." Alvarado was pointing out the gaping hole in the wall where the back door of the hotel used to be. "Looks like a couple of men with torches." He sighted for a long time, then shot as Chance scooted up to the opening. The man with the torch screamed and was thrown backwards into the willows. The torch rolled and tumbled through the dry brush catching it and the willows on fire immediately.

At least a dozen shots rang out from the bushes, some aimed at the hotel, some aimed at those shooting into the hotel. "That you in the hotel, Chance?" a voice hollered following the shots.

"Nice to hear your voice, Hank. Listen close. There are several deputies upstream from you, closer to the livery.

Don't let them shoot you and please don't shoot them."

"I think Cotton just made contact with them, Chance. Looks like Dickson is planning to burn down the town. These willows will burn for hours, Chance, and may catch some of the buildings on fire."

More shots rang out from the street side of the buildings. Chance told Alvarado to stay and shoot anything that moved, and he headed up the hallway toward the front of the building. "See something, old timer?"

"Weren't me shooting, Marshal," he said, pointing toward the saloon. "Shots came from inside the Bucket of Good Hope. Startin' to get light, and those boys know they are trapped. Might get interesting."

"That's a mouthful, old man. Follow my lead now and let's have some fun." He pulled the rifle to his shoulder and just started firing, one shot following the next, then did the same thing with his revolver. The old man fired his five rounds from the rifle, and all at once every one of the men along the river did the same thing. More than one hundred rounds were fired into the saloon walls, doors, and windows.

It was only moments later that the flickering of fires could be seen from within the building. "Looks like that worked," Chance said. "Keep reloading and firing, don't give them a chance to work on putting out those fires. Keep shooting," and he emptied his rifle again. Within minutes flames were seen through the windows, smoke billowed out every crack, and in less than ten minutes the entire saloon was engulfed in flames.

Jerrod Stockton, standing inside the open door of the jailhouse, started cheering like a little kid when the flames could be seen. "That's payback, you bastard. Burn that building to the ground, and I hope you get trapped in there, Dickson." His big booming voice could be heard up and down the dusty street, well lit now by a combination of the burning building and the coming sunrise.

"Been a long time since I have been able to smile," he said to his companion, "but this is good to see. Let's keep sharp. Those boys inside are going to want to get the hell out of there real soon."

***

Dickson and Cooke went back up to the office and heard the first of the torch men get killed, heard the words between Hank Adams and Marshal Chance. Dickson went to his vault. "I think it's time for a hasty retreat, Cooke." He pulled four heavy canvas sacks out of the safe and handed two of them to Will Cooke. "There's a ranch about ten miles south of here, an old couple and screwed-up kid live there. If we can get there, we can get provisions and get the hell out of this mess."

As the two men started to leave the office, hundreds of gun shots rang out, from the town, from along the river, from the front, and from the back. Men were diving for cover, bottles and lanterns exploded, bullets were ripping the entire saloon to shreds, and then the fires started.

"Get those fires out!" Dickson was howling mad, and the men were more interested in protecting themselves than worrying about fires. Another prolonged volley of a hundred or more shots rang out. Will Cooke felt a bullet slam into his chest and he crumpled over, tumbling down the stairs to the saloon floor, the canvas bags coming open, spreading hundreds of twenty dollar gold pieces across the saloon floor.

Several of the men recognized what was about to happen. "You bastard," one of the men hollered. "You are running out on us," and he made a move to shoot Colonel George. Dickson was just a bit faster—two shots rang out, two men fell to the floor. Dickson had taken a round through his leg, the gunman had taken one through his heart.

Between hundreds of rounds being fired through the saloon walls, doors, and windows, fires burning out of control, and now gunfire from inside the saloon, the scene was pure chaos. Another of the gunmen spoke up. "I ain't fightin' for no man what would run out on me in the middle of a fight," and many of those in the saloon seemed to agree.

"I'm all for calling it," one piped up, and grabbed one of the bar towels and moved slowly toward the front doors of the Bucket of Good Hope. Dickson was lying on the floor in a gathering pool of blood, raised his pistol.

"Hold it right there," he said, and the man nearest him kicked the gun out of his hand, then kicked the colonel in the head.

"Shut up, you miserable bastard." He reached down and picked up one of the canvas bags Dickson had with him and emptied it on the floor. More twenty dollar gold coins spilled out. "Let's see if we can get out of this alive, men," and he crawled across the floor to the man with the bar rag. "Here, tie that thing onto my rifle barrel," he said, "and I'll crawl out and wave it. If they accept our surrender, don't nobody get excited and start shooting or we'll all die."

There were only five men left alive in the saloon when Chance, along with Marshal Stone, took control of the situation, including Dickson. "So, you're the Colonel George I've heard so much about," Chance said, putting a bar towel around the injured man's leg. "Maybe we can get Jerrod Stockton over here to tend your wound." At that moment, Stockton, along with men from the jail, from the river, and from across the street at the Crystal Saloon, came into the furiously burning building.

"Yeah, I'll fix him up," Stockton snarled, fingering the hammers on that massive shotgun of his. "Yes sir, Marshal Chance, give me five minutes alone with that varmint and we won't have to worry about trials and things."

"Hold up on that, Jerrod. We'll not have any

lynchings yet." Chance looked into the pleading eyes of Dickson. "At least not til the judge says to hang 'em from the biggest tree in town." Cheers echoed through the flames and smoke and everyone grabbed injured and dead men and got them out and into the street. Ira Stone led Bettencourt and Martinez up from the river and joined the fray.

"Nice war, Mr. Stone. Glad you boys made it for the finale." They were standing in the street, the sun all the way up, watching the Bucket of Good Hope burn to the ground. Jerrod Stockton was piling pieces of wood into the flames, with pure glee in the effort.

"Payback you dirty bastard," he said with every piece of wood thrown into the flames. "Payback." Most of the men who helped get the wounded and dead out of the flaming holocaust also carried a few pockets full of gold coins. Chance gave every indication that he saw nothing.

"Who's down at the jail, Jerrod? We need to protect that fool banker and the others locked up down there. Mr. Stone, will you join me for a cup of coffee or something just a bit stronger?" And the two ambled across the street toward the Crystal Saloon.

***

It was just getting light as Jennifer Stokes led her band out onto the trail that would take them to Preston. Cookie, four cowboys, Sarah Jackson and daughter Georgia, and plenty of guns and ammunition. They left two of the hired hands behind to protect the ranch just in case Dickson sent more men out. As they neared Preston they could see great clouds of black smoke, and could hear tremendous rounds of gunfire. "We have to be very careful now," she said, as it became obvious there was one hell of a fight going on in that town.

It was as if somebody had signaled *End*, and there was a heavy blanket of quiet that settled in—from Jennifer's point of view—ominously. "Something just happened," she said over her shoulder to Sarah. The entourage was stopped in the middle of the trail and the silence continued for minutes.

"Let's just ride in, nice and slow, and be prepared for anything that might happen. Either side could have been the winners here, so let's play it slow." She led the way, the boss of the outfit, with the wagon surrounded by the cowboys—reins in one hand, revolvers in the other—at a slow walk, first past some tied horses in the willows, then alongside the still foul-smelling burned-out hulk of Jerrod Stockton's Livery Stables and Blacksmith shop, and into the area in front of the Bucket of Good Hope Saloon, now a raging inferno. They found the street filled with men and women, the townsfolk, the surrounding area ranch hands, and one big rancher, coming lickety-split up the street.

It was Big Ben Stokes who gave out with the loudest yell ever heard in Preston when he saw Jennifer and the gang arrive. Cotton Phelps was next to holler, and then the streets erupted with people. Jacob Chance, Stockton, all the town defenders, a dozen or more cowboys and Ira Stone and company, flooded out of the Crystal Saloon, what was left of the hotel, and from the jail. It was a celebration of victory, a celebration of life the way it was supposed to be, which hadn't been part of Preston for a long time, and a venting of pent-up emotions, finally let loose.

Chance and Stone went back into the Crystal Saloon while the party raged in the middle of the street. "I'm sure glad to see you, Ira. I had no way of knowing if my letter got through to the Major. For a simple land law dispute, I made a mess of this town, eh?"

"Burned her to the ground, Jacob, burned her down." The two men shared cold glasses of beer, and got down to business. "The Major sent a rider to Carson City to escort the federal judge down here. He felt it would be a lot easier to conduct whatever hearings might be needed here, rather than try to get everyone up to Carson City."

"That was going to be my first question, Stone. We

almost lost the guy I wanted most to see in prison. That bullet through his leg will heal in no time, but I'm afraid the damage he caused to this town, valley, and people won't heal for years, even generations to come.

"Right now, that old jail is filled with men and boys and it will take all of our effort to figure out which is who, and maybe even answer why. You won't believe the story I'm about to tell you." The two men sat at a table, finished off several cold brews and Jacob Chance outlined the story over the next several hours.

Out in the street, men had created a bucket brigade, not to quell the fire in the Bucket of Good Hope Saloon, but to keep the flames from spreading up and down the dusty old main street. All of the buildings in Preston were made of wood, they were tucked up too close to each other, and the threat of losing the town put an urgency to the firefighting.

The old hotel was most vulnerable, and with the saloon fire raging the men also had to fight the fires in the back of the building, moving swiftly through the willows and dry brush. The fight continued through most of the day before anyone felt safe.

***

Cotton Phelps took charge of Sarah Jackson and Georgia, made them as comfortable as possible in the old hotel. "You missed a hell of a show, Sarah. You asked me if I thought that marshal was tough enough to take on the problem here. Let me tell you, he's the toughest man I've ever met. Fearless, Sarah." He had hugged her until her ribs hurt and she didn't care.

"I was so afraid, Cotton Phelps. Don't you ever leave me again." She stopped, moved back a bit from the embrace.

"What's wrong?"

"We have to change the brand. I won't be Sarah Jackson for very much longer. I'll be Sarah Phelps. We have to change the brand." Out on the street, those working with Jerrod Stockton heard gales of laughter coming from one of the hotel upstairs windows, blown out by many rounds sometime yesterday.

"All right, all right, let's get back to work," Stockton said, a broad smile on his big face. "Those two will be making noise up there for a long time. Let's get everything that can still be salvaged from the saloon and what's left of my stables, and then pile the junk up and burn it.

"We got a town to rebuild, men, even if nobody knows who owns what."

Chapter Sixteen

B ig Ben Stokes, his arms filled with daughter Jennifer, had tears running down his cheeks as he tried to tell her what had happened, how it was that her brother was in jail, and would be a hated man by so many when his story got spread around. "He just never grew up, Jenny, never became a man, and has no honor. He turned on me like I was curdled cream, sold out to the highest bidder, that bastard Dickson and his crony Miller." He appeared to be a beaten man and Jennifer eased him down into a chair. They were sitting in the front of the jail, bright sunshine pouring down on them.

Jennifer looked around the town she had all but grown up in, seeing buildings shredded by gunfire, buildings still smoldering from intense fires, and people she had known since she was just a little girl wandering around in a daze similar to her own.

"It's okay, papa," she whispered, and walked inside to pour some coffee. "It will take a long time, but we'll be a family again, sometime down the road. The big thing right now is to protect the herd, get it down from summer grazing, and then work to make sure we still have a ranch." Those were the kinds of words, sentiment, that Ben Stokes had always hoped to hear from Jim and never did.

Jennifer Stokes, the strong one in the family, also had tears running across her pretty face, trying to figure out what might have triggered such a change in her brother. "I'm going to go talk to him, Dad. No, you sit still, drink your coffee. He's my brother, I have a responsibility to him and to you." She patted Ben Stokes on the shoulder as she walked back into the jail and toward the cells in the back. It was an ugly scene, one wall all but blown away by Jerrod Stockton, and the four cells, two on each side, jammed now with prisoners.

"Hello, Jim. Dad tried to tell me what happened, but

it doesn't make any sense. Do you realize just how much trouble you are in? We need you at the ranch, it's your home, not this filthy jail. What happened?"

"Get out of here, Jenny. You're not my family anymore. Get out," and he turned away from his sister, walked toward the back of the cell. Two hands reached out from behind Jennifer, fingers grasping shoulders, neck, breasts, followed by a long scream, and then guffaws from the penned group of men. James Stokes just stood and watched as two men groped his sister.

Ben Stokes came through the jail like an enraged bull and stopped dead in his tracks. "She's dead, Stokes, unless you let us out of here, and I mean now." One man had his fingers laced around Jennifer's throat, the other was busy groping, and Stokes stood still, his revolver clutched in his right hand. Jennifer looked her father in the eye, nodded ever so slightly, and ducked her head fast.

Stokes' gun flashed twice and the man whose fingers had been around Jennifer's throat was thrown back against the men behind him, minus half his head. Jennifer lunged forward, out of the grasp of the other man, and Ben fired twice more, killing the assailant. Jennifer looked into the cage where her brother was. "You filthy pig," she said and stormed out of the cell area.

By this time, men raced to the jail, led by Jerrod Stockton and his massive shotgun. Jennifer helped Ben back onto the chair on the front porch of the jail and told Stockton what had happened. He marched back into the cell area.

"Alright," he said, opening the cell where the two men lay dead. "You and you, move these two fools out of there. Come on, stupid, one at a time, and take the bodies down to the stables for burial. Sample, you walk with them and if either one tries to jack rabbit on you, kill both of them.

"You get that one down there, come back for this

second idiot. Move it," Stockton snarled, bringing that shotgun to what would be called port arms in the military, and the whole jail froze. It looked like another killing real soon. The two prisoners grabbed the first body and hauled it out and down the street fast with Sheriff Sample giving them the proper escort.

There were still two more men in the cell and Stockton turned his attention to them. "Get a couple of pails of water and get this bloody mess cleaned up. No, wait," and Stockton opened the cell where Jim Stokes was standing with a stupid grin on his face.

"Get your ass out here, Stokes." He re-closed the cell door and pushed Stokes into the other cell. "Now, you two come with me and we're gonna get a couple of pails of water, and Stokes, you little shit, you're gonna clean up this bloody mess. It's just a shame I can't take five minutes and spend it alone with you right now." He pushed the two prisoners and they left to get the water.

Jennifer and Ben Stokes were on the porch watching all the activity up and down the main street. "I'm going to gather the men, papa, and then we should head back to the ranch. It'll take days for the marshal to get things straightened up around here, and then we can start to worry about whether we own what we think we own. In the meantime, I have to start into the high country and get the herd down here.

"Do you have any idea where your horse might be?"

Stokes had to laugh at that. "I don't even know where my hat is, Jenny." He took a long draught of coffee and for the first time in his life realized he was physically worn out. "I've been up for a couple of days, old girl, and I'm beat, I'm hungry, and I'm still as angry as I've ever been. My own son, your brother, turned on us like a mongrel dog, those bastards Dickson and Miller have been lying to us for years, and I only want a steak this big and a bed this soft." Jenny thought he was going to go to sleep in the old cane chair.

"I'll get the men and be back shortly, dad. Drink your coffee, that'll help."

"A hefty belt of bourbon would be better," he muttered as she walked back into the jail.

***

"That's the most amazing story I've ever heard, Chance. I hope that judge has a sense of humor because he'll drive himself batty without one. Not one single deed on property filed anywhere, not one paper filed for water rights anywhere, and these folks bamboozled out of everything."

"One thing, Stone. We have to work as hard as we've ever worked to save these people's property. I don't know how yet, but I won't be able to ride away from this mess and just leave it up to some judge or government type to make decisions dealing with what these people have built over many years."

"That's why you've always been among the best, Chance. I take it this saloon is your office?" He had noticed the bartender allowing him full use of the building, actually catering to the marshal. The beer glasses never quite emptied before fresh ones were offered, the cane chairs were the best in the saloon, even with cushions for the seats, and there was a fresh spittoon at each chair. "I think the major would approve."

Chance laughed at the comment but had to agree. "We pretty much shot up the hotel, blew out most of the windows, tore down walls, destroyed furniture, so yeah, this is my office." The two were having a good laugh when Peter Sample walked up to the table, also holding a glass of beer.

"Mind if I join you, Marshal?"

"Have a seat. Sample, this is Ira Stone, lead deputy U.S. Marshal for this district. Stone, this is Peter Sample,

188

the man I told you about who was appointed sheriff by Miller and Dickson. Sample's a good man, Ira, and we'll need his services down the line around here." Chance looked at Sample and gave him a smile, which Sample appreciated.

"What were those gunshots we heard a few minutes ago?" Sample took the next several minutes to explain what had happened at the jail, and how Jerrod Stockton had simply taken control of the situation.

"Jerrod's a good man, a natural leader and not just intelligent but self-educated as well. Preston will need men like him if the town survives this current agony. Keep a close watch on those men in that jail, Sample. With Dickson and Miller still alive, we don't need them to lead a riot or worse, a jail break. Sample, can you spread the word that I would like to hold a town meeting early tomorrow morning, here in the Crystal Saloon? Tiny," and looked over at the Crystal barkeep, "is that all right with you?"

"You bet it is," Bidwell answered, thinking of all the glasses of beer, shots of whiskey, and jingling coins that would be rung up. "Bring 'em all in," and he was smiling.

"I'll get right on it, Marshal. I'll send men up and down the valley to notify the ranches. Some of those folks have to be scared half to death right now." He downed the last drops in his glass and walked out, with Chance and Stone just a couple of minutes behind him.

"Mr. Stone, let's wander over to the bank and see what kinds of paper old Preston Miller kept around. Anything that Dickson might have had is gone now. We will have some fun talking to those two."

"What do you think we'll find at the bank, Jacob?"

"Well, if Miller really is a banker, we should find ledgers going back many years detailing who bought what, how much they paid, and their current mortgage situation. Or, and this bothers me, we'll find nothing."

Stone was looking forward to going through the

banker's paper work, but was also concerned about what Chance had said to the sheriff. "Are you worried about Dickson and Miller trying something at the jail? Is that why you mentioned riot or jail break to Sample?"

"Very much so, Stone. Very much so. I tell you what, let's go down to the jail first and talk with those two fools and then go to the bank. Yes, I am worried they might try something. In particular, Dickson. When we get into his background, we're going to find a lot more than just some paramilitary nonsense during the California statehood war. He's got criminal, con-man, gangster written in bold letters across his face.

"He's no more a colonel than I am a Union general, Ira, and we need to worry about him."

***

"That leg really hurts, doesn't it. I didn't do a very good job setting it, I'm afraid. I hope you don't have too much of a limp when it all heals." Sarah looked deep into Cotton Phelps's eyes, reached up and brushed some hair from his face and nestled even closer into his big strong arms and shoulder.

"You did a fine job, Cotton. Even if it don't heal perfect, what matters is I'll be with you, and that'll make things perfect." The smile was soundly etched into her soft face, hadn't changed since Phelps lifted her out of the wagon and brought her to the hotel. "I like the way you take care of me, Cotton. Just keep doing it the same way."

They had found one room that had most of the windows intact, doors that actually closed, not splintered and ripped apart, and a bed that wasn't covered in broken glass and shards of this and that. Phelps had settled Sarah Jackson on the bed and was sitting alongside, staring into her eyes for minutes on end. "I think we should keep the brand the way it is, Sarah. It's you and Georgia, and what more could any many want besides spending the rest of his life taking care of the two of you."

190

"Do you think my ranch will be okay? I hope Dickson or Miller didn't do something really stupid like burning my home and barns, or killing all my animals. I'm really worried, Cotton. When can we go back?"

"Jennifer left the wagon and horses here for us, so we could probably go back as soon as you want. You need a little rest first, though. Let me find Georgia and get her up here, then I'll round up some food for us, you can take a nice nap, and we'll load up and head back to your ranch."

"You mean our ranch, cowboy."

People up and down the dusty and cluttered main street couldn't help but notice the wide smile spread across Cotton Phelps's face as he started the search for Georgia. "Looks like that old cowboy has found himself a long-time home," Hank Adams said after Phelps walked by. That brought a few outright laughs, and Phelps's face took on a crimson glow.

"Knock it off, now," he grumbled, still smiling, though. "Seen Georgia anywhere?"

"Mrs. Kindle took her over to the café, Cotton. Too much blood and trouble out here on the street."

"She's seen her share of it, I'm afraid," Phelps answered, nodding his thanks and heading to the café to get his soon-to-be step-daughter and grab some food for the three of them.

Chapter Seventeen

"So you're the infamous Preston Miller, land and cattle thief and destroyer of men's dreams." Ira Stone looked over at Jacob Chance, took a long drag on a big black cigar, blew a stream of blue smoke square into Miller's face, wiped a hand back and forth across his drooping walrus moustache, and said, "He looks more like a fat old man who's going to spend the rest of his life pounding rocks in a federal prison to me.

"Not just a fat old man, mind you, Jacob, but a stupid fat old man." Ira Stone smiled at Miller who had been brought out of his cell and into the front office of the jail. They scooted everybody else out, most of whom would have rather stayed for the show. "You couldn't be so stupid that you really thought you could get away with this?" He stopped for just a minute, giving the impression that he was contemplating something, and then continued.

"Listen, Jacob, how many men do you suppose have died since you began your investigation into this man's incredible land fraud scheme? Ten? Twelve?" Stone wasn't looking for an answer. Chance knew that and just stood behind the banker, his hand resting on the man's shoulder.

"Doesn't really matter how many," Stone smiled at Miller, "I mean it only takes one to change the charge from land fraud to accessory to murder. With just the first, the charges involve more than land fraud, more than conspiracy to defraud, now they involve the death of a human being. That would indicate a hanging offense, Marshal Chance. A hanging offense."

"Absolutely would, Marshal Stone. Certain of that, I am. A hanging offense."

Miller's reaction was just as swift as Stone thought it would be. And almost as dramatic. Miller tried to jump to his feet and at the top of his voice screaming "No!" Chance thumped him back down in the chair, and simply said,

"Yes." Miller's eyes were wild with fright, he continued stammering his "no," plaintively, realizing for the first time since all this started that he was in the most serious trouble of his life.

"This isn't my fault," he wailed, over and over, trying several times to get to his feet, every time being slammed back into the chair. "Dickson," he cried. "It was Dickson that did all this illegal stuff."

Stone pulled up a chair, so close the two men's knees were almost touching, and before speaking, took another deep pull on that horrible old cigar, again blowing the smoke directly into Miller's face. Even Chance grimaced as some of the smoke curled up toward him. Stone continued, more sarcastically than as a direct question, "Just exactly how is that, Miller? The colonel, supposed California war hero, responsible for all this misery? Just how is that?" He looked up at Chance, still standing behind the banker. "You think Mr. Miller here is going to hang, Marshal Chance?"

"Seems more than likely, Marshal Stone. Certainly does."

"No. You don't understand," Miller sobbed, again trying to stand, again being shoved down into the chair. "You don't understand."

"Why don't you tell me what it is I don't understand about a man that owns a bank and sells land that he doesn't own, that forecloses on loans on land he doesn't own, who physically evicts people from land they do own by way of the federal homestead act of 1862. Give us a little hint about what it is we don't understand, Mr. Miller, sir."

Miller's eyes, wet, red, still smarting from the cigar smoke, looking all about the room, trying to find an escape from this torture, slumped deeper into the chair, and then, without any warning, bolted for the door. One solid swat from Jacob Chance sent the fat banker skidding the last three feet across the floor, flat on his face. "You're damn near as stupid as you are fat, Miller. Now get up and answer the damn question," and Stone roughed him to his feet and threw him back into the chair. "I mean, sir, talk now," and his fist was cocked, and only Stone and Chance knew Miller wasn't going to be hit.

Miller started very slowly, and Stone held him up. "Wait just a minute, Miller," and he walked to the door. "Is the sheriff around close? No? You, then, what's your name?"

"Adams, Marshal, Hank Adams."

"Good, Chance told me about you. Come in here will you? We need one more person in here to hear what banker Miller is going to tell us. Always good to have another witness to a full confession." Adams walked in, said howdy to Chance and took the chair offered to him. "You know Preston Miller, I believe?" Adams nodded, and Stone continued. "Good. Now, Miller, let's go back to where you were going to tell us all about how this monstrous land fraud scheme and all these dead people are not your fault in any way.

"There are three of us here to listen, Miller, so you may start whenever you're ready, and I mean right now," and that cocked fist reappeared.

Miller straightened himself up, dabbed at the scrapes on his nose and jowls from his face's slide across the rough wooden floor of the jail house, and began, quietly, still giving indications of a crying jag right around the corner. "This valley was claimed by my grandfather back in the early eighteen fifties when it became a part of the United States, you know, from Mexico, and his ranch took in most of the valley. When he died, I was his only heir, and I do own this valley." He said that with the same type of authority he used when throwing someone off their ranch.

"Seems odd to me, Marshal Chance, that no one seems to have ever seen that original claim or deed, either in Salt Lake, San Francisco, or Carson City." He looked at Miller. "If your grandpa did claim this valley, he sure as hell didn't do it legally. And if you claimed it as his heir, you didn't do a damn thing about it legally either. Your grandpa was a fraud, you're a fraud. You can't simply ride in and say, hey, look at this nice little valley with a river and good grass, I think I'll just take the whole damn thing.

"Is that what you did, you and your grandpa, Miller? Just take it? Listen you fat ignorant pig," and he stood up, clenching the cigar between his teeth, clenching his fist in the banker's face, "even under the homestead act, you can only claim one hundred sixty acres, not a whole damn valley." He wiped the sweat from his face, shook his head in disbelief, looked around the room, first at Hank Adams, then at Marshal Chance. "This is just beyond me, Chance. I can't remember seeing this level of arrogance." He shook his head one more time, and continued.

"Okay, we know that part of the fraud. How on earth is Dickson to blame for all this?" While Stone was acting incredulous over what he was hearing, in his heart he really was incredulous. This was a story out of some drunk's imagination, he kept thinking: some wild-eyed drunk, oblivious to reality, finds Golden Valley and says, "This is mine." If Preston Miller actually knew how it happened wasn't known, but the thoughts running through Stone's mind were closer to what really happened, and only the old man really knew that part of the story.

"Dickson. Come on Miller, the judge is on his way, we got to hang you and get on with our jobs, so tell us how all of this is Dickson's fault." Chance didn't dare look at Ira Stone, wouldn't look at Hank Adams, and even so found himself chortling softly at Stone's comments. Hank Adams was trying his best not to spit coffee all over the jail house office. Miller seemed unable to understand the humor or the irony.

It took more than two hours to get the wildest tale

of criminality they had ever heard out of the banker. How Miller had been selling land out of the old ranch house, and how Dickson and another man, possibly Will Cooke, had offered their scheme. Build a real town site, lay out streets, and have Cooke set up an office in Salt Lake and other places in the territory to sell the mortgages and fraudulent contracts, and bring people in. Make that ranch house a real bank, let Dickson open a big gaudy saloon, and just to prove their generosity and love of their fellow man, allow a second saloon to be built.

And because of all that, you see, Miller had said, all of this is Dickson's fault. "I was just selling the land, at good and fair prices, that my grandpa had claimed, that I own. It was Dickson's scheme that created this problem."

"Is that why you threw Sarah Jackson off her ranch? Is that why old Eb Kiefer and his family don't have any water? Is that why you and Raccoon Toby beat the hell out of Randall Beuller in front of his wife?

"Sorry Miller, you're gonna hang." Stone never allowed a situation to just end, and he took this time to put even more fear into Miller. Looking around, first to Hank Adams, then to Jacob Chance, he said, "Do we really have to wait for the judge? I mean, it's pretty clear to me that Preston Miller needs to hang. Why not do it right now? What do you say, boys, let's hang the bastard right now and save the government a couple of double eagles?"

Chance jerked Miller to his feet and said, "Okay, let's go. End of the line for you," and marched him out of the office, into the street, still filled with people trying to find out what had happened to their town. Miller was screaming. "No. It was Dickson! No!" at the top of his lungs, and finally, Chance, laughing right out loud, marched the man back into the jail and slammed him into his cell.

"Maybe we need to have a chat with this Colonel Dickson before we hang you, Mr. Miller. Do you know where we can find that distinguished gentleman? Oh, look, there he is, in that cell over there, still bleeding all over everything." He walked over to Dickson's cell, opened it and grabbed the large man, stood him straight up and drove a fist into his belly.

"Sorry about that, old man. Let's go have a chat, shall we?" Stone was still laughing, chomping on the stub of a big black cigar and he, Adams, Chance and Dickson waltzed into the office and closed the door.

***

Jenny Stokes had Ben all tucked in, in the back of the wagon where Sarah and Georgia had ridden, and was driving the team with the five cowboys from the ranch riding along behind. "Never could find your horse, Dad, so just make yourself comfortable in all those blankets and we'll get you home for some good food and a long sleep."

"How about if we make one stop along the way? I'm worried about Sarah and Georgia, been tied up in all those problems in town and been worried sick that Dickson and Miller might do something horrible to them."

Jenny smiled as she answered him. "All taken care of, Dad. Cotton Phelps and Hank Adams got her out of that camp, and right now she and Georgia are in town under the full protection of Mr. Cotton Phelps. When that judge gets here he'll have more to do than just a land fraud case. Those two will be getting all hitched up, dad."

When she looked back over her shoulder, he was already asleep. "Good," she smiled to herself. "He deserves that."

It was a long, slow ride back to the ranch and Jenny was in a hurry to get started on the fall drive. She motioned one of the cowboys over to the wagon. "We need to get that drive underway, Sanchez. Take the boys back to the ranch and get started lining things out so we can pull out before sunrise tomorrow. Make sure the grub is packed right, make sure the remuda is ready to move, make sure we have everybody." With all the ruckus in town, she wasn't sure if she had lost any of the Stokes' hands, if any had bolted and joined Dickson and Miller, or if any had just bolted.

"It will probably take us at least two weeks to get those animals gathered and brought down to winter pasture. Damn," she said all at once, then catching herself. "Sorry, but I just remembered that Cotton Phelps and Hank Adams were supposed to be on our crew." She came very close to saying damn one more time, and then, with a smile, she mumbled, "Okay guys, get haulin' and when I get back with Dad, we'll finish up."

Her mind was trying to put together just how many men she might have for the long drive out of the mountains. "These five, for sure," she knew, "and no Adams or Phelps. Five just ain't enough for this drive. Those horse wranglers are going to have to pull some double duty, and I might even put cookie on a bronc or two." She knew she didn't have enough time to get Ben back to the ranch, ride like hell back to town to round up a crew, and still make it out in the morning. "What am I thinking? Dad isn't hurt or sick, he's just tired. He can go into town in the morning, put together a crew, and bring them along behind us. That's why I'm the boss of this outfit," she smiled, just a bit of a smug look across her pretty face.

"Of course if I let Dad take the crew up I could ride back to town and maybe have a nice chat with that marshal. I think I'd like that." There was a definite redness showing across her cheeks and along the back of her neck, and then she found the humor of it and laughed, gently nudging the team into a trot.

***

"Mr. Dickson, I'm Ira Stone, deputy U.S. Marshal for this territory and I'm placing you under arrest, charged with multiple crimes, the least of which are conspiracy to commit fraud, accessory to murder, arson, and, oh hell, we'll find more. Sit down, please."

"It's Colonel Dickson, sir, and I'm telling you right now, you are not welcome here. You are on private property. This is not public property, it is private, and you are not welcome." Stone's right hand, palm open, fingers spread wide, slapped the side of Dickson's head so hard the men in the street took immediate notice.

"Now, Mr. Dickson, do I have your attention?" Anger boiled across Dickson's face and he tried to get up. Stone wasn't going to be denied, and a big ham of a fist slammed into the colonel's face. "Sit down and listen, you ignorant fool. It's over, Dickson. You're finished, you and your fat ugly banker friend are going to prison for a long time," and he took a long pause, "unless, of course, you hang first.

"If you're even half way smart, you'll tell me your part in this damned mess you call Preston. What's your part in this scheme?" He had his fist cocked for another shot at the man's face. "Miller has told us his part, we even have a contract drawn up between the two of you, so if you lie, I'll know it, and I don't much care for liars. Give it to me straight or I'll bring Jerrod Stockton in here to help your memory along some."

That should have done the trick, but Dickson, suffering a gunshot wound, suffering bruises and bumps from his own men beating the hell out of him when it was apparent he was going to run out on them, then the slam to his stomach from Chance, and now being beat by Stone, he just wasn't in a thinking mood.

His walrus moustache quivering, blood spatters on his face and clothing, and now being humiliated by this federal marshal was almost more than he could take. He tried to summon the old colonel into action, what came out was more of a whimper. "We own every inch of this valley and you're not welcome here," is all he could get out.

"How can we keep Miller and Dickson from being able to talk, Sample?" Stone asked when the sheriff came back to the jail. "Those cells are too close together, and they will conjure stories even more radical than the truth."

"Before Miller built this jail, if those two needed to hold someone, they had a room at the back of the hotel, down that back hallway, that doesn't have any windows and just the one door. We could put one of them there, and all it would mean would be one man to stand guard in the hallway."

"I saw that room during the fight," Chance piped up. "It would be a good spot. Sample, you and Adams here, take Dickson over there and lock him up tight. Sample, you take the first shift watching him, and we'll get a plan underway to have guards here at the jail and at the hotel."

Stone reached out and grabbed Dickson by his shirt front and jerked him to his feet and slammed a fist into the large man's stomach. "Wasn't fair that you got to do that and I didn't," he said to Chance, laughing as Sample and Adams escorted the man out of the building. "March that fool right down the middle of the street, Sheriff. Let everyone see for themselves that when the federal marshals come to town, things get done." The old black cigar was chewed to bits as he flipped it onto the dusty street and reached for a new one.

Dickson's marching wasn't up to par, what with a bullet in his leg and his ribs aching from the fists of Chance and Stone. Sample took great pleasure in pressing the man, nudging him along with the end of his rifle barrel. Several of the townsfolk taunted Dickson as they walked toward the old hotel.

***

Cotton had only been gone about half an hour when he got back to the hotel room with a tree limb that had a V in it at the top. "Stand up for a minute, Sarah, I need to measure this thing." She was laughing as she saw what he had cropped together, the crotch in the V wrapped with sheets and other padding, the whole thing almost six feet in length. "Stand still now," he said, "and lift your arm out to the side." He realized that he was going about the thing all wrong, and Georgia, wide awake and with a huge smile on her face told him so.

"You got it upside down, Cotton. You can't measure from the bottom, you gotta measure from the top, so turn it over, put the V on the floor, and then measure to under mama's arm.

"Look at him, mama. That's why women do all the measuring, to get it right," and you could hear the laughter out on the main street of Preston. "Golly, Cotton," and she wanted to keep needling the man but a scowl sent her way shut things off.

He got it measured, took his big knife and carved away at the limb and had Sarah try it out. "Think you can walk with that?" he asked, and grabbed Georgia, tickling her as he dumped her on the bed. "Take a couple of steps and see if it works. I can make it a bit shorter but sure can't make it longer."

Sarah had the crutch under her arm pit, put some weight on it, and took a few steps around the messed up hotel room "This is good, Cotton. This is good," and she moved her broken leg around with little effort and no pain.

"Okay good, now. You practice with that, I'm going to try to find Jerrod and see if he has a horse and buggy for you and Georgia. Seems Jennifer already took the one I was planning on using. We're moving you back to your ranch where you belong." Again, the cheering could be heard out on the street, and Sarah almost lost her balance trying to walk to Cotton for a kiss and hug, and clap her hands at the same time. "Easy girl," he said, holding her tight, "don't break the other leg." He gave her a long, gentle kiss, took a little quick poke at Georgia, and walked out of the room.

"Mama, is Cotton going to be my daddy?" There was a grand smile that went with the question and Sarah answered, very softly, "Yes."

Cotton started at the jail in his search for Jerrod Stockton, then went to the Crystal Saloon, and finally, to the burned out livery stable. "There you are," he said, finding the smithy trying to clear out some of the rubble. "You okay? I sure heard that shotgun of yours bark a few times when we were back in the trees. Glad that bangs on your shoulder and not mine."

"It's all in how you hold it," Stockton answered, feigning holding it up and pulling the triggers. "Gotta pull 'em both to get the full effect," he laughed, poking at Cotton. "You on a mission or something? I seen you prancin' around town."

"Looking for you. I'm gonna take Sarah and Georgia back to their ranch, but with her broken leg she can't ride. You got a wagon or buggy and a spare horse or two?"

Jerrod Stockton has been known as the man to go to for so many years, and now here he was standing in a burned-down old livery, dead horses just pulled out, and he didn't know if he could help or not. "Damn, Cotton, I know I got that big freight wagon, because it was outside when the fire ran through. Let's take a walk around and see what I got left." He had been putting this part of the program aside for as long as possible, didn't want to know how much he had lost, and found himself fighting back tears as the two old friends started through the soot and grime.

"Both those fools are behind bars for right now, and you can bet I'm gonna give that judge an earful when he gets here. Chance said it would be next week sometime. Coming down from Carson City. They say this is gonna be a state someday soon. How about that?"

"Gold and silver under the ground, sweet grass on top of the ground, sounds like the perfect spot for a couple of old guys like us to spread a blanket. Me and Sarah are going to get married when that judge gets here, so don't be scarin' him off." Cotton Phelps wasn't an old man at all, neither was Jerrod Stockton, but they had been close friends from the day they met in Golden Valley, had hunted together, fixed broken equipment together, and drank whiskey together. It was a good relationship.

"Married? That's a thought didn't cross my mind. Married? You, Cotton? Next you'll be wanting me to make you a plow or two, then buy some mules so you can be a farmer. Married." And he just stood looking at the man.

"Yeah, probably not much farmin', but we will be building up that herd. Sarah tells me that I can also homestead a hundred and sixty acres, and that would give us half a section, Jerrod." Stockton just looked at him and turned to walk through the burned-out livery.

"That freight wagon would take a big team, Cotton, so let's find something a bit smaller. So many animals died just because that bastard Dickson doesn't like me." Again, tears were near the surface and he tried to keep his head turned away from Phelps. "There's a nice little buggy. Singed some, but looks like it's okay. There's a couple of horses in the outside corrals that should work." Then he added, "Not the big black Morgan. That's Chance's horse."

As the two worked to pull the buggy out of the burned shell of the stables, Chance walked in. "Looks like you two are up to something," he said, heading back toward the corrals. "Just had a long talk with Miller and Dickson, and that judge is going to have a field day, I think."

"I'm taking Sarah back to her ranch, Marshal."

"Good idea, Cotton. Have her get all her paper work in order. Her claim will be settled right away since it is completely legal, then we'll have to deal with the mess of all the others. Jerrod you need to do the same with your paper work and receipts. Spread the word, too, so as many people as possible have every shred of paper work on their leases and mortgages. What a damn mess." He went on back to have a long talk with Mr. Morgan. "I want to ride out to see Eb and Adelaide Kiefer. Bring them up to date. They're in bad shape. Miller is in the jail, Dickson is locked up at the hotel. Jerrod, do you know where I can find Stone and the other marshals? I want to make sure everyone is up to date on where we stand right now.

"Oh, and Jerrod, I'm really counting on you. Keep this town together. You're the one person that lives here that everyone looks up to, and I know that's a huge responsibility, but I also know you're the man to do it." Chance mounted the big horse, reached down and shook Stockton's hand, and again said he had to find Marshal Stone and the others.

"Will do, Marshal." His battered face and body still aching from the beating, Stockton knew the marshal was right, and hoped that he really was the man Chance thought he was.

Chapter Eighteen

A mos Brady, a bullet hole in his foot, had managed to get out of the saloon during the melee and down to the river, and was hiding in the willows, his bloody boot off and the wound cleaned out. "Went all the way through the boot and foot, and hurts like hell," he muttered, ripping part of his filthy shirt into a bandage. "What the hell kind of a war did we ride into? I've got to get out of here." He was slowly moving through the willows when he spotted the sheriff and another man shove Colonel Dickson into a room at the back of the hotel.

Brady was going to need all the help he could get to be able to live through what was happening. He hunkered down along the river bank, and with the back door of the hotel blown to dust, he could see right into the hallway. He watched Hank Adams bring a chair from the front of the hotel, watched the old sheriff shake Adam's hand, watched the old sheriff sit in the chair and Adams walk toward the front of the building and not come back. The outlines of a plan began to form.

He knew he could sneak close to the open door without the sheriff seeing him. What he was worried about were the men moving around trying to put out the fires in the willow stands and those piling trash and other material on the still-smoldering saloon.

"That colonel must have some horses, probably some money stashed somewhere, and if I get him out of there, he'll owe me." Brady had tried twice to get his boot on and it wouldn't go, not from the pain, but from the bandage. He almost let out a cry from the sharp feeling in his foot, and finally he just ripped the bandage off and this time, even with the pain, he got the boot on. As he moved through the willows, to get closer to the hotel back door, the pain almost stopped him. It was the fear of being caught by the mob that kept him going.

Sheriff Sample was sitting in the old cane chair, his back to the wall, and seemed more interested in what he could see down the hallway than what he could see out the broken up doorway. Brady was able to creep right up to the side of the hotel, was catching his breath, fighting off nausea, and waiting for the right time to strike. "Can't make any noise," he said to himself, "and can't let that old man make any either."

The minutes seemed to drag as Brady stood outside the hotel and Sample sat in the chair inside. "If I shoot the old man, then shoot the lock off that door, I don't know how many people there are in the front of that building. Damn," Brady said. "One shot, maybe, but two or three— bring the whole town running." He heard some noises and plastered himself against the wall. Footsteps, a long yawn, and Sample was standing at the doorway, starting to stretch when Brady's revolver crashed into his skull, taking him down instantly.

Brady grabbed Sample's rifle and hand gun, stepped into the hallway and blasted the lock on the door. "Come on Colonel, now," and pushed the man out the door, both running as fast as their wounds would let them toward the willows. In less than thirty seconds men were pouring out the back door of the hotel, some trying to help Sheriff Sample, others searching for Dickson and whoever it was had helped him escape.

Hank Adams took charge of the mob right away, sent one man to the jail to find Chance and the other marshals, and split the seven or eight into groups to find Dickson. One man came back with the scrap of shirt Brady had used as a bandage. "At least we know somebody's bleeding," Adams said. "Look for footprints in the mud along the river bank. They can't have gotten too far away. Remember, we know Dickson is wounded, and maybe whoever is helping him is also. A wounded man fights the hardest, so be warned."

As Adams said that, men near the river heard pounding hoof beats and set up a howl. "They have horses, heading south," one hollered to the group just as Chance and Stone came running out of the hotel.

"How many are there?" he asked Adams.

"I think just Dickson and one man who broke him out. Sounded like two horses going south." They walked over to where Sample was spread out on the ground. "He got hit awful hard, Marshal. I don't think he's going to live."

Chance shook his head and motioned for Stone and Adams to come with him. "Hank, I want you and Jerrod Stockton to put some order to the town. Protect the hell out of Miller and the men in the jail. Stockton is there now. Help him do whatever needs to be done.

"Stone, get Bettencourt and Martinez and meet me at the stables. I'm going to get Mr. Morgan. He's already saddled, and I think I know where Dickson is heading. Let's hurry," and the men moved through the people standing around, through the hotel, and out onto the street. "If I'm right, the Kiefer family is about to find themselves in a lot of trouble. We need to ride hard, Ira, hard and fast."

Chance sprinted to the livery, mounted the big stud and rode back to where Stone and the group had formed. "Let's go. They have a good head start on us, but I'm pretty sure I know where we'll find them. Dickson has a real hate for the Kiefer family, maybe because they are able to make things work even when he did everything possible to run them off." As the four rode out, Chance reminded them that the ranch was about ten miles out, so don't destroy the horses. "We'll find that fool, you can bet on that."

***

As Brady and Dickson limped into the willows lining the Good Hope River, Dickson took immediate command and led them to several horses tethered near a clump of cottonwood trees. "Will Cooke left these for us,

Brady. Let's go before that gang finds us. There's a ranch south of here where we can get food and supplies and get the hell out of this valley."

"I'm with you, Colonel." And the two men rode out fast, just seconds before they would have been spotted. They moved onto the south trail at the edge of town and kept the horses at a full gallop for the first several miles then pulled them into a trot the rest of the way to the Kiefer ranch.

"We get to that ranch, Colonel, you pay me my money, get me some grub for the trail, and I'm out of here. You picked the wrong fight this time, I think."

"You aren't running out on me, Brady," and the Colonel used the rifle Brady had taken from the sheriff to blow him right out of the saddle. "I'll take this horse, too, thank you." Dickson continued south, a grim smile on his face. "Dumb bastard," he mumbled. He reached behind the saddle and opened a flap on a saddle bag. "Good, Cooke had most of the gold from the Salt Lake business with him. Lost those two bags at the saloon. Damn," and he continued toward the Kiefer ranch.

Old Eb Kiefer was out by one of the irrigation ditches when he saw Dickson coming up the ranch road, riding one horse, ponying another. He was slumped in the saddle like he was hurt, and Kiefer started walking toward the ranch house. Dickson got there first.

He was still in the saddle when Eb came up the walkway. "What do want, Dickson? You hurt?"

"I need some help, Kiefer. Get me some food, I need some trail gear like a bedroll and ax, maybe a knife or two. Come on, get that stuff, don't be getting me all riled up at you."

Kiefer started toward the house and Dickson yelled, "Not in the house, old man. That stuff would be in the barn or shed. Move it," and he lowered the rifle, pointing it at the old man. Dickson got down off his horse and tied the two horses to the rail as Kiefer's son Bruce came onto the porch, a shotgun aimed at Dickson.

Dickson whirled and fired the rifle, knocking Bruce back into the house, but not before he pulled the trigger on the scattergun, knocking Dickson to the ground with birdshot in both legs. The Colonel still had his rifle at the ready, and when Bruce crawled toward the door for a second shot, Dickson killed him.

Dickson was still sprawled in the dust, both legs bleeding bad, and he leveled the rifle at Eb Kiefer. "All right, old man, in the house," and he was barely able to get to his feet and hobble toward the porch. "Move it." He led the man in, had him pull Bruce's body out of the way so he could shut the door, and then Dickson fell into one of the overstuffed chairs in the living room. "Where's your wife, Kiefer. Get her out here."

Kiefer was on his knees, cradling his son's head, quietly sobbing when Adelaide came into the room. When she saw Bruce she started screaming and ran across the room and attacked Dickson. She was hitting, scratching, kicking, and Dickson raised the rifle and smashed her across the face with the butt of the gun, bringing Eb to his feet to join the fight.

The rifle was leveled but not fired and Eb Kiefer stopped in his tracks. "That's enough now. Cover your boy's body, get your wife in a chair, and then do as I told you. Get me some trail tack, some food, and some extra clothes, and if you even make one little fool mistake, I will take it out on your wife. Any wrong move, she dies a long painful death. Move it, old man." Eb had tear stains across his weathered face, eyes red and angry, but did as he was told. After he left for the barn to get what Dickson wanted, he saw dust on the trail, riders coming from town.

He was too old, his joints too stiff to allow him to run very fast, but he limped and hobbled as fast as he could, down the ranch road toward the main trail, knowing that

Dickson would hear the riders soon and come out on the porch. *Hurry old man*, he said to himself, now being able to see four horses coming down the main trail at a fast trot. He started waving his arms and saw the horses move from the trot to a gallop.

The four reined up as Eb Kiefer reached the trail. "Marshal, Dickson's here, shot Bruce, beat up Adelaide, and is in my house now," and the first rifle shot went off, tearing through Kiefer's leg, knocking the man to the ground. Chance, Stone, Martinez, and Bettencourt were off their horses and flat on the ground in half a second, crawling toward the brush growing alongside the trail.

"Doesn't look like the man wants visitors," Chance drawled as they settled in. "Martinez, swing down and around the side of the building to the north there, and George, you swing out to the south, get along that irrigation ditch and see if you can put yourself in good shooting range of that cabin.

"Ira, looks like it's us gonna storm the fort one more time," and he cracked one of his famous grins. "Eb, you okay?"

"Hurts like hell, Marshal, but it's not bleeding heavy. I got a rag on it," and he stayed as low as he could get in the dust of the main trail. "Save my Adelaide, Marshal. He hit her awful hard, and she ain't well anyway. Please," and his voice trailed off into great sobs.

"We'll get her safe, Eb, you just lie still there, don't try to move. He can't see you, so you're safe. Marshal Stone and I will make her safe, so you stay safe, too." He looked over at Stone, then the cabin. "He came in on two horses, so that body up the trail was probably the man that helped him escape. He must have been truly grateful, eh?"

Stone had been searching the area closely and started pointing things out to Chance. "Looks like the ranch road makes a little cut over there, and those bushes and trees could hide a man. Windows on that cabin look right out on us, here, so we'll have a hard time moving straight toward the place. Have to come in from the sides, so Martinez and Bettencourt are going to be in the right place. We need to get somewhere that we can back their play. We're too far out for our hand guns, Chance. Good rifle range, but we need to get a lot closer."

***

Stockton had taken control of the town, had the men who helped clear and hold the hotel move up and down the streets, knocking on doors, making sure people were all right, making sure they understood that the town was again safe, they could move about if they wished. He put people to work cleaning up the mess at the livery, at the Bucket of Good Hope, at the hotel.

"Damn, saving the town almost meant destroying it," he said to Hank Adams. "Look at this mess." They were standing in the street in front of the jail, and looking to the north all they saw were burnt and burning buildings. "I better get some men in the back of the jail too. I really tore that wall to pieces back there." Alvarado came up about that time and passed on the word that Sheriff Sample had died from his wounds.

"Damn shame," Adams said. "He got himself all put back together, and then died for the effort. Damn shame." He moved back up the street toward the destruction to see what he could do to help, and Stockton walked into the jail to pass the word on to the men in there.

"Sample has died," he said, pouring yet another cup of coffee. "See if you can get that back wall put together, and let's move those prisoners into separate cells. Chance says the Territorial Judge will be here in a day or so, so let's make this right. Probably have to hold court in the Crystal Saloon, I don't think the café will hold everyone." He put the coffee down, wiped his mouth and continued.

"That thought of the Crystal Saloon sounds pretty good. I could handle a cold beer right about now. I'll see

211

you gentlemen a little bit later," and with that huge scattergun cradled under his arm, he marched right up the street, waving to townspeople coming out of their homes and businesses.

***

"If we lay down a barrage, there's the possibility of hitting Adelaide, Ira, and we sure don't want to do that. I'm gonna move back out of range and then circle around behind the home, see over there, where the barn and equipment sheds are. I might be able to get close enough to pick off that fool."

"That's good, Chance. I'm going to try to sneak up to that crook in the road there, and that might give me a good shot also. With four guns from four angles, Dickson will have a hard time trying something.

"Damn, I hate these hostage things. They never turn out right." Chance was already moving back from their position, got across the main road, back into a line of brush and trees, and started moving north so he could circle around to the back of the small ranch house. There were no shots taken so he was assuming that Dickson hadn't seen him make his move.

He was several hundred yards to the north when he came back across the main trail, and staying in the brush, he moved toward the back of the house, near the barns. He could see Martinez, on his belly, crawling, bush to bush, closer to the house, and figured he would be in a good position to take Dickson out if he came anywhere near one of the windows.

***

"You ain't hurt, quit your blubbering, old lady. Get some hot water and some clean cloth so you can fix this wound."

"Fix it yourself, Dickson. I ain't doin' nothin' for you. Killed my boy, hit me with your rifle. Hurt my husband. Ruined our ranch. No, sir, I ain't doin' nothin' for you," and she got up to walk out of the room.

"One more step, you're dead, woman," and the rifle was leveled right at her. She stopped dead in her tracks, turned and glared at the man.

"Hope you bleed to death." And she sat down in a chair across the room from him.

Dickson found himself in a bad position, with a woman who would gladly slit his throat and didn't really fear him anymore. He was wounded badly enough that he couldn't force her to do anything, and the house was surrounded by U.S. Marshals. "Damn you, woman, get some bandages and hot water, or so help me, I'll blow your head off," and that rifle came up again.

"Go ahead, Dickson. Go ahead, shoot me, and those men will be in here, guns blazing before the bullet hits. You need me, and I ain't helpin' you none at all. Get your own damn bandages, you think you're so high and mighty. Go ahead, let's see the powerful Colonel George walk all by hisself," and she cackled and clapped her scrawny hands.

Dickson brought the rifle to his shoulder, knew he wouldn't pull the trigger because she was right. He needed her more than she even knew. Between the fire, the beating he took from the men in his saloon, the gunshot wounds, and the extra effort some took to put him in custody, Dickson was almost out of the game, physically. He checked his leg and most of the bleeding had stopped, but the pain from the first gunshot--that was a bullet, not birdshot—was fierce, and he could almost feel one or two of his ribs scratching against each other at the fractured ends, pain tearing through his chest with every move.

He tried twice before he was able to get to his feet, and then almost passed out from the pain. One step and he felt searing pain, another and his head swam, so he almost lost consciousness. But he got alongside the living room window. He used the rifle barrel to break out the glass and hollered out to whoever was outside.

"I'll kill this woman," he yelled, "if you try to stop me. We'll be leaving in a short time. Try to stop me and she's dead."

"Give it up, Dickson," Bettencourt yelled from his position directly across from the window. He was hidden behind a buckboard wagon, less than twenty-five yards from the house. If Dickson walked in front of that window, he'd be dead, if he tried to come out the front door, woman or no woman hostage, he'd be just as dead.

"There's seven of us out here, Dickson. You're surrounded, you're wounded, and you're not going anywhere. Send the woman out, alive, and we'll talk some more. Give it up now, you might come out of this alive yourself." Bettencourt upped the ante, and when Dickson heard that seven men were outside, he knew it was over.

He slumped down onto the floor, noticed that just moving across the room opened the gunshot wound in his leg, and he was bleeding heavily. He motioned to Adelaide Kiefer and said, "Go. Get out of here before I change my mind." She moved cautiously to the front door, not trusting the man who tried to destroy their ranch and killed her son.

Bettencourt saw the front door come open and saw Mrs. Kiefer step out onto the porch. "Hurry, lady," he said to himself as he watched her move off to the side of the porch, away from the doorway, away from the window. "Hurry, you're not safe yet," and to make the point he put two shots into the front of the house.

Adelaide Kiefer heard the shots and bolted into a full run toward the barn where Jacob Chance grabbed her and got her out of the line of any gun fire that might cut loose. "You're safe, Adelaide. You're safe, just sit down, take it easy. You're safe now."

"Where's Eb?"

"He's safe, too. Relax, it's almost over now. You're ranch is safe, you're safe, Eb's safe. Take it easy, try to relax." The big man who killed with such ease, who took out bad men for a living, had a soft side that surprised many. He eased her down into the dust and straw on the barn floor, and moved back to the doorway. "You just stay right there and relax. We're gonna get the rest of this finished off." He looked around, then remembered the two horses tied up in front.

"Is he alone?" When she nodded yes, he took a deep breath and moved toward the open doors of the barn. Chance could see Bettencourt, knew where Martinez was, and knew that both men had good shots into the house, Bettencourt with the best one. "George," he hollered, "you know where I am now?" He answered back and Chance continued, "Martinez is on your left very close to the house and a good shot at that side window. Let's try to take that fool alive if we can, but kill him if he does something stupid. You hear that too, Stan?" Again the affirmative, and Chance moved out of the barn and toward the side of the house.

"Dickson, this is U.S. Marshal Jacob Chance. You are surrounded by federal officers. You can live through this if you surrender immediately. If we have to come in to get you, we will bring you out dead. Did you hear me?" There was silence for about a full minute, then a weak voice cried out to the marshals.

"I'm hurt. I can't move," and the rifle was thrown out the front window.

Chance motioned to Bettencourt to move closer as he also moved toward the front of the house. "Careful, George, this guy's been a jackass all along. He might still have another gun in there."

Dickson heard Chance and answered back. "I'm not armed, Marshal. I'm bleeding bad. I give up." It was almost a cry for help.

With Adelaide's and Eb's help, they spent the next several hours doctoring Dickson's many wounds, got him tied tight. "I'll drive this fool into town for you, Marshal," the old man said, bringing an old horse out of the barn, already harnessed. "I want the town to know I'm bringing him in."

All four marshals agreed to that, spent another hour or more digging a grave and burying Bruce, Adelaide beside herself at her loss. "Eb, I want to ride into town with you. I want to watch when Marshal Chance puts this horrible man in the jail."

"I would be proud to have you sitting next to me on the seat, Addie. Very proud," and he helped her onto the high seat of the wagon, and went one step further. "Here, you take Bruce's shotgun, and if that fool even looks at you wrong, you pull both them triggers."

The men hustled Dickson into the wagon and Chance jumped in the back with him. "No need for that, Adelaide. I'll ride back here and make sure there is no mischief." It was a long, slow ride back to town, with one stop along the way to pick up Brady's body.

"We'll find you a room at the hotel," Chance told Eb, "and get you a good supper at the café. On the government," he smiled, as they pulled into the village, night coming on fast. "Been a long day."

Chapter Nineteen

"When is that judge coming? This town is a shambles, the people are still afraid to move around much, and some of the ranchers need to get their herds down out of the high country." Jerrod Stockton had become the leader in Preston, organizing cleaning parties, making sure the town folk and the ranch owners knew what was going on.

"He probably left Carson City yesterday," Chance said, "so, figuring at least three, four days to get down here, we have a little wait." They were at Chance's saloon table office in the Crystal, enjoying a cold beer. "Ain't nobody taken a shot at me for this whole day, so far, Jerrod. That's pretty nice," he said, taking a long slow poke at the blacksmith. "I still haven't met Sarah Jackson, and I want to talk to Ben Stokes some before the judge gets here. You have the town pretty much under control, don't you?"

"Clean up is going good. I put two men in the jail to keep control of the prisoners, every cell has two or three men in there, and we haven't had any indication that Dickson has more men coming or has men waiting to break him and Miller out. And besides, Chance, I have Ira Stone and company for deputies." That brought a round of laughs, even from the two old guys at the end of the bar.

"Dickson's gunshot wounds are festering up pretty bad and he's in a lot of pain, but I think he'll live. I've got him and Miller as separated as I can get them." Stockton finished that statement, almost as a question, then continued. "Are you still giving thought to separating them even more?"

"I felt good about moving Dickson to that hotel storeroom, but that sure didn't work out very well. If Dickson or Miller try to get together or start talking back and forth, we'll have to separate them, but for right now, just keep an eye on them." Ira Stone walked in as they were talking.

"Glad you're here, Ira. Before I ride out to see Sarah Jackson, let's go over to the bank like we talked about. Damn, things happen around this little village, don't they?"

Stone laughed, and the two went across the street to the bank. "This will be a mess for these people, Jacob, but if we find some kind of paperwork that talks about the conspiracy, it will sure be a big help." The door of the bank, blown to bits like so many doors in Preston, had been standing wide open since Chance got in the gunfight with the three Dickson men.

"For a town run by criminals, the regular townsfolk seem to be pretty honest, Ira. Nobody has tried to rob the bank," and the two men gave some serious guffaws over the comment. "The vault is back here, and we also want to go over Miller's private office carefully."

The two marshals plowed through files and records for the next two hours, finding most of the money matters of Preston well documented. "Miller is very systematic in his bookkeeping, but so far I haven't found anything that ties the two men together. They had to have an agreement, and Miller strikes me as the kind of man that would want it in writing."

"I'm not so sure of that, Chance. He never filed deeds on any of this property his grandfather supposedly left him. He does keep complete records on his land sales, the payments made, foreclosures, but he is also cunning."

"I really want to see Sarah Jackson and Ben Stokes, Ira. I'm going to leave you to the rest of this and head on out. Use Bettencourt and Martinez if you think you need them. Martinez went back out to the Kiefer place with Eb and Adelaide but should be back in a few hours. I'll be back this evening. Let's have supper and go over our plans for when the judge gets here." They shook hands and Chance left the bank and walked down to the corrals, all that's left now of the livery, saddled Mr. Morgan and rode out of town toward the Jackson ranch.

"Well, Mr. Morgan, looks like we got the first half of our job done and these next few weeks are going to be mighty hard on some of these folks." The miles went by quickly, and the lawman saw some of the most beautiful land he could ever remember.

"Can't get old Eb and Adelaide Kiefer out of my mind. Water taken from them, denied any opportunity to make that little ranch work, and they still did it. Eb showed me how many times he had repaired that old plow of his, how many mends in the harness for his mules, and fences for the corrals just tied together. What do you think, Mr. Morgan? Think I'd have that kind of fortitude?" Thoughts of running a large cattle and horse operation were still dancing in his head, along with pictures of Jenny Stokes.

"Maybe I don't really want to see Ben Stokes. Maybe just Jennifer," he mumbled, then turned a bit red in the face and put Mr. Morgan in a long trot.

Grasses were turning brownish as the fall temperatures cooled things off in the valley, trees more and more into the yellows and reds, and on many of the fields he rode past, he noticed that most of the crops had been taken in. "Looks like folks in this valley eat well. Potatoes and onions, beans and carrots, lots of squash and pumpkins, cabbage and green peas. Put a venison or two along with some beef and lamb and pork, and a man could get fat on a long winter." His conversations, mixed with questions for the horse, kept him in light and friendly spirits as he rode onto the Jackson ranch.

He stepped down from the big stud, tied him off, walked up onto a broad porch to the front door of a solid cabin. One good knock on the door and little Georgia was standing there, hands on hips, demanding to know who he was. "Well, little one, you must be Georgia Jackson. Howdy to you, my name is Jacob Chance, U.S. Marshal. Is your mama home?"

"You come with me right now, Marshal," and Georgia jumped out onto the porch, grabbed Chance by the hand and pulled him along. "Come on now, don't be slow," and it took another step or two to get the two of them into a little lope across the front of the house and toward the barn and corrals.

"Mama, Mama," Georgia was howling as they ran into the barn. "Look who I found. Mama, come here. Where are you?" and she dashed first one way, then another, all the time pulling Chance along with her.

"Okay, little one," Chance finally said, "I think I see some movement out that way," and he steered the two of them out the back end of the barn where Sarah Jackson and Cotton Phelps were working a load of hay into winter piles under the shed.

"Mama," Georgia howled again. "Look who's here. Mama, this is the marshal," and the two, still hand in hand, walked up to the hay rack. "Look how big he is, Mama. Just look."

Chance slipped his hand out of Georgia's and shook hands with Sarah, then Cotton Phelps. "It's taken awhile to get to meet you ma'am. Your letter certainly has stirred up some dust around these parts. Someplace we can sit and chat for a spell. Have a lot to go over with you, I'm afraid."

"I'll finish the hay, Sarah, go ahead on in the house with the marshal. Georgia, you can earn your keep by helping me with this hay," and he shook hands again with Chance. "Sure glad you came to Preston, Marshal Chance. Sure glad."

Sarah poured cups of coffee as the two settled in chairs at the kitchen table. "Jerrod Stockton made this table and these chairs, Marshal. Cotton, Jerrod and I built this cabin and the barn, and Jerrod did all the iron work around this place. It's home, Marshal Chance, it's home," and Chance could see tears forming.

"It's a beautiful home, too, Sarah, and one I'm sure you and Georgia will be living in for a long time. I think your claim is the only valid land claim in the entire valley, so don't worry too much about that." The two went through another pot of coffee, talked about claims, looked over legal paperwork involving her homestead, and talked, almost as old and dear friends for the next two hours.

Georgia led Cotton into the house—she covered in hay, and he still laughing from her tumbling around in the winter feed. "Mama, Daddy Cotton threw me in the hay, and just look, just look at what a mess I am." She went out on the porch and shook herself off, Sarah, with her crutch operating fine, walked Chance to his horse.

"Thank you, Marshal. Thank you," she said, and he gave her a good hug, shook hands with Cotton one more time, tousled Georgia's hay filled hair, and stepped into the saddle of Mr. Morgan.

"Judge will be here in the next few days and I'm sure everything will be fine. I'll make sure you're kept up to date on everything that will be happening." He tipped his battered old sombrero, and rode out of the ranch toward the main trail. "Good people, Mr. Morgan. Good people," he commented, and turned toward the Stokes Ranch.

***

"What exactly did that fool Dickson say?" Ned Thompson was sitting in the Old Corner Saloon in Virginia City, watching a couple of the dancing girls work their magic on a drunked up miner. Thompson, known in many circles as the best man with a knife since the bad man Sam Brown was killed, said, "I don't like that man, Walters, and I sure as hell don't trust him."

"He said he's in trouble and needs help. It took me three days to get here, and he said to promise you anything you want to get you to come down to Preston and help him out."

"Anything? Sure, Walters. He makes those kinds of

promises, then conveniently forgets all about them. Well, you ride back and tell him I'll be along soon, and I want that saloon of his." He laughed out loud, smacked one of the girls on her cute little bottom. "You tell that pig that's what I want.

"I have a little business here, and I'll leave out in the morning. Now, get out of here, cuz I'm gonna be busy," and he pinched the lady, gently, as she eased into his lap.

Terrible Sam Walters, once a bad man himself, now just a stove-up old man with memories, walked up to the livery on 'B' Street, packed his old mule and saddled his tired horse, ready for the long ride back to Preston. "Colonel George isn't gonna like this," he grumbled making his way back down to Eagle Valley and the trail south.

Walters spent the first night on the trail, and late the second arrived in Body, found the hotel and slept till late the next morning when he started the search for Arnold Whitman, gunslinger, card shark. He hit his third saloon before finding the bad man.

"That's all I know, Whitman. Dickson said to promise you anything you want, that he needs help. Ned Thompson is on his way south right now, and Dickson says he needs you."

"All right, old man. That fool cost me a lot of money last time I was with him, but I guess I do owe him one more shot. I'll be mighty angry if he doesn't come through. You know how he lies and cheats. I almost killed the man once before, and it wouldn't take much to get me riled at him."

Walters left town the next morning. Whitman had left well before him, and Walters made a detour over to Ione before heading back to Preston. "Dickson has cheated so many people over the years," he muttered, "I don't want to be there when those two get to Preston. He paid me before I left, maybe I won't go back."

***

"Another hour and you would have missed me, Marshal. Glad to see you." Ben Stokes was standing on the porch of the large ranch house, fitted out for a cattle drive in full bat wing chaps and carrying his weather coat which would be tied behind the saddle, over his bed roll.

"I wanted to let you know the federal judge should be here in the next day or two. I fully understand how important it is for you to get your cattle out of the high country, but you already know your entire life is in the balance here. Your testimony, your paperwork, and your knowledge of the law is going to have an impact that will be felt by everyone in the valley." Chance laid it on the line for Stokes, and he was sincere in the effort. "I really feel it's imperative that you stick around, Ben."

"That's where I was headed, to tell Jenny that I have to be in town. She's very good on a drive, I know I should be there with her, and I know I have to be in town. Damn. I'd love to ride into town with you, right now, Marshal, and slit those two men's throats. Cut their heads off."

"We can't do that," Chance smiled saying it, "But we can work to save your ranch and send them to prison. Will you come back to town as soon as possible?"

"I'll spend two days with the crew, make sure Jenny has everything lined out, and I'll come back down. I'll be in your office four days from now."

"That's perfect, Ben. Thank you." Chance paused for just a minute. "When you see her, say hello for me, will you?" There was a rise in color to Jacob Chance's little boy grin as he said that.

"I'll be sure to do that, Marshal. Yes I will," and rode off, giving Chance a big wave of his hand. Two other cowboys rode out from behind the barn and joined Stokes for the ride into the high country.

"Wish I was going with him," Chance said, turning

the big stud and riding off toward the main trail to town. "I have never thrown a lasso, I've never branded a calf, I've never even seen a cattle drive, and here I am thinking about being a rancher. I better have a long talk with Jerrod Stockton and let him pound some sense into my thick old head," and he was chuckling to himself as he rode off, but thoughts of Jennifer were dancing about, making the ride a little more pleasant.

It would be several hours before he got back to Preston and he put the horse into a nice trot to eat as many miles as possible. "I wonder if Ira was able to find something that might look like a contract? Dickson would want one so he could hold it over Miller's head, but would it be at the bank, or up in smoke at the saloon. I'll just have to wait till I get to town, eh Mr. Morgan?"

All the colors of fall were on display as the sun moved slowly behind the mountains to the west, and Chance finally rode into town. He put up the big horse and his tack and walked over to the Crystal Saloon for a cold beer. "Long time in the saddle today, Tiny. How about a cold one or three. Seen Stone or the others recently?"

"I think they're down at the jail, Marshal. They haven't been in here all day. You think something's up?"

"No, they're probably going over all the paperwork we found this morning. I'll finish this and head down there. Did Stone talk to you about holding court in here?"

"Sure did and I'm all in favor of that. You bet I am."

Chance quaffed the beer and headed down the street to the jail, watching a lone rider come into town. He rode over to Chance and said, "I thought there was a regular livery and stables here, and a saloon called the Bucket of Good Hope. Is this Preston?"

"Yes it is, mister, but there's been a problem. That pile of rubble across there is what's left of the saloon, and at the end of the street there, that pile of rubble is what's left of the livery.

"There are corrals behind the mess there."

"Thanks, mister. Quite a problem, I'd say," and he rode off toward the corrals. Chance went on up to the jail, thinking that he may have seen that gentleman sometime in the past. He couldn't put a finger on it, but he thought he recognized him.

***

Ned Thompson rode toward the stables and had the same thoughts rolling through his mind. "I've seen that man somewhere. So Dickson's saloon is burned to the ground, the livery is burned to the ground. I wonder what kind of problem I've ridden into?" He put his horse up, threw some hay into the corral and made sure there was water in the old tank, and walked back out onto the main street.

Thompson wasn't a big man, maybe five feet eight inches, maybe one hundred forty pounds at best, but he carried two knives at all times, one big bladed and heavy, one almost a stiletto. Coupled with a revolver, he was known as a killer in many parts of Nevada and the west. "Looks like at least one saloon is still standing," he muttered, walking toward the Crystal Saloon.

"Howdy stranger, welcome to what's left of Preston. What's your pleasure?" Tiny Bidwell thought that his saloon would finally be a paying venture if people were already arriving for the big court showdown. Miller and Dickson would make his little saloon successful, and the irony of that was pure pleasure.

"Whiskey and a cigar," Thompson growled. He downed the first one, poured a second, took time to bite off the end of the cigar and get it lit before saying another word. Bidwell moved down the bar toward the two old guys at the end. "Where would I find Dickson?" Thompson said, blowing blue smoke into the air. "Thought he owned a saloon here."

"Dickson's in jail, down the street there, and those ashes across over that way are what's left of his saloon. You here for the trial, mister?"

Thompson just grunted, poured another healthy shot. "Got a hotel in this camp?"

"What's left of it's right across the street there. Be a dollar for the drinks and two bits for the cigar, mister. Yes sir, gonna be some kind of trial with Dickson and old Preston Miller heading up that cold river of justice. Some kind of trial." Thompson just laid some coins on the bar, turned and walked out the door. Bidwell turned to the old guys. "Wonder if I said the wrong thing. Didn't seem very friendly, did he?"

One of the old guys said he thought that maybe Chance should know about the stranger. "He might be here to help Dickson, not watch him sent off to jail, you know, Tiny. That marshal's a pretty sharp boy, and he might want to know about the stranger."

Tiny Bidwell still had thoughts of a full saloon for days on end, what with the trial and all the people coming in and hadn't given any thought to Dickson and Miller having help coming in. "Damn, you're right. Keep an eye on things, I'll be right back," and he untied his well-used bar apron, came out from behind the bar and headed down the street to the jail.

"Marshal, Marshal," Bidwell said as he hurried into the building. "They's a stranger just came into the Crystal looking for Dickson. I may have spouted off some and told him Dickson is in jail and they's gonna be a big old trial. Hope I didn't do wrong."

"No," Chance said, "you didn't do wrong, Tiny. I saw him when he rode in." Chance looked over to Stone and Bettencourt, sitting along the back wall. "Had the feeling I knew the man, Ira. Not too tall, almost thin, with long scraggly hair and a pencil moustache. Ring a bell?"

Stone shook his head no, but Bettencourt just

simply said, "Ned Thompson." Chance smiled immediately and nodded agreement.

"Let's take a little walk, George, get some fresh air. Ira, we still going to have supper tonight? Need to know what was in all the rest of the papers you might have found after I left. Hope there was a contract."

"Almost a contract, Jacob. Almost. How about if I walk with you and George, and then after we spook up good old Ned Thompson we can have a big steak with sour dough biscuits. I watched Henrietta make them this afternoon and she wouldn't even let me have one." The three were laughing and Stone was grumbling as well as they walked out on the main street of Preston.

They picked up sounds of arguing up the street and headed that way, toward the hotel. Voices were raised, and then there was silence. The three hurried their steps, and found Ned Thompson, bloody knife in hand, standing over the dead body of the hotel owner. "Don't move Thompson," Chance said, revolver in hand. "Drop the knife, and I mean right now." The big gun was cocked, Chance had a finger on the trigger, and he had his pistol pointed at Thompson's right eyeball. "Do it now, Thompson," and the little man slowly let go of the knife, let it clatter to the floor. "Step back, slowly," and he stepped up to him and slammed the pistol across his forehead, knocking him unconscious.

Bettencourt stooped down and relieved Thompson of the dagger-like knife and his handgun, rolled him over, and slipped a set of cuffs on. "Alright, fool, on your feet," and he jerked him up just as he was coming to. "Heard you're in town to see Dickson, well, my stupid friend, you're gonna meet him in just a minute or two." And the four men walked back to the Jail.

Chance sent a couple of men to take care of the hotel owner's body, and bring whatever Thompson had with him back to the jail. "This will be the third time we've tried to have supper, Ira. Let's really do it this time. Find Martinez, George, and join us at the café in a few minutes. Steaks are on the major tonight. If he could, he'd be here right with us.

"Listen, Ira, if Dickson sent for Thompson, and we heard he sent for hired guns, then we can probably expect more coming in over the next couple of days. We don't need a town full of hired guns when the judge gets here."

Chapter Twenty

Two riders flanked the small delivery wagon pulled by two mules, and two saddle horses were ponied behind. The mounted riders wore badges and the man sitting alongside the driver was in a black suit, white shirt and string tie, and black felt hat. "Well, judge, looks like we'll be in Preston some time tomorrow, 'less of course we break somethin' else."

"There isn't much left to break, Dusty," the elderly man said. "It's a wonder to me anyone even lives in this country." On the trail the old wagon had split its tongue, thrown a wheel, which caused considerable delay, and one mule threw a shoe. It was getting that iron rim back on the wooden wheel and then soaking the wheel to tighten it that took lots of time and effort. The judge was much more a city man than a trail-wise jurist, and he did tend to complain some.

"Just sage brush and jack rabbits as far as I can tell." Fred Davenport was in his early sixties and had been a United States Territorial Judge for the last five years, spending most of his time in Salt Lake City. He was a big man, mostly out of shape today, but with remnants of his earlier years when he was known as a bar room brawler of an attorney in Philadelphia.

"You left out one thing, Judge. Yer right, there be sage brush and jack rabbits, but they also be silver and gold. Those are the best reasons to be in this country," and Dusty cackled over his little joke. Judge Davenport harrumphed, but did give a short little smile at the comment. "These trails are good when you're on horseback, but they ain't so good for wagons. We'll get there, don't you worry about that."

"We got water ahead, 'bout three miles up the ridge there. Might be a good place to make our camp. Get started early, we'll be down in that valley and into Preston in just a few hours." Dusty had made this trip from Nevada's Territorial Capital to Preston twice a year for several years and knew the trail well. "I'm liking this trip, Judge. Don't get a chance to talk much on most of my trips."

"I'd say you're catching up, Dusty," the judge grumbled. "I've certainly heard a lot of stories these past few days." The two outriders came up alongside the wagon and pointed out some dust being kicked up a mile or so ahead. Both riders wore badges naming them Deputy U.S. Marshals.

When President George Washington created the marshal service, the purpose was protection of federal courts and judges, and in the territories, many of the judges needed that protection. Rule of law was a concept not accepted by everyone once outside the more civilized areas of the country. Sean McComber rode up alongside Dusty.

"Going to jog up the trail a bit, Dusty. Pete Samuels will stay with the wagon. Keep your eyes open wide 'till I get back," and he spurred his horse into a gentle lope. About three or four hundred yards up the trail he noted that the dust was mixed with some blue smoke, probably from an early camp fire. He settled his horse into a slow walk as he neared the area of commotion, and coming around a large granite boulder saw a man whipping his horse.

The man had raised bloody welts and the severe lashing had broken the skin on the horse in several places. The man was drawing his revolver when Sean McComber drew his first. "Stop right there, mister. That's all the whipping that horse is gonna get today." Pistol in hand, he stepped off his gelding, dropped the reins, and walked to the man with the whip. "Drop the whip, very slowly drop the gun."

"Who you telling me what to do?" and he whirled, only to find a forty-five slug tearing through his chest. The impact drove him back several feet, and even though mortally wounded, he tried to fire his pistol. One more round of heavy lead took him to the ground, dead.

With the sound of gunfire, Pete Samuels told the judge to climb in the back of the wagon and lay down. He had Dusty put the mules in a trot, and he pulled his rifle out of its scabbard, jacked a round into the chamber, and rode hard toward McComber. As he neared the large boulder, McComber stepped into sight and gave an all clear signal.

"Look at that horse. Look what that fool did to that horse. Dusty, can you doctor him up, and we'll see if we can figure out who this fine upstanding piece of rot is." McComber's family, back in Tennessee, bred and raised some of the South's finest horses, and for him to witness someone mistreating a mount was a hanging offense in his mind.

"I know that man well," Judge Davenport said, climbing down from the back of the wagon. "Name's Johnny Phillips. I sent him to prison two years ago."

"That might have been his name then," Samuels piped up, "but I bet Sean and I know him as Arnold Whitman, one of the most cold-blooded killers I've ever had to deal with."

"You're right, Pete. I didn't recognize him in the furious little fight we just had, but I sure do now. That's Whitman for sure." He shook his head as he watched Dusty work with Whitman's horse, blood still dripping from whip wounds. "That horse is going to be man-shy for a long time, I'm afraid."

"Well, let's gather up Whitman's gear and get the fool buried. Might as well make camp right here, Dusty, since there's water and grass. Can't ask for much more than that." McComber and Samuels grabbed shovels and moved many yards from the trail to dig a shallow grave for the gunman.

"Not a lot of people on this trail," McComber said. "Wonder if Whitman was headed for Preston? Whipping a horse like that, damn. I'm sorry I killed the bastard, because if I had just wounded him then I could take that whip to him."

Samuels had to laugh at the comment. "You'd die to help a horse, wouldn't you?"

"Got more horse friends than people friends, Pete. Yes, I think I would."

***

Chance, Stone, Bettencourt, and Martinez were at the café even before the doors were open, before the sun splashed across the Golden Valley. "You boys hungry or something? At least let me get the stove hot."

"Sorry, Heather," Chance said with a smile. "Gonna be a busy day I think and we need our strength. Got any of those big pork chops left? And some of those sour dough biscuits? And a couple of bowls of gravy?" The four clattered into their chairs, Heather talking to herself as she made her way to the kitchen. She also gave Chance another one of her special smiles, which both Stone and Martinez picked up on immediately.

"Got something going there, Jacob?" he joked, kicking Martinez under the table.

"Just never mind, Ira. Business first." And those at the table gave some pretty hearty laughs. "That judge should be arriving today, if I can calculate anymore, and I'm worried there might be trouble on the trail."

"He should be coming in with U.S. Marshal protection, Chance. You want one of us to ride out and add to that protection?" Judicial protection was first priority for the Service, and Ira Stone was fully aware of that.

"I want you to stay here in town, Ira, with me. We need to talk to these people, make sure they understand the long-term problem, but I am worried about extra guns being around. Hired guns. Martinez, you and Bettencourt ride out, right after we eat, and meet with the judge's party, and finish the escort in. He should have two deputies with him, and with you two added on, that judge will be as safe as safe could be."

"I'm just amazed at how much you boys can eat," Heather said, picking up empty platters and bowls. "Want more coffee?" and her smile went straight to Chance. The other three were grinning like little school boys about to pull a pig tail.

"No, Heather. I think we're fine, thank you. George, Stan, do you want Heather to make up a couple of saddle lunches for you? Don't know how far you might have to ride before you meet up with the judge."

While those two waited for their trail food, Ira Stone and Jacob Chance walked down to the jail. "Ned Thompson was here to meet with Dickson and we know, because Hank Adams was there when Dickson sent people out to hire guns. This could get dicey, Ira. We need to get together with Jerrod Stockton. He knows everyone in town and would spot a stranger faster than anyone." The two stopped, turned, and walked straight back toward the stables.

***

Ben Stokes had a large binder filled with records, notes, and letters, had them tucked neatly in saddle bags, and was on his big ranch horse, headed toward the main trail to town when he spotted the wagon and riders coming down the trail. He waited for them, more out of curiosity than anything else. "Mornin'," he said as they approached. "You gentlemen are out early."

McComber rode out in front of the wagon, very defensively, and made sure his badge could be seen for miles if necessary. Stokes spotted it right away. "I'm Ben Stokes," he said, and motioned toward his ranch. "This is my place. You must be riding in to help Jacob Chance. I'm heading into Preston myself. How about I ride with you?"

"Ride in front of the wagon with me," McComber said, still in defense mode. "So, you know Chance. Is he okay?"

"He's fine. Town suffered some, but he has the bad guys in jail, those that lived through the problem. Ira Stone and two other deputies arrived to help settle things down. He's just waiting for the federal judge to arrive and clear up this horrible mess."

"That man in the wagon behind you is Judge Davenport, so Chance's wait is about over." They spotted two riders coming toward them and McComber again ordered the judge into the back of the wagon, told Dusty to hold up, and Samuels rode up front to join McComber. "Busy trail this morning," he said, almost smiling.

Stokes recognized the two right away. "Those are the deputies that rode in with Ira Stone. Bettencourt and Martinez." All the tension eased immediately and the group had a sort of homecoming, the judge climbing back onto the seat of the wagon.

"Looks like you're going to have more protection than you have ever had, Judge. Four deputies, a personal driver, and rancher. Well, let's get this procession to Preston before we make it into a parade." McComber wasn't trying to be funny, and the group headed out, Martinez and Bettencourt leading, Stokes riding alongside the wagon, and the others trailing the wagon.

"Are you one of the land owners that will be facing problems because of this dispute?" the judge asked as they got underway.

"Yes, sir, I'm afraid I am. Marshal Chance has had all of us that bought land over the years from those crooks put all our paperwork together so you would have a good idea of the depth of the problem." Ben Stokes had never spoken to any kind of judge, more or less a federal judge, and felt a little overwhelmed. "I don't mind saying I'm very much worried about what I've enjoyed building for all these years. That ranch is my home, it's where I raised my children, it's what we've built from just a range full of scrub brush."

Judge Davenport, contemplative for a couple of moments, said, "Cases like these can become so complicated. I'm a fair man, Mr. Stokes, and I'm glad you told me about Marshal Chance making sure everyone has as much paperwork as possible. So often in these land fraud cases, there isn't any paperwork, just a worthless handshake or a deal at the saloon. This will make my job a little easier, and, as I said, I'm a fair man." They rode on in silence for several more miles, both men deep in their own thoughts.

"Tell me about this little town of Preston, Mr. Stokes," the judge piped up as they continued down the trail. "What are the people like?"

"Well, judge, Preston has been under the thumb, the fist actually, of Dickson and Miller from the beginning, but the people that have moved there, built their homes, opened their businesses, are good people. Many were enticed by sweet talk and blue skies, and many have been treated awfully bad, but for the most part, they are strong, law abiding, good people just looking for justice and to be treated right." He was thinking to himself that he hadn't talked this much in a long time, and he's talking to a federal judge.

Stokes spent the next hours discussing the valley, its people and ranches, with the judge. By the time they reached Preston, Stokes felt good the prospects he and the community might be looking at.

***

Jerrod Stockton had most of the residents of Preston in the Crystal Saloon for a quick meeting with Chance and Stone. He was still nursing his bruises and wounds, but his mood had changed from foul to just slightly angry. "I walked from one end of this little village to the other this morning, Chance, and talked with just about every person I've known for years. They're scared, Jacob, just plain scared. It would be so easy for me to walk into the jail and shoot those two bastards. So easy," and he just let his voice trail off.

"Well, you might be able to justify something like that to yourself, but you know you would be wrong. The law will take care of those two." The saloon held about thirty people, old Tiny Bidwell smiling at everyone, pouring a beer here, a glass of stronger stuff there. Chance walked to the center of the large room.

"I'm glad you're all here. Settle down some and we'll get this over with as quickly as possible. You have businesses to run," he said with a full Jacob Chance smile to those around him. "I think the federal judge will be here sometime today and the first order of business will be to bring George Dickson and Preston Miller to trial." There was a solid round of applause at the comment. "None of the lease and purchase questions can be taken up until those men are tried.

"One of the things the judge is going to be most interested in are your records. Deputy Stone and I have found many records that Preston Miller kept, but any that Dickson had were burned when the saloon went up in flames. Miller kept some pretty good records and notes and the judge will want to correlate them with what you have. I cannot say for sure what is going to be the final outcome but I can say that everyone will get a fair hearing, the judge will want to know everything you have been forced to do.

"Go home and back to your businesses and spend a lot of time putting your records together. Deputy Stone and I will be available just about any time if you have questions or need help. When this is all over, it will be time to make Preston a real town, with elections and leaders, real law, a real town. We're here to help you get that." Again, the large room filled with applause and Stone, Chance, and Stockton were surrounded by people with millions of questions.

Chance walked over to his own table, motioned to Bidwell to pour a cold one and sat down with Stockton. "Jerrod, you're a born leader, you know everyone in Golden Valley, and I hope you're planning to rebuild that livery." He caught himself, took a deep breath and continued. "That is, after the judge makes all the decisions on who owns what around here," which brought smiles to both men.

"Anyway, this is a fine town and it will need men like you to make it a better little town. One of the things the judge will have to do is create a town government. Right now, Preston is just a name. It doesn't exist because of all the fraud and deceit brought about by Preston Miller and George Dickson. With your permission, I'm going to recommend to the judge that you be named interim mayor, and you're going to need to bring these people together as a genuine community.

"You'll have a lot of help, from the judge, from Ira Stone, and from me. Preston is lucky that you are here and you can put it on the map. It's actually a part of a Nevada Territory county, but no one in the county even knows there is a town. Will you do this?"

This was the biggest question the big man had ever had thrown at him, and he sat in silence for a long time. Finally, after downing a full glass of cold beer, he answered. "Jacob, when you came to town that morning, and it seems like years ago, I knew things were going to get better.

"You're giving me a chance to do what I've wanted so many others to do. I'm telling you yes, but that is going to be codged to a point. The people will have to be involved in the decision." Chance could see a hint of worry in the big man's face.

"The town must be put together first, Jerrod. To do that, it has to have someone in charge. After the town is organized, and this might take a year, it might take two, then elections can be held, and then, the people will make their choices, their decisions. But right now, Preston needs you."

"All right," the big man sighed, rubbing a bruised if not broken rib, and smiling through his black eye and cut lip, "All right. Shake hands with the interim mayor of Preston, Nevada Territory."

After the pep talk, and after at least one more cold beer, Jerrod Stockton got up and took the long walk to his burned out livery. He realized this was the first time he had been able to visit the stables and blacksmith shop, and actually take inventory of all the damage and loss since the fire, since the horrible beating he had taken. "What a damn shame," he mumbled, as he began the long process of finding tools, discovering what could be saved, what had to be discarded.

"All those beautiful horses," he said, over and over, tears streaming down his cheeks, as he moved charred wood into piles to be burned or hauled away. He found the forge, and knew he could make it work again, found many of his tools, found a burned out leather apron, discovered that the rooms he had lived in all these years, destroyed, along with his personal papers, his clothing, his books, his life.

After two hours of intense work, sweat pouring off him, Jerrod Stockton took a break, sat on a pile of leather goods, and came to grips with the situation. "I have almost nothing left except myself, and Chance wants me to give myself to Preston. I can do that. I can bring all this together into a real community, rebuild my business at the same time, because God knows these people are gonna need a damn blacksmith," and he grinned for the first time in hours, "and besides, I kind of like the name, Mayor Stockton. Kinda like that," and the smile continued for minutes.

It was a town-wide celebration of sorts as Judge

Davenport and the entourage rode into Preston late that afternoon, Chance standing in the middle of the street welcoming them, people gathering around, almost cheering their arrival. All the marshals renewed their friendships, introductions were made amidst the hullabaloo, and after almost a half hour, Davenport and Chance were able to move off to the jail for their first meeting.

"Looks like one hell of a fight, Jacob," Davenport said as they walked down the dusty street. "You really did walk into a hornets nest. Major Randall sent me a long letter outlining the basic problem, but it's seldom that land fraud turns into a war."

"War is a good name for it, Judge. War it was. George Dickson and Preston Miller are two very dangerous men and they were willing to kill anyone to protect what they stole. I'm very lucky that I've been able to keep them alive to face you," and he opened the door to the jail for Davenport.

Chapter Twenty-One

The two men met for dinner, met for breakfast, and met for a cold beer in the middle of the day for at least a week, planning what had to happen. During all that time, deputy marshals were interviewing all the prisoners, and many of the townspeople, putting together reams of testimony that would be heard in open court.

The judge wanted to have Dickson and Miller tried first, and if they were convicted of all the land and water rights fraud that seemed to have taken place, then the questions of land ownership could be addressed.

Judge Davenport had many legal questions that he had to answer before any trial could even take place. "I'll tell you, Chance, this is a mess. These people have broken federal law, territorial law, and any other law you might conceive of. I can only address the federal portion of this problem. We need a territorial judge down here, and soon."

It was this separation of federal and territorial law that complicated matters in the minds of many of the local people. Jerrod Stockton brought it to the attention of both Chance and Davenport. "Some want to see Dickson and Miller hanging from a scaffold, judge, for the murders and killings, for the way they were treated."

"Hanging might happen, Mr. Stockton," Davenport told him, "but that matter will have to be handled by a territorial judge and court. I can only try these men on federal charges, and believe me, they won't ride away from territorial charges."

Dickson's gunshot wounds were seriously infected and a rider had been sent to Salt Lake City to bring a doctor, and another rider to Carson City to bring in a territorial judge. "If he dies, it will complicate this case, Jacob."

"As I mentioned earlier, Judge, he has also sent riders to find hired guns to come to Preston. We know of at least two, you met one on the trail, we took care of the other, but we don't know if any others might be on their way."

"I had the idea of trying the two together, but now, I wonder." He sat silent for a couple of minutes, seemingly staring off into the dust outside the door. "No, I think it best to try them separately. We'll try Preston Miller first. You know, I can only hold court on the federal land fraud charges. Other criminal activity, you know, murder and the like, will have to be heard in territorial court." He took another couple of minutes to contemplate all that dust outside the jail door. "We'll discuss land fraud, water allocation fraud, banking fraud, and of conspiracy to commit all those frauds.

"I'll convene court Monday morning, ten o'clock in the matter of the United States versus Preston Miller. Have your deputies aware of this. I want absolute protection, Jacob, and I don't want to hear about witness intimidation. Right now we have five deputy marshals in town and one on his way to Salt Lake and another to Carson City, both to return as quickly as possible.

"I don't want anything to interfere with the court proceedings. Are we clear on this?"

"Could not be more clear, Judge. You'll have complete protection at all times. I have two men that I can depend on to notice any strangers arriving in town, one of whom you already know, Jerrod Stockton. He has taken over the position of town leader, and was a tremendous help in our little war." The two men walked out of the jail and started down the street.

"Will you be putting a structure to this village before the trial? There is no town of Preston, it isn't even on the county maps, and these people need a town."

"That they do, Jacob, but again, that would be territorial business. The county would have to declare it a township then the people would have to declare it a city if that's what they wanted. That's not a question I will be answering."

"There is one other thing that has been bothering me," Chance said. "Almost everyone in this entire valley has been affected by the actions of Dickson and Miller. How will you be able to seat a jury of their peers?"

***

"There may be a steer or two left up there, Dad, but I think we got just about everything, and it looks like we got things done just in time. Look at those clouds building in. There'll be a foot of snow up high by tomorrow." Jennifer Stokes was caked in trail dust. The five cowboys, two horse wranglers, cookie and his wagon, and three hundred steers and cows were flowing onto Stokes's winter pastures. "Good feed all winter and we'll take the steers to Carson City come spring. We'll all go on that drive," she said, the smile from one side of her pretty head to the other.

"Good job, Jenny. Good job."

Jennifer spent the next several hours getting the herd spread out into the open grass land, got the men and equipment taken care of and found her way to the main house. "First, papa, a hot bath, then a dinner at a table sitting in a chair, then we can talk."

"That's what I want, too. The judge arrived, and things are happening in Preston. Lots to talk about."

It was an evening full of lively conversations as Jennifer related the week-long drive and Ben talking up a storm about his meeting with Judge Davenport, and about the trial of Preston Miller. "I think you'll like this guy, Jenny, he's a real brawler. Grew up on the bad side of Philadelphia, even worked in the stockyards to pay his way through school. He's one tough gentleman, and he and Jacob Chance are all but drinking buddies now."

"Is the marshal okay?"

"He's looking forward to seeing you again, I know that." Stokes had to think for a minute before he continued, asking himself if he even should. "He's been asking a lot of questions about running a ranch like ours. He grew up in Missouri on a dirt farm, hated it, and doesn't know much about ranching."

Jennifer blurted out, "I can teach him," then realized what she had said, blushed about as deeply as possible, and got up, took two quick turns around the living room, and mentioned that it was probably bed time, and slipped out of the room, accompanied by her father's laughter.

He knew there would be a ride into Preston in the morning, and from Jennifer's reaction and Jacob Chance's questions, there might be more than one ride. "I lost one son," he mumbled to himself, straightening out a chair or two, "and I wonder if I might be gaining another? Chance is one tough hombre, but I wonder if he's a cowboy?"

He thought about that for a minute, then all to himself said, "Of course I was a cabinet maker before I got this place started," and headed off to bed with irony written across his weathered face.

***

"Cookie can bring the wagon any time today, Dad. Why don't you and Hank Adams ride in with me. We'll make good time that way." Ben Stokes gave her one of his knowing smiles, which brought on another blush from the girl, and the group was mounted and on their way. "That summer pasture was really good this year, Dad. We should get top dollar in Carson City come spring. Do you think we should send someone up there now, or wait for a couple of months?"

"Wouldn't hurt to find out what the market is in the capital. I think down the line we will have to have a full time agent doing our business there. Too far to drive them to Sacramento, and they lose too much weight driving them to Salt Lake. I keep reading about railroads in the east, we could sure use a solid rail line in the territory."

The ride into Preston was filled with Stokes Ranch

business talk, and it wasn't until the burned-out hulk of the livery came into view that Hank Adams was able to get a word in. "Ben, you were talking about an agent in Carson City and I've been pondering on that for a couple of hours. There are several very good ranches here in the valley along with some farms that produce a lot of vegetables, far more than are eaten on the farms.

"Would I be out of line asking that I be considered for that position? I know cattle, I know what it will take to drive herds north to Carson City, and I had a fair amount of number learning when I was younger. I think the whole valley would do well with a full-time agent up north."

"That's the kind of thinking I like, Hank. When we get back to the ranch, you, me, and Jenny need to spend a lot of time putting something like that together. Represent the whole valley, not just one ranch. I like that."

They dismounted and tied off at brand-new racks in front of the old blacksmith shop and walked to the Crystal Saloon. "Chance and the judge have set up an office right in the saloon, and that's where the trial will take place as well," Ben said, holding the door for Jennifer. "There they are in the back there. Hello, Judge, Chance, lots of activity out there on the street today."

The two men at the table stood, shook hands all around, and bade the three to sit. "I think I better go find Jerrod," Hank Adams said, feeling Ben and Jenny would have a lot to discuss with the judge and the marshal. "I'll set up a camp in the willows, Ben, when Cookie gets here with everything. Guess the hotel is pretty breezy still," he said, walking up to the bar to get a beer first.

"Glad you made it back safe, Jennifer," Chance said, holding a chair for her. "Judge Davenport, may I present Jennifer Stokes. Jenny, Judge Davenport." They nodded to each other and all four settled into their chairs. "It's going to be mighty busy around here for the next few weeks. Along with all the others that believe they own property here in the valley, we'll need lots of in-court testimony from you and your father."

"I'll have to go back to the ranch from time to time, but I'm planning on being in town for the duration," she said, offering a beautiful smile, which was returned immediately. "Dad said Colonel Dickson is in bad shape. What happened?"

"During the big shoot out he was hit in the leg, and then when we captured him, he was shot again, in the same leg. Both wounds are festering bad, and there is some concern that he might not live to his trial."

Judge Davenport said, "That's why I want Preston Miller on trial first. Even if Dickson croaks, Miller's testimony will be on the record, and if Dickson lives, will be used against him." He gave a long appraising look at Jennifer. "So, Mr. Ben Stokes, this is the daughter you were telling me about, and U.S. Marshal Jacob Chance, this is the lovely lady you have been telling me about." He nodded to Stokes and to Chance, and gave a welcoming smile to Jennifer. Jennifer and Chance each had a moment for a bit of embarrassment.

"I'll be holding pre-trial hearings starting at ten tomorrow morning, right here," and he looked over at Tiny Bidwell, "and you'll have this set up as a court room." It wasn't a question, and Bidwell gave his full guarantee. "Ben, I'd like to spend about an hour or so with you, right now. There are some questions that have come up, and I think you might be the only man in Preston that can answer them. Okay with you?"

"That's fine, Judge, because I've had time to put a few questions of my own together. Want to do that now, that's fine. Jennifer, make sure that Cookie gets our camp set up right, will you, and Jacob, will you have supper with us tonight? Cookie is bringing in the tenderloin from the tenderest calf we had."

Before Chance could answer, Judge Davenport said

he would be glad to join the group for dinner. "And bring this blacksmith, Jerrod Stockton, in too. I want to talk some more with him."

Chance said, "Looks like we've been thrown out, Jennifer. Need any help getting that camp set up?" He gave her a big smile as they walked out of the Crystal Saloon. "One thing I know how to do is set up a camp." This kicked off an internal conversation dealing with living in a permanent home, being home on a regular basis, having a family, and he couldn't stop the questions.

"When you get quiet, you really get quiet, Marshal. Are you worried about something?" Jennifer assumed he was thinking about the coming trials and the possibility of more gunmen coming into town.

"No, not worried," he lied, "I'm just not very good at small talk I guess. I've spent most of my life being alone, and when I'm not alone, too often the others are criminals and such." He smiled, saying, "I've been looking forward to being able to talk with you, and now that I have the chance, I don't know what to say."

She laughed, gave him a long look as they walked toward the willows on the north end of town. "When you're not chasing criminals or solving crimes, where do you live?" She knew nothing about the man other than he was very interesting, handsome enough to set her heart thumping, and apparently single.

"Well, actually that was one of the things I was thinking about when you commented on me being quiet. My jurisdiction extends from the Sierra Nevada Range, through Nevada Territory to the Wasatch Range in Utah Territory, and I spend most of my time on the trail, traveling from place to place, based on who is breaking federal law and where in the area they might be."

"Are you saying you don't have a home?" The thought hadn't occurred to her at all and she was taken back somewhat. "Really? That's terrible, Jacob Chance, just terrible. No home? Terrible." She had stopped as she said this and turned to the big marshal, taking his hands in hers. "How can you live that way?"

Her hands wrapped around his gave his system a good jolt of warmth, and he stammered a bit, saying something about living on the trail wasn't bad at all. "Jenny, I've been a marshal for a long time, I've been carrying a badge and fighting criminals for many years, and I guess I've just gotten used to it. I'm not sure I would know how to take care of a home or property.

"I grew up on a farm, and I have to be honest, I didn't like that life at all. Have you always lived on the ranch?" He all at once realized he was having a real conversation with the lady, and he smiled a bit to himself. She caught the little smile and returned it.

"I was born in St. Louis but Jim and I were pretty young when we moved west. I grew up on the ranch and I guess it would be safe to say it's the only life I really know." They stayed quiet for a few minutes, crossing into the deep willows half a mile north of town, getting their boots wet crossing the river, and moving up onto the flat plain on the other side. "I guess we really do live very different lives, Jacob Chance. I want you to tell me all about your life, and I want to tell you all about mine."

Chance talked about living on the trail, sleeping under the stars far more often than in a hotel room, eating rabbits and birds, fish, biscuits, and beans cooked over an open fire, bathing in cold streams and rivers. He didn't go into much detail on fighting criminals, didn't tell her about the gunshot wounds he had suffered, didn't tell her about killing men.

"You love living on the trail, don't you?" she asked. They were helping cookie get the camp site put together. "And you've never married?"

He had fallen in love once, many years ago, but decided this wasn't the time to talk about that. "I have to admit when I do spend some time in a town I enjoy a soft warm bed and a hot bath, but, yes, I do enjoy living on the trail. Watching the sun come up, feeling that sunrise chill trying to get a fire started, hearing the birds chatter their greetings to the day." They got quiet for a spell, and finally, it was Jennifer's turn, and she was anxious about telling her story after hearing his.

"There's a huge amount of work on a ranch, Jacob, and dad has always felt that Jim and I needed to know that. Jim always balked, he hated it, but loved telling people that he was a rancher. I'm just the opposite." They settled down on some camp chairs, and Chance could see the sparkle in her eyes as she told of ranch life.

"The cattle really keep us busy. The breeding, then the spring time calving. There's so much work. Getting the calves weaned is a chore, then doctoring, branding, castrating. Every spring we have to separate the steers that will be driven to market, then drive the rest of the herd into the high mountains for the summer, and bring them back down in the fall." She was smiling all the time she was talking.

"Sounds to me like you spend a lot of time on the trail and working in the outdoors as well," he said. "You just got back from a trail ride. You look pretty healthy to me."

"I love the trail rides, love working with the cattle, love working outdoors. I'm afraid if I ever do fall in love and get married, I won't be a typical ranch wife. Give me some canvas pants, high boots and chaps, a good horse, strong rope, and healthy cattle, and I'm one happy little girl."

They laughed together, actually spent a little time just looking into each other's eyes, and Chance finally had to say he needed to get back to town. "We'll have supper together, Marshal Chance," she smiled at him, "and maybe I'll even wear a dress."

***

It was a big happy camp that night, with two or three of the Stokes Ranch cowboys on hand with guitars and fiddles, a roaring fire warming everyone in the early fall chill, steaks broiled on the open coals along with other fine food from cookie, several U.S. Marshals, a federal judge, and one large and gregarious blacksmith. It was late when things broke up and people headed back to town.

Jennifer walked Chance back to his horse. "I'm glad you didn't wear a dress, Jennifer," he said, holding her hand as they walked. "I think that would have scared me half to death."

"The big strong U.S. Marshal is scared of a little girl in a dress?" and she laughed long and hard. "Now that's something I will have to see." He was a bit embarrassed and glad it was dark. She held tight to his hand, and finally had to let go. "I'll see you tomorrow, Jacob Chance," and he squeezed her hand, stepped into the stirrup and mounted the big black stud.

"Tomorrow it is," he said.

Chance and Stockton rode together going back. "What's the attitude of the town, Jerrod? Are we going to have trouble?"

"I don't think so, Jacob. Just about everyone has been hurt in some way by those two bastards, but they seem very willing to let the court handle things. Also, while I'm thinking about it, a couple of ugly men rode through town late this afternoon. Didn't stop, just kept riding, looking at everything. I've never seen either one as far as I know."

"I think maybe we can take a little ride in the morning. Join me for breakfast and we'll take a ride out to the Kiefers'. That's where Dickson went, and I wonder if your strangers would also go there." The two men corralled their horses and walked to the hotel.

As usual, Chance was at the café before anyone else and was soon joined by Stockton and Ira Stone.

"It looks like you've already started rebuilding the stables. That's a good sign, Jerrod. A good sign," Chance seemed to be in a very good mood. "You and the judge had a good time last night. I think he surprised you with his strength."

"Damn near beat me, Chance," Stockton said, smiling. "I got some strong arms, but that judge almost beat me. You still planning on going to the Kiefer ranch?"

"Soon as we're finished here. Ira, you make sure that trial gets underway on time and with no problems. Jerrod here spotted a couple of drifters come through yesterday, and I'm worried about that old couple out there."

It was a quick breakfast and Chance and Stockton headed for the corrals for their horses and the ride south. "Cold this morning," Chance said, cinching his saddle down. "Sure feels like a storm to me." The clouds had been building all the previous day, the wind came up overnight, and it was bitter this morning as the two men rode out.

"Old Eb and Adelaide have had enough problems because of Dickson and Miller. I hope we don't find more when we get there." The two put their horses in a steady trot most of the way, only slowing the last mile to let the horses cool out some.

"'Mornin', Eb, everything okay out here?" Chance and Stockton spotted the two extra horses as soon as they turned onto the Kiefer property. "Got visitors, do you?"

"Howdy, Marshal. Yes sir, we have visitors. Come on in and meet 'em." They dismounted and tied their horses off, and kicking dust off their boots, they followed Eb Kiefer into his old cabin.

Two large men, still in their trail clothes, dirty and unshaved were sitting at the kitchen table with coffee mugs in front of them. Adelaide had just filled the cups.

"Marshal Chance, what a nice surprise, and Jerrod, you don't get out here very often. We always have work for you. Want you to meet my nephews, this big one is Johnny, and this here little scab is Henry." Big Johnny stood up and he was big, and little scab Henry stood up and was just shy of the same size as Johnny. They had broad smiles on their faces, sticking grubby paws out for a shake.

"Aunt Addie told us all about you, Marshal," Johnny said. "Thank you for taking care of my family. Uncle Eb sent for us several months ago, but we had a hard time getting out of Texas. They wouldn't be here without your help. Thank you."

It was a morning filled with coffee and sweet breads, conversation, and the retelling of keeping the Kiefers safe and well. "I'm glad you men are here," Chance said as he and Stockton got ready to leave. "There could still be trouble and from what I see, it will be taken care of if it heads this way." All the goodbyes were said and the two started the long ride back to Preston.

"I'm glad we came out, Marshal. Glad too that we won't have to worry about old Eb and Adelaide. Sure a shame that Bruce had to die." He got silent for a couple of minutes, then started up again.

"Just how many men did Dickson and Miller kill? Seems like the best thing to do would be to just hang the bastards."

"We're a civilized society, Jerrod, and that's why we have laws and courts and justice. Hanging may end up being what will be done, but following a trial in a lawful court. There are many ways to kill a man, my friend. Dickson and Miller killed many with their guns and their hired thugs, but they also killed men by way of their greed and fraud. Old Eb and Adelaide were on their way to a kind of death, probably having to give up their ranch and all.

"That's the kind of death that folks have to live with, and that's the kind that this trial is going to be all about." He gave the big blacksmith a smile and continued. "You had a taste of that kind of death as you watched your livery burn to the ground. Dickson and Miller are responsible for both kinds of death, and many people have suffered because of it."

Their conversation continued all the way into Preston, arriving about midafternoon. "Damn, Jerrod, I really messed up."

"How's that, Jacob?"

"Putting that court room in the Crystal Saloon means no beer to wash down the trail dust until after court," he said, tying off his horse. The two were laughing as they entered the courtroom.

Chapter Twenty-Two

On the morning of the third day of Preston Miller's trial, Jennifer Stokes found Chance at the café with Ira Stone. "May I join you for a minute, Marshal?" she said, pulling out a chair. Both men were on their feet, and both tried to help with her chair. "Easy, boys," she said, "You'll have me shoved into the kitchen in a minute." The laughter came easy and everyone sat back down.

"I have to make a run out to the ranch this morning, Jacob, and I was hoping you would escort me. All the hands are already back and cookie will be bringing the wagon so we can re-supply our camp. We'll be back late this evening. Can you do that?"

There was no hesitation as Chance said yes. "I want to make sure everything is set for court this morning, and then I can do anything you want."

"Go ahead and take off now, Jacob," Ira Stone said. "I'll take care of court for you. You two need a little time together." He gave Chance a big horse smile, looked over to Jennifer, and said, "He's been kind of grumpy lately," and got up from the table, and left the café. *Probably saved my life,* he thought, walking back to the jail.

"I'm not grumpy," was all Chance could say and Jennifer smiled knowingly. "I'm not."

The walk to the livery was quiet as Chance was putting two and two together, and not understanding the equation in the least. "I'm not very good at making small talk, Jenny, but I am glad for this opportunity to spend time with you. You have the advantage, I'm afraid."

"What advantage, Jacob?" she asked, knowing full well she did.

"You have been raised and spent your entire life surrounded by men. In my entire life, I've never talked with a woman as much as I've talked with you. Deep inside, I want to be more than your friend, and I don't have the

253

slightest idea how to do that."

They had their horses saddled and as Jennifer Stokes swung into the saddle she simply said, "You already have," and spurred her little cow pony into a gentle lope, leaving Chance in the dust.

On the ride to the ranch, Jennifer talked about roping, branding, calving, doctoring, and driving cattle. Talked about building and keeping irrigation ditches clean and running, about raising and training good ranch horses with plenty of cow savvy, and just about everything else that took place on a ranch.

"Ever built a house?" she asked as they rode onto the property several hours later.

"I've never done any of the things you've talked about since we met, Jenny, more or less built a house."

"Dad built our house, our barn, our outbuildings. In fact, he even built all our furniture, tables, chairs, beds, everything. Jim and I were pretty young when we moved here and dad had to do it all."

"When I was a boy, back in Missouri, after my folks died, an old man, we called him Pappy, took us in and raised us on his farm. He did all the things you have been talking about, tried to teach me how to be a dirt farmer, and I hated it." He got quiet again, remembering those days, trying to put in his mind the consequences of what seemed to be happening right now. They tied their horses off, pulled the saddles and bridles, and then walked them to one of the corrals.

"There's water in the trough, but let's throw some grass in for them," he said, grabbing a pitch fork. "They need their strength," he laughed. She watched as he tossed a few forks full into the corral and stepped close as he set the fork down.

"You're a good man, Jacob Chance, and, as you said, I too want to be more than just a friend." He put his arm around her waist and pulled her in to him, feeling every inch of her body. "Just hold me like this for a few minutes, let me feel all that strength, all that good."

He brushed her hair back and looked into her eyes, just a few inches from his own. "I've never been this afraid ever in my life," he said, and their lips came together and stayed together for long minutes.

They spent the rest of the day talking, hugging, kissing, and doing ranch chores. One time Jennifer pulled a long lariat off a hook in the barn, made a loop, played out some rope, twirled it two or three times, and put that loop right over a barrel, thirty feet in front of her.

"Here, cowboy, you try it," and she gathered in the long rope. "That loop on the end is the hondo, and you develop your big loop using it. See?" and she twisted and turned a loop. "Then, when you get it big enough to do something with, you roll it around your head like this," and she had the loop going in a big circle over her head. "Then you throw it at your target. Bingo. Here, now, your turn."

There were gales of laughter from both of them when he knocked his hat off the first time he tried, and then threw the entire rope the second time. With more than a little frustration, U.S. Marshal Jacob Chance actually hit the barrel on about the fifth shot, and put a loop over the barrel by the seventh. He had a triumphant look on his face until she reminded him that he would have to do that on a horse going at a full gallop chasing a steer or bull also at a full run.

She was getting off a good laugh, walking out the door of the barn when a loop from that lariat dropped over her head and she was jerked off her feet. He fell on top of her, and the laughter from the two of them slowly turned to noises of pure pleasure. "Just roped your first heifer, cowboy. Now you gotta tie her off and not let her get away."

***

"Before we get underway this morning, I want to

make a couple of announcements," Judge Davenport said, getting settled behind his cocktail table judicial bench. "First, I reached a couple of decisions that will affect just about everyone in Golden Valley. In the matter of water and its distribution to those ranching, farming, or using water from the Good Hope River, its tributaries and ditches, and the ground water located below the surface, at this time, no one owns that water, nor does anyone have rights to use that water.

"Now, let me explain. Neither George Dickson nor Preston Miller filed any claims on water rights in this valley. Those claims will have to be filed with the Territory of Nevada. They are not a federal issue. Sarah Jackson, you are the only land owner in this valley at this time, I recommend you file your water rights claims as soon as it is possible. By territorial law, only a land owner can have water rights for the land." He smiled at Sarah and Cotton, sitting in the gallery, and she almost let out a cry of relief.

"Let me go on, now. As far as land ownership in this valley, again, this is purely a territorial decision. A territorial judge will be here soon, and all the land issues will be straightened out. I am making myself available to that judge to help along the way. With the documents I have in my possession, I'm sure the problems will be ironed out rather quickly.

"So, that being said, let's bring to trial the case of the United States of America versus one Preston Miller," and he went on to spell out the charges against the banker and noted that there would also be state charges filed when the territorial law enforcement arrived in Preston. "I'll hear the prosecution's opening statement first. Mr. Miller has refused to discuss any of the issues with the U.S. Marshal Service investigators and has refused to take the stand during trial, therefore there will be only comments from the Marshal Service Investigators on behalf of Mr. Miller. Mr. Stone, let's break for lunch, and then you may begin your opening statements as the acting prosecutor." He banged the gavel on his table, the crowd stood as he did, and there was a general move toward the bar.

Sarah Jackson and Cotton Phelps walked up the street to the café for lunch. "I don't think I've ever had better news in my entire life, Cotton. We own our ranch. No one can throw me off that ranch again, ever," and she reached around, in mid stride, and threw her arms around the big buckaroo. "We need to file for water rights as soon as possible, we need to purchase those heifers from Ben Stokes that we talked about, we need to have Jerrod make us a new plow.

"I have a list in my head that I've been adding to ever since that marshal came to town," she laughed, giving Phelps another hug and kiss, then realizing they were standing in the middle of the street. "I love you," she said, and they walked into the café.

***

The afternoon went by quickly with witness after witness describing how the banker stole money, sold land he didn't own, held mortgages through the bank, all based on federal law. Many of the witnesses wanted to talk about the brutality, the beatings, and Judge Davenport had to continually remind them that that would be handled by the territorial judge.

Davenport didn't want the trial to drag, wanted things done quickly, and get out of court early. He had a signal system worked out with Tiny Bidwell, standing behind the bar, had told him to start polishing glasses just before four o'clock, and he saw the sign immediately.

"Well," he said as Randall Beuller finished his testimony, "as it's just about four o'clock, I think we'll fold our cards for today and resume this case at ten tomorrow morning. Mr. Miller is to be returned to the jail and tomorrow's witnesses are reminded to be here on time. That's it for today folks," and he banged the gavel on the table, winked at Bidwell, and stepped to the bar for a cold beer. Ira Stone and Jerrod Stockton joined him.

"That was some pretty devastating evidence, Mr. Stone. More of the same tomorrow?"

"I'll be wrapped up before noon, judge," he said. "The conspiracy to defraud, not just these people, but the government as well—that is, selling government land and water—is pretty strong. Eb Kiefer will talk about water in the morning, and I'll wrap it up." He took a draught of cold beer and said, "I wonder when that territorial judge will arrive?"

"If my trip is any indication, he should be here tomorrow as well. Good, Ira, we can then finish with Miller in the afternoon and start right away on George Dickson." He paused for just a moment, then asked about Dickson's condition.

"He's bad, Judge," Stockton answered, "but I'm sure he's going to live. Wonder why those people from Salt Lake haven't arrived yet? Anyway, Dickson's fine."

The three spent the next hour or so discussing the cases, and eventually made it to the café for supper. "Haven't seen Jacob all day," Davenport mentioned, taking his seat.

"Went out to the Stokes Ranch early this morning with Jennifer Stokes," Stone said with a wicked grin on his face. Laughter and knowing smiles preceded their supper.

Chapter Twenty-Three

It was dark when the two riders approached the town, stopping along the line of willows. "It's been the most wonderful day of my life, Miss Jennifer Stokes, and far more scary than I've ever had to face. If you'll give me time to figure out what happened, sleep long and warm, and meet me for breakfast in the morning, we will need to have a long talk." The two horses were close enough for the two to be holding hands as Chance was trying to say goodnight.

"I'll have a smile on my face all night, and it will still be there in the morning, Marshal Jacob Chance. One of us needs to say it, and I want to be first." She gathered herself up, put her weight in the stirrups, squeezed his hand hard, and declared, "I love you, Marshal Jacob Chance." Chance couldn't see it for the darkness, but great streams of tears were running down the lady's cheeks.

"The only people I've ever loved were my sister and Pappy, and what I'm feeling right now is far stronger than that. There must be levels of love, Jennifer, and if that's the case, I must love you very much." They parted, she to the camp, he to the livery to put Mr. Morgan up for the night. *"What have I done?"* he said to himself, walking down the street toward the hotel, his smile almost lighting up the street.

He was thinking all kinds of crazy thoughts as he stepped up onto the boardwalk in front of the hotel. Thoughts of being a rancher, being a husband, being a father flowed through his mind, with pictures accompanying each thought. He almost missed the sound of a boot heel scraping through the dirt and gravel. He spun, pulled the forty-five, and dove onto the boards in one quick move, feeling the draft of the bullet knocking his hat off. Two quick shots from his revolver and a dead man fell next to him.

In less than a minute the town was alive with

Marshal Ira Stone first on the scene followed immediately by Jerrod Stockton. A lantern was brought out from the hotel and Stone rolled the dead gunman onto his back. "You know him, Jacob?" Stone asked, everyone peering at the body.

"Don't believe I do, Ira. You seen him before, Jerrod?"

"Nope. Not from around here. How'd he get this close, Chance?"

"Had my mind on something else," was all Chance said, shuffling his feet a bit. "Let's get him down to the jail and see if we can figure out who he is." Several men picked the body up and the group headed for the jail. Chance spent the time chewing himself out for not having his mind on his job.

Back at the hotel, after figuring out the dead man was a Dickson hired hand out for revenge, Chance found himself in a major argument with himself. "All these years," he mumbled, pulling his boots off, turning down the covers, "and that's the first time I've allowed someone to get that close." He pulled the covers back up, took off his gun belt and tucked the forty-five under the pillow, his rifle leaning up against the night stand, and sprawled, fully dressed across the bed.

His dreams were vivid, lovely scenes of Jennifer, open pastures filled with fat cattle, strong boys on horses calling him pa, and then changes, with ugly men holding smoking guns coming up behind him, scenes of riding into ambush after ambush, and finally, sunrise.

***

"I'm glad you're here early. Let's take a walk, Jenny, before we have our breakfast," and he led her across the street and into the willows behind the hotel. "My job here is almost done, it's time for me to leave and meet with my people in San Francisco. I have the biggest decision I've ever faced staring at me right now, and I'm not sure I

260

want to have to make it." He let the silence drag for a minute as they continued to walk.

"I'm a law dog, Jenny, from the word go, and last night, after spending the most wonderful day of my life, I let a man sneak up on me. He took a shot before I did, and that has never happened before. I don't know if you're understanding any of this, but I was thinking only of you and it almost cost me my life."

She squeezed his hand tight, stopped, turned to him, and said very softly, "I'm terrified of what you're going to say next, Jacob Chance."

He put his arms around her and held her as tight as he dared, and just stood in the damp ground along the Good Hope River, rocking back and forth, hanging on. "What I'm about to say, you'll have every right in the world to say no to, every right to be very angry, but please let me say it all before you shoot me.

"I wasn't lying or leading you on last night, I love you very much, and more than that, I want to spend the rest of my life with you, I want a home, I want a family, but it might be just a little ways down the road. I already have a huge obligation to the Service, and I'm not the kind of man that walks away from something like that.

"What I'm asking isn't fair and you can tell me to go to hell, but I'm going to ask. It may take a little more time than we can suffer, but will you wait for me? I can't simply ride into the federal complex in San Francisco and quit. But I will quit, and when I do, will you be there? Will you wait for me? Will you marry me?"

Jennifer Stokes was bawling like a newly weaned calf, great gushes of tears washing her face, and she was hanging onto Chance with the strength of a very strong ranch girl. She tried several times to say something and couldn't, just cried more, hung on tighter. It was several minutes before things calmed down and Jennifer could talk.

"You promise you'll come back, Jacob Chance?"

"I not only promise I'll come back, Jenny, I also promise I won't be wearing a badge."

They walked up and down that river trail for another hour, talking, stopping to hug and kiss, talking some more. "When will you leave, Jacob? When will you come back?"

"The territorial judge should be here today, Judge Davenport has the federal case wrapped up and I'm sure he'll ask me to escort him back to Carson City. He'll probably want to leave in the next couple of days. Will you wait until spring, Jenny?"

"I was afraid you were going to say years, and even if you did, my answer would be yes."

"Along with what we've done here," he said, "I have other pending cases that I will have to settle. I'm sure I can be back by April, maybe May at the latest."

***

"Missed you for breakfast this morning, Chance. Everything okay?" Ira Stone was giving the marshal a fine leer coupled with a knowing smile. "Sleep late, did you?"

"No, Ira, it was a fine sunrise indeed, today. Morning, judge, looks like you have the federal end of this problem just about cleared up. Think Dickson will live long enough to be transported to prison?"

"Not a chance. Both men will die in custody, Dickson probably right here in Preston. Miller will be behind bars for the rest of his life. Doubt he'll make it in prison with his attitude.

"Judge Stanfield will be here later today, I'll spend a day or two with him, then I want you to put together a detail to escort me back to Carson City. Oh, and get me a good horse, I don't ever want to see that foul old wagon again. Dusty? He was fine, the wagon, no."

That brought a good round of laughter in the jail, and Chance went into the cell area. He had the marshal open the cell where Jim Stokes was being held. "Come on out here, Jim, we gonna have a nice little talk," and he escorted Stokes into the jail office, ushering the others out.

"Sit down. Had your coffee?"

"What do you want?"

"I'd like to say, 'you' out behind the barn, but I won't just yet. You took a chunk out of your father's heart with your bad-man attitude, and that attitude is going to get you in far more trouble than you can imagine when you spend your first few nights in a federal penitentiary. Those guys in there are looking for some new, young meat, and if you snarl once, you'll never snarl again."

"You tryin' to scare me, Marshal?" he sneered, and Chance bashed him across the side of the head, knocking him half way across the office.

"Sit back in that chair and shut your stupid mouth, boy," and he jerked Stokes up and slammed him into the old wooden chair. "I had it in my mind to give you a shot at doing the right thing, since I'm now almost family," and he gave the kid a nice smile, catching him fully off guard, "but I guess you're too far gone. Wipe that blood off your mouth, you look like a fool.

"One last shot, James Stokes, and this is it. Will you testify for the prosecution in the upcoming territorial court?"

"Go to hell. What do you mean, 'almost family'?"

"It means you won't be at the wedding, dear brother-in-law-to-be. Back to your cell now, boy. Come on, move it, you stupid fool," and again Chance jerked him to his feet, pushing him out the office door and back into the cell block.

***

Amos Stanfield arrived about noon with a large party of officials from the territorial offices, and some from the county that Golden Valley sat in. Judge Davenport was there to meet the group, along with Jacob Chance, Jerrod Stockton, and Ira Stone. "Welcome to Preston, Judge

Stanfield," Davenport said, "and the beautiful Golden Valley."

"Thank you," he said, "it's a pleasure to finally get here. Most out–of-the-way place I've ever been to. Some of these people represent Esmeralda County and didn't even know this existed. Where is this Marshal Jacob Chance?"

"Right here, Judge. What can I do for you?"

"Two things. I have a letter for you from Major Randall, and I want you to meet Esmeralda County Sheriff Harvey Dawkins. He has quite a few questions for you." He reached inside his dovetail coat and pulled out a large envelope and handed it to Chance.

"Nice to meet you, Dawkins. Let's go down to the jail to talk. Judge Davenport is about to reconvene court, so we'll be mostly alone."

Dawkins was a big man, not just tall, but one might say, his girth was filled. He wore a gun belt with a large caliber revolver and carried a rifle as well. "Heard stories that you shot up the town and killed most of those that could have testified. Even allowed evidence to burn. Not the best actions of a lawman, I'd say," and he poured a cup of hot coffee, pulled a flask from inside his vest, and added some flavor to the cup. He did not offer any to Chance.

"Part of what you say, Sheriff, sure is true. Sure is." His eyes were narrowed, his jaw was set as tight as possible without busting a tooth, and he sloshed some coffee into a cup, sat down on the edge of the desk, and glared at the big man. "Yes sir, we burned old Dickson's saloon to the ground, and no doubt at all that we killed many a bad man, but you better listen very close to what I'm about to say.

"You take that gun belt off, rest that rifle in the corner over there, and you tell me again that I'm a bad law man, and we'll have a go. Do it now, or apologize. Your choice." His hands were in plain sight on the top of the desk and Dawkins was eyeing that, glancing up to see the burning anger in Chance's eyes, and slowly took a sip of his laced coffee.

"A little touchy are we, Marshal? A real lawman doesn't make those kinds of mistakes." That's as far as the big man got. Chance went from sitting on the desk to slamming a fist into the face of Dawkins in half a second, coffee cups flying in all directions.

Dawkins was big and heavy, but also fat and lazy, and after splashing the big man's nose across his face, Chance spun the man around and slammed his head into the wall, once, twice, couldn't do a third time as the man collapsed onto the bare wood floor. The jailers in the cell area rushed to the office and found Chance standing over Dawkins hulk, fists balled into knots of fury.

"Chance, what happened?" one of them said, pushing their way through the door.

Chance gathered himself up, let his anger settle some, then helped one of the other marshals get Dawkins off the floor and into a chair. The man was slow to come around, but he did eventually. "You ever talk to me again like that, Dawkins, I'll see to it that you never wear a badge again, ever. You get your swaggering butt out of this office right now." He made a move to smack the sheriff again, and Dawkins staggered to his feet and left the jail. The two jailers went back into the cell area with much to discuss back there.

Chance straightened himself out some, picked up his own rifle, slung on his worn out old serape, and walked out of the jail, running into Ira Stone. "Don't know what's going on, Jacob, but those county people have their tails in a wringer of some kind. Judge Davenport wants you down at the saloon right away."

"They are here to cause trouble, Ira. That fat sheriff just called me a bad lawman, and he has a broken nose for the effort. Get your people together and quickly, and come down to the Crystal Saloon. Davenport himself might be in danger there."

Chance strode into the saloon, itching for a fight. "Judge, are you all right? I don't know what's happening, but you stay close to me. My only job is your protection, so stay close." First almost getting blindsided the previous night, now being challenged by a fat sheriff, Chance was as taut as a piano string.

"Marshal, I don't think these people that say they are from Esmeralda County are legitimate. Dusty told me about this county on our trip down here, and these people aren't who he was talking about. That man with the badge, I don't know why, but I've run into him somewhere."

Chance had his thoughts flowing again, back being a full-time marshal, not a bride-groom to be. "Let's get Judge Stanfield in here then call those county men in and get this straightened out." Davenport motioned for Stanfield to join him at his table in the back of the saloon, and Chance found Stone and the two of them gathered up the county men, including Sheriff Dawkins, and brought them in. Davenport took immediate charge and had everyone sit down, spread around the table.

In the meantime, Davenport asked Stanfield how the Esmeralda County officials came to join his party coming south and was told they had intercepted the group two days before. "You mean, you don't know that they are really who they say they are?" the judge asked.

"That's right, Davenport. I have no reason not to believe them."

"I'm afraid I might," the federal judge replied. "I don't think this man Dawkins is a sheriff anywhere, and these other people seem to want to take control of everything in sight, my court, your court, this valley, and its precious land and water."

"I've had a chance to talk with Jerrod Stockton since arriving, just briefly, mind you, but do you think these people might be trying to take over what Miller and Dickson had going for them? That's a long shot,

Davenport."

"It is indeed, and after you've read everything I've prepared for you, you won't think it's such a long shot at all. These people could very well be working for Dickson." He saw that Chance had the county people in, had U.S. Marshals spread around the saloon, and called the group to order.

"First off, I think, we need to get our credentials on the table," and he was immediately interrupted.

"No, judge, first off, as Esmeralda County Sheriff," Dawkins said in an overly loud voice, "I need to see Colonel George. This is a kangaroo court, has no legal authority, and this county is now taking charge of the valley and all its affairs."

It was Ira Stone who stepped forward first, then Chance from the opposite side. Chance leveled his rifle at Dawkins while Stone, revolver in hand, lifted the pistol from Dawkins gun belt. "That was the give away, Judge Davenport. If he had said he wanted to see Dickson, he might have bought a little time, but calling him Colonel George gave it away."

Chance turned to the others at the table. "Gentlemen, please stand," and the other marshals relieved them of their weapons. "You are all under arrest for conspiracy to defraud the government, for actions that would endanger a federal officer, and for threats to a federal judge. Take them down to the jail, Mr. Stone, and sort this out with them behind bars."

"That was fast, Jacob. Looks like I'll be in town for a while longer. What did Major Randall have to say?"

"Haven't even had time to open the envelope yet, sir. It's back down at the jail. Everything all right with you? If so, I'll head back down there and send a couple of the marshals up here."

"I'm fine, Jacob. You go ahead. Court is obviously done for today, so we'll get started again in the morning."

He headed to the bar for a needed cold beer. "Let me know what Randall has to say."

***

He sent Stone back to the Crystal Saloon, checked on all the prisoners, found Dickson in deep conversation with one of the men purportedly from Esmeralda County and had the jailer separate them. "Looks like Dickson is feeling better. That's good. Maybe the territorial judge will find a hanging offense somewhere in his background."

He sat down at the sheriff's old desk and opened the envelope from Major Randall. There was a good smile on his face when Jerrod Stockton came into the office to join him. "Good news, Marshal?"

"Good and bad, Jerrod, good and bad. Sit down for a minute, will you? There are some things I need to talk about, and they definitely concern you." He stretched his arms as wide as they would go, motioned that he could use a cup of that boiling coffee, and gave Stockton a generous smile. "Seen Jennifer Stokes today?"

"She and Ben went out to the ranch when the territorial judge and that bunch came into town. Cookie went with them to bring in more supplies. I thought that's what you two were supposed to do yesterday."

"We got a bit busy, Mr. Stockton. A bit busy," and the smile got considerably bigger. "That's pretty much what I want to talk to you about." He took a long draught of the hot coffee and settled deeper in the chair, finally sitting back and putting his feet up on the desk.

"Jenny and I are getting married." He caught himself, but then continued, "And, I'm going to quit the service, move into this beautiful little valley, and settle down for the first time in my life."

If he could, Stockton would have fired both barrels of that monster scatter gun of his. "Well, damn me," is all he could say. The two men, sitting on opposite sides of the desk, just stared at each other for long moments. "Well damn me," Stockton said again. "That's wonderful Jacob. When does the shindig start?"

"I have this situation here in Preston pretty much wrapped up, I think, and Major Randall wants me in San Francisco to put the final stamp on another project, and I should be back in the spring and we'll do all the planning from there." He thought for a minute, then went on. "Only you and Jenny, and probably Ben know about this right now. It's not a secret, though. I can see it in your eyes, Jerrod, you want to run up and down that street out there and howl the news."

They got a good laugh out of that, Jerrod shaking his head, yes, and they got quiet for a minute. "These men that rode in with Judge Stanfield this morning are criminals, Jerrod. Keep your guard up. There very well be more behind them. That fool last night almost got me, so don't let up now. If you or Ira Stone need me, I'll be at the Stokes' camp on the other side of the river for a while, then back at the hotel."

Chapter Twenty-Four

"I was going to be escorting Judge Davenport back to Carson City, but with these new developments, he's going to stay here in Preston for probably another couple of weeks." Chance and Jenny were sitting in front of a big fire at the Good Hope River camp site, lingering over a final cup of coffee after a big supper of steak and potatoes. "Major Randall needs me back in San Francisco, so I'll be leaving at first light."

"Isn't there any way you can stay?" she asked, knowing of course he couldn't. "This is going to be the longest winter of my life, Chance." For weeks she called him Marshal Chance, now, it was just Chance. She didn't like calling him Jacob, he had told her not to call him Jake, and she appeared comfortable with Chance. "You promise you'll be back. Promise."

"I promise, Jenny. I will be back, we will be married, and we will start a new life together." It was very quiet for some time as they sat, holding hands, looking into each other's eyes, thinking their own thoughts. "Ben is going to have to teach me how to be a carpenter, so we can have a house to live in, you're going to have to teach me how to be a cowboy so we can have a herd to maintain, and old Jerrod is going to be busy tending to all our iron needs." Gentle laughter from both, followed by hugs and kisses, and finally a long goodnight and goodbye.

"I don't want to see you leave, Chance. Let's let this be our goodbye," said with tears streaming down her face. Chance had his arms wrapped tightly around her, kissed her gently on the lips, then her forehead, patted her on her bottom, and slipped away into the dark of night.

It was a slow ride back to Jerrod Stockton's livery. With Mr. Morgan put up in his corral, Chance made his way to the hotel to pack up what little he had, followed by a fitful night's sleep. He was up before light, saddled the big stud, and left Preston for the long ride to San Francisco. Passing by the Stokes' camp, he murmured a goodbye to Jenny and repeated his promise to return.

During the ten-day ride to Sacramento, he thought about building homes, barns, corrals, fences, knowing that he had never in his life hammered a nail or sawn a piece of wood. He thought about trailing cattle to summer pasture, trailing them back in the fall, thought about trailing them to market, knowing he had never done any of that even once. And, he thought about the whole idea of being married and raising a family. "I hope I'm man enough to do this," was a continuing thought, almost chilling at times.

***

In Preston, things were busy. Preston Miller was convicted of all the federal charges, then bound over to face charges leveled by Nevada Territory. Dickson was brought to trial but made only the first week, getting weaker as each day passed. The doctor brought in from Salt Lake could not stop the massive infection from the two gunshot wounds, and Dickson was found one morning dead in his cell.

"Mr. Stockton, I understand you have taken the position of mayor of this little community," Judge Stanfield said one morning. "I need to talk to you about that." They had run into each other at the café for breakfast. "Holding court in a saloon will work for these trials right now, since there is nothing else available, but you need to build a real courthouse and town center.

"Now that Preston is going to actually exist, not just be a major land fraud conspiracy, you will need to create a town board, make laws and rules, elect a sheriff and justice of the peace, and these people will need somewhere to work. Not a saloon," and he offered a full-fledged harrumph.

"We've decided to convert Mr. Miller's old bank into the town hall and court house, Judge. Lots of room, well built, and free," and he gave a good natured laugh at

271

that last comment. "When will you be able to begin your hearings on the territorial charges, and particularly on the land ownership questions?"

"I don't need a courtroom to settle the land questions, in fact, I've already got a good start on many parcels. People bought this land in good faith, that's a big part of how I'm going to have to look at the questions. Money changed hands in good faith on one side, and to take that away now would be wrong." He paused, putting some thoughts in order.

"I'd like to have a town meeting, in two or three days, but there isn't any place to do that."

"Actually, Judge, there is. I have my livery cleaned out, ready to rebuild, and that area is large and open. It would mean an outdoor meeting, but that shouldn't hold anything up."

"Very good. Put out a notice that I will be holding open court in your stables to air my findings on land ownership, and what will be necessary for all concerned to do. Spread the word, and we'll meet in two days, ten a.m. sharp."

***

"We really do own the ranch, Jenny. It's ours." Ben Stokes had ridden hard from town to the ranch to spread the good news. "Judge Stanfield allowed those of us who had been making our payments to own the land we're settled on. Deeds will be filed with the Territorial offices when he returns to Carson City."

"What about the land that people like Toby and some of Dickson's other gangsters took over? What happens to that land?" The question had first been broached by Jacob Chance and intrigued Jennifer. "There are ranches out in the valley, poor in every respect, but sitting open and vacant. In some cases, with livestock."

Ben Stokes had moved into the kitchen and was pouring a hot cup of coffee. "Stanfield answered that too.

He said since that land was never considered by Miller or Dickson as having been sold, it was simply vacant land and under the federal Homestead Act, claims could be filed and they would be legal."

"All right," she almost bellowed. "Chance and I will have our own ranch, Papa. I want that forlorn old piece of land that Toby almost destroyed. There's good water, good grass, and I'm going to file on that tomorrow." She gave Ben Stokes a grand smile, continuing, "The best part, it backs right up to this wonderful ranch, so we can share pasture, share water, and grow lots of big fat cows." Jennifer Stokes was almost dancing, almost spilled Ben's coffee trying to hug him, and it was several minutes before calm was restored in that kitchen.

"I'm going to send a letter to Chance tomorrow. This is wonderful."

***

Furious activity was taking place in Preston, with Jerrod Stockton leading several operations, including the rebuilding of his stables and blacksmith shop, turning the Preston Bank into Golden Valley Community Center, and putting together various committees to work on laws, rules, taxes, and possible elections within the year. Judge Davenport had wrapped up all the legal business that entailed federal law, saw to it that water rights issues were well understood, and was ready to make the long trek, first to Carson City, then San Francisco.

Stanfield on the other hand had a long list of court sessions facing him. "Looks like I'll be here all winter," he said one morning over breakfast with Jerrod Stockton. "There are literally hundreds of criminal cases stemming from this outrage. I ought to just declare everyone currently in jail guilty, and get on with the hangin'," and there was another harrumph, as he continued.

"That Stokes boy is a case, Jerrod. Is he as stupid as I'm seeing and hearing?"

"His father gave him every chance to get out of this mess, Marshal Chance begged him to understand the severity of the situation, and I threatened him with my double barrel shotgun, Judge. I think stupid is a good word."

"He doesn't have to go to prison," Stanfield said. "All he did was assault a federal marshal. If he would show just a hint of remorse, I could give him probation, or just set him free with a hefty fine. I don't want to send that boy to prison.

"You take care of that, Mr. Stockton. Your first 'do-good' as acting mayor of this fine little village." He gave every impression of feeling very good about himself as he clapped Stockton on the shoulder and left the café. Stockton said something like 'thank you so much,' and he too walked out on the street and right into Jennifer Stokes.

"Good morning, Jerrod. Well, I did it. Chance and I now have our own homestead, the old Toby ranch, and I've filed for water rights on the one hundred sixty acres."

"That's great news, Jenny. Great. Let's go back inside and have a spot of coffee. Judge Stanfield just gave me a job that I'm going to need help with."

They spent more than an hour discussing what would happen to Jim Stokes and if either thought there was any way to save the boy. "He's my brother, Jerrod, and I love him, but when I talked with him, and the terrible things he said about me, about dad, and about Marshal Chance, I don't think he can be saved."

"If we go to him together, would it make a difference?"

"Dad will be here this afternoon, let's wait for him and all three of us get on that fool's case. He's not stupid, Jerrod. He's not."

***

"Company, Stokes," Stone hollered, coming into the cell area of the jail.

274

"Go away. I don't want no company."

"Too late, Jim, we're already here." Ben Stokes, Jennifer, and Jerrod walked into the cell area while Ira Stone unlocked the cell. "Let's go for a walk, Jim," Stokes said, holding the cell door open.

"No. I ain't going nowhere."

Ira Stone reached inside the cell and grabbed the boy by the shirt and yanked him out. "You're going for a walk, young man, and I mean right now. You took a poke at Chance, and look what that got you. Want to try me on for size? Didn't think so." Stone looked over at Jerrod Stockton. "If he gives you any trouble, just slap him up the side of the head. Works most of the time." He jerked Stokes over to Jerrod who took him by the arm and led the group out of the jail and onto the street.

"Where we going?" he demanded, fighting to get Stockton to let go, forcing the giant blacksmith to grip tighter.

"Just going to take a nice stroll down to the river, Jim. Been awhile since I just took a nice walk like this," his father said. "How about you, Jenny? Been walking along the river lately?"

"Oh, yes. Chance proposed to me on a walk just a short time ago. The most wonderful day of my life."

"How about you, Mr. Mayor?" he asked.

"Yup, shot two fools right over there, the last time I walked along here. They worked for Dickson and Miller. Shot 'em dead with this old scatter gun of mine," and he held the shotgun up for all to see.

"Got the paper work done on your ranch, Jenny?"

"Finished the Homestead Act paperwork yesterday, and filed the water rights paperwork this morning. Chance and I now own a quarter section of land right along the north east border of the Stokes Ranch, and have access to the summer range we always use. You know dad, it's a shame that Jim can't file on a ranch, too."

"They don't let prisoners file homestead papers, Jenny. He'll be in some hard time prison back east for a long time, I'm afraid." Ben gave young Jim a scowl, saying that.

"Doesn't have to be," Stockton said. "I had breakfast with Judge Stanfield and the only charge against him is the assault on Marshal Chance. He said if Jim would show some remorse, maybe say he was sorry, he could let him off with probation, maybe a nice hefty fine to pay for all this time down here.

"No, sir. He said that to me, and that man is as honest a fellow as I've dealt with in a long time."

"So," Jennifer said, not even looking at Jim, "you're saying if he could indicate that he was sorry for breaking into Chance's room, for taking a swing at the marshal, and the judge might let him off? No prison time?"

"That's what he said," Stockton muttered. They continued their walk along the Good Hope River, past the burned-out hulk of Dickson's saloon, past the rebuilding stables and blacksmith shop, and in just a few minutes walked into the almost permanent camp set up by Ben Stokes.

"Hey, Cookie, nice to see you. You remember Jim, don't you? How about rustling up something for us. A nice walk along the river makes a man hungry," Stokes said, watching Jerrod force young Jim onto one of the chairs. "We've just been walking and talking, Cookie, and I'm hungry."

Jim Stokes couldn't stand it any longer. "You've been lying to me. You just want me to get the other guys in more trouble."

"No, Mr. Stokes, they haven't been lying." Judge Stanfield stepped out from behind the large tent, and walked up to the young man. "Unless you're very, very stupid, you'll look me in the eye, right now, and tell me you are sorry for what you did and have been doing. And, young man, I'm not a patient person." He sat down next to Jim, watched as Jerrod Stockton let go of the boy's arm, for the first time since they left the jail, and almost smiled.

"Say it, Jim," Jenny said, as softly as she has ever said anything. "Come back to the family."

It was a jaunty group that filed back into town, walking along the main street to the jail, no one having hold of anyone else. "Alright, set up the table over there, Jerrod, put that chair behind it, and bring Ira Stone in here. James Stokes, sit in that chair, please. Good. Ira, stand to Mr. Stokes's right, and Jerrod, to his left.

"Now, Mr. Stokes, do you swear to tell the truth?" He didn't wait for an answer. "Good, are you sorry for breaking into Marshal Jacob Chance's hotel room? Good. Are you sorry for taking a swing on the Marshal? Good.

"Therefore, as Territorial Judge for this district, I find you guilty and sentence you to three years' probation, and fine you one hundred dollars. You are to remain on the Stokes Ranch and work for your father for those three years. If I find out you have broken probation, I will sentence you to hard labor in the territorial penitentiary.

"This court is adjourned."

***

"So, Jacob, you're sure this is the right thing for you?" Major Randall was holding Chance's letter of resignation from the U.S. Marshal Service. "You'll leave a large hole in our operation, one that may not be filled for some time." The two men had worked together for many years, on many operations, even shared hospital rooms, and Randall was having a hard time holding in his emotions.

"If this question had been brought up six months ago, Major, I would have laughed long and hard. Today, yes, this is the right thing for me to do. I have concerns, of course, questions, you bet, even a slight amount of fear, but all I have to do is conjure a picture of Jennifer Stokes, see visions of that beautiful valley and the Good Hope River, and I know I'm doing the right thing."

"You're eligible for a slight pension, Jacob, and I'm going to hold you to your original contract with the service. In times of desperation, you may be called back for short amounts of service. You have been one of the finest members of our service that I've had the pleasure of working with. Go in peace, my friend."

"Thank you, Major. I've never worked with a finer bunch of people in my life. You will be missed."

"When will you leave, then, for the journey back to Preston?"

"The snow in the Sierra Nevada is melting fast now, and I just sent a letter to Jenny that I would be leaving in two weeks. I'll take Mr. Morgan and two pack mules for my last trail ride, and then," and he had a big smile on his face, "I'll be living in a house with solid walls and a roof."

-End-

About the Author:

I've had a wonderful and varied time along this bumpy highway called life. I spent my early years in Santa Cruz, California, swimming, fishing, and wallowing in the splendor of redwoods, the Monterey Bay, and a loving family. Then, my four years of high school were spent living on the Island of Guam. That was back in the early 1950s Yes, Virginia, I am that old, but only in body, not spirit.

My first job in radio was in 1958. I bought the Virginia City Legend newspaper in that old western mining community in 1971, and retired from having a job in 2010. That's when I changed from being a reporter of news to being a writer of fiction, and over these last few years have found my western and crime/mystery short stories published in magazines and anthologies, around the world.

My beautiful wife Patty and I live on a small hobby farm about twenty miles north of Reno, Nevada, sharing space with a couple of fine horses, a flock of egg-producing chickens, and some breeding rabbits. You're always welcome to visit. I need help cleaning those corrals.

Social Media Links:

Facebook: https://www.facebook.com/johnny.gunn.31

Blog: http://johnny-gunn.blogspot.com/

Twitter: https://twitter.com/johnnygunn11